MAKE SHIFT

TWELVE TOMORROWS SERIES

In 2011 *MIT Technology Review* produced an anthology of science fiction short stories, *TRSF*. Over the next years *MIT Technology Review* produced three more volumes, renamed *Twelve Tomorrows*. Beginning in 2018, the MIT Press will publish an annual volume of *Twelve Tomorrows* in partnership with *MIT Technology Review*.

TRSF, 2011

TR Twelve Tomorrows 2013, edited by Stephen Cass

TR Twelve Tomorrows 2014, edited by Bruce Sterling

TR Twelve Tomorrows 2016, edited by Bruce Sterling

Twelve Tomorrows, edited by Wade Roush, 2018

Entanglements: Tomorrow's Lovers, Families, and Friends, edited by Sheila Williams, 2020

Make Shift: Dispatches from the Post-Pandemic Future, edited by Gideon Lichfield, 2021

MAKE SHIFT
DISPATCHES FROM THE
POST-PANDEMIC FUTURE

EDITED BY GIDEON LICHFIELD

THE MIT PRESS
CAMBRIDGE, MASSACHUSETTS
LONDON, ENGLAND

This book was set in Dante MT Pro and PF DIN pro by New Best-set Typesetters Ltd. Printed and bound in the United States of America.

Library of Congress Cataloging-in-Publication Data

Names: Lichfield, Gideon, editor.
Title: Make shift : dispatches from the post-pandemic future / edited by
   Gideon Lichfield.
Description: Cambridge, Massachusetts : The MIT Press, [2021] | Series:
   Twelve tomorrows
Identifiers: LCCN 2020040801 | ISBN 9780262542401 (paperback)
Subjects: LCSH: Science fiction—21st century.
Classification: LCC PN6120.95.S33 M35 2021 | DDC 808.83/8762—dc23
LC record available at https://lccn.loc.gov/2020040801

10 9 8 7 6 5 4 3 2 1

CONTENTS

INTRODUCTION   vii
Gideon Lichfield

1   "A VEIL WAS BROKEN": AFROFUTURIST YTASHA L. WOMACK ON THE
    WORK OF SCIENCE FICTION IN THE 2020s   1
    Wade Roush

2   LITTLE KOWLOON   11
    Adrian Hon

3   PATRIOTIC CANADIANS WILL NOT HOARD FOOD!   27
    Madeline Ashby

4   INTERVIEWS OF IMPORTANCE   43
    Malka Older

5   JAUNT   57
    Ken Liu

6   KORONAPÁRTY   77
    Rich Larson

7   MAKING HAY   91
    Cory Doctorow

8   THE PRICE OF ATTENTION   105
    Karl Schroeder

9   MIXOLOGY FOR HUMANITY'S SAKE   123
    D. A. Xiaolin Spires

10   A NECESSARY BEING   143
    Indrapramit Das

11   VACCINE SEASON   159
    Hannu Rajaniemi

CONTRIBUTORS   173

INTRODUCTION

Gideon Lichfield

IF YOU LIVED THROUGH THE YEAR 2020, YOU'VE EXPERIENCED COVID TIME dilation—the phenomenon by which the immense gravity of a global pandemic distorts temporal reality, making events in its vicinity seem to last much longer than they actually did. When I first proposed this anthology to the MIT Press in early April, it was less than three weeks after the first US states had begun going into lockdown, and the presidential primaries that had dominated headlines in February already felt like last year's news.

As I write this a mere sixteen weeks later, the global death toll has climbed from some 65,000 to 650,000, the United States has spent weeks being roiled by protests over racism and police brutality, US-China tensions are at an all-time high, President Donald Trump is promoting the views of a physician who believes many diseases are caused by sex with incubi and succubi, and early spring feels like a different decade.

By the time you read this, thanks to the schedules of book publishing, at least another six months will have passed. It feels almost incomprehensibly far off. Will the United States be tipping over into civil war over a flawed election? Will war have broken out somewhere else? Will there be millions dead from the virus; will a second, even deadlier pandemic have appeared? Am I being clear-eyed and rational, or feverishly apocalyptic? I really can't tell.

For perspective, it's worth remembering that COVID-19 is still small on the scale of the past century's tragedies—the 1918 flu, AIDS, the world wars, the Cultural Revolution, Stalin's terror, and the countless other wars, genocides, massacres, natural disasters, and disease outbreaks that have wreaked far more destruction on the places they affected than this virus ever will. The coronavirus kills people and ravages economies, but it doesn't flatten cities, dismember bodies, or leave its victims bleeding from every orifice.

What makes it so unsettling is in part that it affects the entire planet at once, leaving nowhere safe to run to (and those places that are now safe are wisely not accepting visitors). Another reason is that the outbreak has laid bare the fragility of the so-called developed world's economies and healthcare systems. The 2008 financial crisis, the subsequent resurgence of nationalism, Brexit, the election of Donald Trump, and the rise of China have all knocked chunks out of the West's post-1991 narrative about the ultimate triumph of capitalist liberal democracy, but the coronavirus has ripped open a gaping hole in it that may never be closed up. We are fearful not so much of dying young and alone in an isolation ward as of growing old with absolutely no idea what kind of a world we will grow old in.

That, of course, is where science fiction comes in. In early April, when it became clear that a long and painful pandemic journey was just beginning, it occurred to me that after a few months of scrambling to adapt to social isolation and economic upheaval, people would be ready to forget the present for a moment and start dreaming about the future.

The world we live in now feels uncannily like a sci-fi dystopia, but there is also a strong tradition of inspirational (without being utopian) sci-fi about a world made better by technology. It runs all the way from the writings of Isaac Asimov and Arthur C. Clarke to more recent projects like Neal Stephenson's 2014 *Hieroglyph* collection—developed in deliberate opposition to the dystopian tendency—and *Twelve Tomorrows*, the series of anthologies from *MIT Technology Review* and the MIT Press of which this volume forms a part.

In that spirit, I suggested, the MIT Press should commission an "emergency *Twelve Tomorrows*," a set of stories plucked from the darkest hour of the pandemic that imagine we've come through it and out the other side. What, ideally, would we have learned about building a more resilient, more just society, and how might technology help us do it?

The authors who responded to our invitation are all well-established, known for their ability to imagine a plausible future in realistic detail. Most write about a post-COVID-19 world, but they vary in how far in the future it is set; some, like Karl Schroeder in "The Price of Attention," treat the current pandemic as just the first of several, while in Rich Larson's sweet and melancholy "Koronapárty," the disease is still raging. In "Little Kowloon," Adrian Hon deftly plays out the consequences of two present-day disasters, the pandemic and the Chinese crackdown on civil rights in Hong Kong, while Cory Doctorow's "Making Hay" is a climate-change story. Fans of Hannu Rajaniemi's *Quantum Thief* trilogy will enjoy "Vaccine

Season," which is set in that same universe. In addition, there are terrific, imaginative stories from Madeline Ashby, D. A. Xiaolin Spires, Ken Liu, Indrapramit Das, and Malka Older.

A shortcoming of this collection is that none of the stories focuses directly on how a post-pandemic society might also become less racially unjust. It's a shortcoming because the protests that spread across the United States after a white police officer, Derek Chauvin, murdered a Black man, George Floyd, in Minneapolis, are directly related to COVID-19. Black Americans have, up to this point, been 2.5 times as likely to die of the disease as white Americans, because they are more likely to be poor, lack good healthcare, and work in jobs that require contact with a lot of people. Though it's a coincidence that Floyd was killed just as the United States was about to cross the threshold of 100,000 COVID deaths in late May, it cannot be entirely happenstance that the protests took off as they did. Magnified by that grim statistic, the Trump administration's clear indifference to the racial disparities of the pandemic surely played a part in driving people to the streets.

Those events came too late for us to commission a story explicitly looking at racial justice. But we were able to touch on the topic by including an interview, "A Veil Was Broken," with Ytasha Womack, one of the leading experts on Afrofuturism, about the potential science fiction has to reshape cultural assumptions and the increasingly diverse range of writers who now form part of the contemporary canon. The interviewer is Wade Roush, who edited a previous edition of *Twelve Tomorrows*.

In mid-March, just as the lockdowns in the United States were beginning, I wrote an article in *MIT Technology Review* titled "We're not going back to normal." It argued that not only would the pandemic last much longer than most people at that point realized, but also that even after it was over, some of our social norms and structures would be permanently changed. At the time, some readers criticized me for fearmongering. Within a few weeks, the piece seemed prescient. Now it seems blindingly obvious. All the stories in this collection predict that the future will be very far from "normal," but that the new normal, though forged in pain and suffering, could be a healthier, more robust, and in some ways more creative society. May you enjoy them and take some solace from them in these dark times—if, that is, the times are still dark when you read this, which I sincerely hope they won't be.

1 "A VEIL WAS BROKEN": AFROFUTURIST YTASHA L. WOMACK ON THE WORK OF SCIENCE FICTION IN THE 2020s

Wade Roush

ONE TASK OF SCIENCE FICTION IS TO KNOCK US OFF-KILTER—TO TRANSPORT US TO altered times and places, the better to question our own world. But sci-fi has renewed competition in that department from reality itself. The quickening storm of events in America in the last half-decade, culminating in 2020 in the COVID-19 pandemic, the uprisings against systemic racism, and (as I write this) the strangest and most divisive presidential election in memory, has unmoored us from old norms and expectations with a suddenness that societies witness perhaps once or twice per century. The future is upon us in its full uncontrolled ferocity, and it takes all our resilience just to adapt from week to week and keep steering toward hope.

But at least one movement within sci-fi may be equal to this moment, in part because it grows out of a history of displacement, atrocity, and instability. It's Afrofuturism, the effort to explore technological and social change from the point of view of people of African descent and members of the African diaspora.

Ytasha L. Womack, a Chicago-based author, filmmaker, scholar, and dance therapist, helped explain and popularize the genre in her widely cited 2013 volume *Afrofuturism: The World of Black Sci Fi & Fantasy Culture*. And she explores and expands it in her own fiction, including the "Rayla Universe" series, about a resistance fighter on a future Earth colony that's fallen into dictatorship. She is a former reporter for the *Chicago Defender*, the nation's oldest Black-owned daily newspaper, and in 2010, she wrote *Post Black*, which celebrated the huge range of African American cultural, social, and political identities overlooked by mainstream media portrayals.

In an email interview in late July 2020, Womack told me she believes the year's tumultuous events are finally awakening white Americans to the ways they consciously or inadvertently contribute to the invented hierarchies that overlook or oppress people of color. In one sense, therefore, the pandemic, the resulting economic upheaval, and the explosion of resistance to violence by the state against private citizens are more material for the kinds of social change that Black people have struggled to promote for centuries. And from this larger perspective, Womack says, Afrofuturism is simply one modern manifestation of the age-old "resilience tools" that help Black communities enact and navigate that change.

WR: It's been five months since the coronavirus pandemic exploded in the United States, and two months since police murdered George Floyd in Minneapolis, and I think it's fair to say these are difficult times. So I wanted to ask first: how have you been coping with 2020?

YW: 2020 has been revelatory, insightful, and I found myself thinking on resilience, particularly in the content of Afrofuturism. In December 2019, I had the deep urge to complete the draft of a graphic novel I was writing before March 2020. I had the very strong feeling that spring 2020 would be fluid. I had a lot of speaking engagement requests for that period and some other possible work, and I just felt like I had to finish this first draft of *Blak Kube*, my story about Egyptian gods and creativity, before March or else. I wasn't aware that this ethereal nudging was speaking to a greater societal shift.

Nevertheless, the day I finished the draft was the same day I led a live dance and music improvisation experience at the Adler Planetarium to bring the *Rayla 2212* utopia to life for "A Night in the Afrofuture." I coordinated freestyle interplay between DJ/sound healer Shannon Harris; Leon Q, my cousin and a trumpet player; Kenneth "Djedi" Russell, a tap and West African dancer; Discopoet Khari B, a poet and a house music dancer; another conga player; and myself. I was a space dance conductor of sorts and we did these interactive shows utilizing call and response dance with an unsuspecting audience in a 360-degree visual dome usually reserved for sky shows. I led audiences in dance movement with an array of Afrobeat, Chicago house, samba, and South African house music as our music of the new utopia.

The event felt like a vortex of energy. I like using music and dance to create multidimensional spaces as a metaphor for exploring both inner and outer space. African/African diasporic dance at its core has functioned as interdimensional. People were so happy. It felt like the beginning of one thing and the end of something else.

The following morning I flew to Atlanta to speak at Planet Deep South, a conference on Afrofuturism. The conference is designed to highlight southern voices and works in Afrofuturism. The conference took place at the Atlanta University Center, an amalgamation of historically Black colleges. I'm a Clark Atlanta University alumna and my initial experiences with Afrofuturism took place on that campus. The conference was organized by Dr. Rico Wade and Clinton Fluker. I gave a keynote speech on Afrofuturism literally at noon the day after the "Night in the Afrofuture." Ruha Benjamin spoke that evening on discrimination in computer applications and algorithms.

Dr. Wade gave me a tour of the rampant gentrification in Atlanta. Within two or three days I was in New York City for an event for Kehinde Wiley. As soon as I landed I learned the event was canceled. The next few days, I was in New York going to the Brooklyn Museum for Kehinde's show with my friend Ravi. Talk of the virus was mounting. Then South by Southwest was canceled and it felt as if a door was shutting and I had to slide through a window of time to get back home.

Three days later, I was back home in Chicago buying bags of nonperishable groceries, reading how to survive the apocalypse guides, and hunkering down for the Illinois stay-at-home order that was in effect. Somewhere in those moments before lockdown, I remember being in a health food store with mostly African American patrons. People were stocking up on garlic, ginger, echinacea, and every herb or vitamin people knew of to build their immune systems. People were walking around with lists of supplements and teas that family members gave them to buy. In that moment, I grew angry.

Simultaneously, my stepdad was trying to schedule appointments with his doctor. He believed he had the virus. His physician wouldn't see him. When he went to [the] emergency [room], he was told he had acid reflux. In order to get a COVID-19 test in the early weeks, one had to have a letter from their physician. We tried to get other physicians to meet with him. None returned calls. By the time we got him to a clinic with a physician who would give him a test, he had to be rushed to the hospital and placed on a ventilator immediately. My mother had to go into self-quarantine. We couldn't see my stepdad. I was quarantined because I spent time with both in the previous day. For the next two days, I'm reading nothing but news from futurists posting dire scientific information for the world. During the period I'm thinking, outside of the information that's recommending masks and cleaning processes, where are the tools of resilience?

Where is the inspiration to keep one fed and their soul enriched during tough times? I literally found myself thinking on spirituality, food, family. Who are the people I talk to to keep my consciousness vibrating highly? What music has the ideal lyrics and frequencies to keep me uplifted? What combinations of food are best to enhance my immune system? What candles do I light? What scents and colors keep me feeling vibrant? How do you hold a healing consciousness for others? What dances keep me refreshed? Am I engaging with nature enough? I was so thankful for all the people who wrote books, created music, and made movies in the past that I could engage in during that bizarre period. I was so thankful for deejays like DJ D-Nice, Questlove, and others who claimed the role of the deejay as a musical shaman.

Within two weeks my stepdad was off the ventilator and back home. The experience was a miracle and I had a very transformative experience putting to practice basics around spiritual grounding, food, and consciousness. The following week, at my brother's urging, I started a weekly Instagram Live called *Utopia Talks*.

These epiphanies were, literally, my month of March. When the atrocities with George Floyd, Ahmaud Arbery, and later Rayshard Brooks took place I had a conscious awareness of tools to work with around resilience. I had an uncle who was murdered by a police officer in New Orleans in the 1970s before I was born, so my family has created practices of remembrance and healing around such atrocities. I spent a great deal of time in May and June devoted to a daily processing of the politicization of the daily shifts, some of which were in line with incidents of the past, others of which were not.

3

So many of the core issues go back to our nation's Civil War and the creation of the Constitution itself. I found myself doing a lot of ad hoc history lessons. I had several conversations with friends about how the Founding Fathers were quite comfortable with the institution of slavery when they were creating the Constitution. There were a number of people quite uncomfortable with its end and not supportive of the protests for civil rights that followed or the BLM [Black Lives Matter] protests today.

Nevertheless, it became overwhelmingly obvious that many Americans in the midst of the BLM protests just didn't know history. Many were clueless around the history of Africans in the Americas in a way that was shocking. The Iroquois Nation was heavily borrowed from in the creation of the US Constitution but you almost have to be in a graduate-level history course to know that. Unless you're a history major in a school that values diversity or a life-long reader on a quest, one can completely miss the basics, and become quite defensive about it. Then you have others who present history in this bizarre propagandized fashion that has people ready to fight you when you tell them it's not true.

For many, pop culture is the lens for understanding history, which means that Black history for much of the populace hinges on the rise of a new music subgenre created by Black people or an unknown moment like [the] Tulsa massacre referenced in a popular television show like *Watchmen*. Fortunately, the Internet is a great source to get the basics if you can follow the social media bread crumbs that led you there. Many people are looking for references for books, films, and documentaries to get some framing for what's going on. I started doing history lessons on my *Utopia Talks* because you can't talk about futures without knowing histories, which were futures for their predecessors. However, in Afrofuturism, time is treated as nonlinear, so it becomes a healthy way to explore histories, futures, and resilience.

Nevertheless, I've had daily conversations around everything from the philosophy behind the politicization of masks to Indigenous frameworks to marketing pivots to mass manipulation to Maroon societies of Africans in the enslaved Americas. In some ways, this period was about processing everything you'd ever learned, reassessing philosophical frameworks, and getting grounded in what's important.

That said, I've become vegan for the season. Between work, Zoom birthday parties, and virtual lectures, I've developed quite a few story ideas. I completed my graphic novel *Blak Kube* for Megascope. I did the edits in June 2020, miraculously. When June was over so much had happened from protests to looting to Juneteenth to virus surges nationwide, I couldn't believe it all happened in four weeks. I've been watching a lot of Korean cinema with my best friend and making an unusual amount of soups with garlic and ginger. I just learned that the current president is sending troops to my city. I prayed about it and I'm fine.

WR: You're both a practitioner of science fiction and futurism, in the form of works like the *Rayla 2212* books and your *Bar Star City* film project, and a chronicler of the field through your groundbreaking survey *Afrofuturism.* In your mind, what good can sci-fi and futurism do for readers and audiences in the here and now? And do these forms of expression take on a different importance in times of crisis?

YW: I would like to see more visions that reflect what a healthy society looks like. I would love to see more schools of thought around healthy futures that were created as worlds that people can read [about] in a book or watch in a film. Healthy societies can have issues, conflict, and all the drama required of a story. I'd like to see more that reflects a kind of world we'd like to live in. I'd like to read a sci-fi story and say, "Gee, I'd like to live there. This place seems like it treats people fairly or at least values doing so." I'd like to see more stories where resilience tools from the past are put to use. Obviously, there's sci-fi that does this, but I'd like to see more. Perhaps that's why I write in the genre, as a way of problem-solving futures, or as Toni Morrison said, to write stories you'd like to read.

I understand that a world moving through or in a dystopia makes the hero's journey a fundamentally high-stakes one. I think many creators are more inclined use history to frame their dystopias than to frame utopias or protopias. But for many, writing in a dystopia is a form of problem-solving, and for others it's a release valve.

WR: **COVID-19 deaths among African Americans have been two to three times higher than what you would expect based on their share of the US population. It's not as if the SARS-CoV-2 virus has *revealed* disparities in healthcare and health outcomes; rather, it's exploiting this longstanding form of injustice and making it worse. Can sci-fi writers and other artists and creators do anything to help call attention to this nightmare?**

YW: I don't know if they need to call attention to it. The news, the protests, the outrage, and the data are doing a great job of exposure. If someone doesn't feel a gut reaction to at least say, "I don't want this in our society," then it's not a question of exposure to information, it's a question of empathy. It's a question of, well, if you're not Black, Latino, a front-line worker, living in a nursing home, or a crowded city, why should you care? It's a question of why should I wear a mask to protect someone else? It's a question of why are so many in our society quick to otherize people as if we aren't connected? This is beyond individualism. Is it mass narcissism? In that respect, sci-fi does write about otherism and how it functions using both the alien and cyborg metaphors. I would love to read more sci-fi that demonstrates how we are all connected. I would like more stories on protopias or with idealized societies in the backdrop. We need more visions of the future that aren't so reliant on technological innovations but also reevaluate human organizing systems and the philosophies that undergird our world.

WR: **When you published *Afrofuturism* back in 2013, part of what made the field so exciting was that, as you wrote, it "combines elements of science fiction, historical fiction, speculative fiction, fantasy, Afrocentricity, and magic realism with non-Western beliefs," often in the service of a message of self-determination. But 2013 already feels like a different era, when we'd somehow leapt into the future by electing and reelecting an African American president. It turned out we had no idea what challenges were coming, all building up to the traumas of 2020. Do you feel like current events are changing the conditions under which Afrofuturist work gets produced?**

YW: Afrofuturism existed long before the term was created and will exist beyond this period. I don't see the times as dictating its necessity. People of African descent and the African diaspora will have a relationship with the future, space, and time and will pull from culture, experiences, and the resilience tools to navigate it in part because that's what humans do.

WR: Has it become harder to sustain the genre's trademark mix of "imagination, technology, the future, and liberation," as you described it in the book?

YW: Black people don't have the luxury of abandoning hope and dreams because of shifts in politics. W. E. B Dubois wrote the sci-fi story *The Comet* in the 1920s, and while there was a literary cultural renaissance afoot, I wouldn't call that the best of times for Black Americans. Ezekiel's wheel as a spaceship reference was in Black spirituals during enslavement. People looked to hope because they had to. Sojourner Truth in the early 1880s said she's "going home like a shooting star." When François Mackandal led a six-year rebellion of self-emancipated Maroons against plantation owners in Haiti in 1752, nearly forty years before the Haitian Revolution, people claimed that during his capture he turned into an animal and flew away.

Many African cosmologies from the Dagara to the Yoruba are inherently interdimensional, as evident in the symbolism of the art and architecture. The narrative of hope that often threads the tougher times is about moving forward. That said, I think Afrofuturism, the term itself, was popularized during Barack Obama's presidency in part because it gave some people context for him existing. Shortly before his presidency the idea of a man of African descent being president of the United States for too many felt like some distant utopia or creative science fiction. To paraphrase a quote in Afrofuturism by longtime activist Jesse Jackson, Sr., you can't move forward with cynicism. That said, there's a big demand for more stories and works by Afrofuturist creators.

WR: From your standpoint, is it getting any easier over time for people of color and LGBTQ voices to find an audience and make a living in sci-fi? And under sci-fi, let's count TV, movies, books, comics, music, and all the forms through which the future is explored. Is the publishing and editing establishment in sci-fi becoming any less white and less male?

YW: There's definitely a greater interest in diverse stories because the audience of sci-fi lovers are demanding it. People want to see stories that provide other insights into the human experience and the realm of the imagination. Independent creators on both the comics and literary side have been self-publishing works with diverse voices consistently to new audiences for the past decade or so. Publishers are responding to that demand.

WR: I'm a Marvel fan, so I have to ask you a question about *Black Panther* (2018), which had a Black director and a nearly all-Black cast and introduced mainstream audiences to Afrofuturism in spectacular and dazzling fashion. Has *Black Panther* made it easier to explain what Afrofuturism is?

YW: The success of *Black Panther* has made life easier for Black sci-fi creators. It was a gamechanger and gave everyone's work a bump up. All these creators who were viewed as niche or fringe were suddenly at the center of this fascinating conversation around "Afrofuturism." Creators could make very edgy experimental music, like composers Nicole Mitchell, Moor Mother, or Angel Bat Dawid, and could flourish in new ways because new audiences had a way to frame their work. Visual artists, writers, and theorists suddenly had a larger world to play in with their works.

WR: Do you ever worry that in the hands of a giant media conglomerate like Marvel/Disney, Afrofuturism might become *too* mainstream and begin to shed its more radical or leftist elements?

YW: We'll see more mainstream works utilizing Afrofuturist ideas and creatives. There will be more people with a desire to create pulling from ideas in that arena. We've seen that in the past two years with both Marvel and DC. Whether people are doing work with large corporations or independently, both scenes ultimately complement one another. Black people will have a relationship to space, time, and the future regardless. Every Afrofuturist story isn't *Black Panther* and I don't think people expect it to be.

WR: Outside the United States, which regions and communities are producing the most notable and exciting science fiction? Are there any international sci-fi authors or books you're enjoying right now?

YW: Brazil has a robust Afrofuturismo scene of theory and works. There's a book called *Afrofuturismo* written in Portuguese that I've just ordered. I'll have to translate it via Google until an English edition comes out. I spoke at a virtual conference of Brazilian Afrofuturists recently and I'm really excited by the depth of their work. Jelani Nias of Toronto, Canada, has a cool book called *Where Eagles Crawl and Men Fly*. Toronto has a robust scene and is home to the annual art show *Black Future Month* curated by Danilo McCallum and Quentin Vercetty. It's also home to A Different Bookstore which has a great Black sci-fi and fantasy selection.

　　Afro SF: Science Fiction by African Writers edited by Ivor W. Hartmann is a good anthology. The book came out a few years ago and has a wide range of works from authors across the African continent, including Nigerian American Nnedi Okorafor. I've seen some great Afrofuturist short films and features from African creators from Kenya, Nigeria, and Cameroon. I've had some great conversations about dance theory as Afrofuturism with dancers from Ivory Coast, Senegal, and Cuba. The ideas in Afrofuturism are fairly understood within the African continent/diaspora, it's just a question of whether people utilize the term to frame their works or not. In many parts of the world, the United States included, many within the diaspora just see what we're calling Afrofuturism as life.

WR: Is Afrofuturism a potential template for other culturally inflected futurisms—say, Latinofuturism or Sinofuturism?

YW: I don't want to say it's a template. People all over the world have relationships to space, time, and the future with a unique cultural lens. However, the term has created ways to narrow the focus on literary works, music, and more from specific cultures. I think it's given rise to conversations on the shared aesthetic and philosophical thought within other cultural lenses. It's pretty exciting. Within African/African diasporic communities, the term "Afrofuturism" helped people to anchor and frame the works they were creating or ideas they were tossing about. I think terms like "Indigenous Futurism" and others are doing the same for Indigenous creators and helping audiences to find them.

WR: George Floyd's killing became the tipping point in a national movement for police reform and seems to have led to a recognition that in this country, racism and policing are two sides of the same coin. Can Afrofuturism or other forms of sci-fi help us imagine a world where policing isn't necessary, where mass incarceration is a thing of the past, or where the law is finally enforced equally without regard to skin color?

YW: Yes.

WR: In *Afrofuturism*, you quote activist Adrienne Maree Brown, who says abandoned urban communities like her home town of Detroit or post-Katrina New Orleans can feel like the post-apocalyptic places we see in sci-fi. But she adds that if you look deeper, you see how communities are rebuilding from within. She writes, "It's not the end of the world, it's the beginning of something else." At the risk of sounding like a Pollyanna—since there's nothing redeeming about a pandemic, or police killings—I wanted to ask whether you think there's a prospect that the traumatic events of 2020 will challenge American communities to find creative ways to repair inequality, rebuild the healthcare and public health infrastructures, and end racism once and for all?

YW: To quote goddess practitioner Lettie Sullivan, a veil was broken during this period. Many have awakened to the fact that there are grave disparities and that they could consciously or inadvertently be contributing to [them]. In a very real way, people are thinking on how they are contributing to systems with hierarchies that kill people or complicate their lives. The widespread protests and the demands for more books to give historical framing around how we got here are all a part of that.

One lesson from COVID-19 is that yes, there are racial disparities in treatment and stress. However, walls, gentrified neighborhoods, and gated communities can't protect people from a virus. It's literally our ability to care for other people by wearing a mask that protects us all. The same can be said about racism. No one, in the end, benefits. Minneapolis is not a highly diverse city, and this mostly white city was in the midst of protests, fires, looting, and police attacks when people challenged the murder of a Black man by police officers. Who benefits from that?

A white, Midwestern science fiction professor told me once that he prided himself on going to the best schools, reading the best books, and later in his adult years stumbled across Octavia E. Butler. He fell in love with her works and was disgusted that he'd never heard of her before. Why hadn't he studied her in his classes coming up? Why was she not mentioned as one of the greatest writers of his time in his literature classes? He literally said that all this time he thought he'd been to the best schools and was introduced to the best writers only to discover that there was a whole world of amazing Black creatives alive during his lifetime from the same country he's come from that he'd never heard of. Were these schools the best? Did he receive a good education? He can't even call himself well read due to racism, and this is just the tip of the iceberg.

Frantz Fanon said that racism didn't benefit the victim, perpetuators, or those who found themselves complicit in it all. Martin Luther King, Jr. said that injustice anywhere is injustice everywhere. Why? Because we're all human beings living on a shared planet. Yes, this is a moment to create or enhance our systems so that they care about the well-being of people. It's an opportunity to center humanity and the planet.

Yet, I do see people caring for one another. There's an abundance of "neighborliness." I had three neighbors pass away during this period. After one neighbor's funeral, the procession of cars came to my block. The cars were led by a purple and gold carriage carrying the body. Yes, I wrote that correctly. A carriage. A fairytale Cinderella-style carriage with gold trim. A minister on a remote microphone asked if any neighbors wanted to say a few words. Some said prayers. One guy came to the mike and gave this rousing inspirational prayer for the block, all followed by a balloon launch. Over a hundred balloons were sent into the sky in honor of this man who most in our society would describe as ordinary. Despite this, he made an impact. Here we were, literally two days after the first wave of protests and looting, and we're doing a balloon launch. People who didn't even know the guy were participating in this shared respect for life. This moment of humanity was heartwarming. We did this as a celebration of life. We did this as a recognition of a new ancestor. But the collective acknowledgment of life elevated us all. We, as a block, were all uplifted. In that moment, I said, "We're going to be okay."

2 LITTLE KOWLOON

Adrian Hon

I WAS TWELVE YEARS OLD WHEN I LIVED THROUGH MY FIRST PANDEMIC. THE RULES were exciting at the start, like a new game to be navigated. No touching the mail, wearing home-made masks like bandits, assembling miniature mountains of rice and flour in the cupboards. But the weeks and months dragged on, and I got headaches staring at my friends through the cracked screen of a tablet. I'd cry with boredom during our walks to the same park and along the same roped-off playground every day.

My boredom was accented with the fear of being near others. My brother had asthma and my mum didn't want to take any risks. "If they get close enough, you lose a point," she said. That kind of game wasn't as fun to play. For one thing, she never told us what would happen if we ran out of our unspecified points, although my brother and I agreed we would probably die.

Some called it a dance. Even as a child, this struck me as yet another cheerful evasion, one of those romantic lies adults tell children and themselves to elide the awfulness of our new reality. A dance should be joyful, something entered into voluntarily, not forced upon you.

Most dances have rules. This dance had only one.

THE EDINBURGH FESTIVAL STUBBORNLY REFUSED TO BE POSTPONED OR CANCELED. It was all my friends could talk about during those early months of the second pandemic, barely a decade from the first. No one understood how the festival planned to safely corral thousands of visitors without breaking the law, but damn it all—they promised the show would go on.

"That means it's in VR. And if the festival's in VR, it'll be shite. As if they can compete against Epic and Disney," said Cindy, warming up a safe two meters away. We were in Holyrood Park for our daily exercise appointment under the crags encircling Arthur's Seat. Cindy had joined North Point the same year as me, which meant we'd been furloughed at the same time. Even though the company worked its artists hard, the job was nothing compared to the twelve-hour days she'd once pulled in Hong Kong.

But if work was a cakewalk for Cindy, furlough was heaven. She had dug up the garden in front of her flat, excited about swapping herbs and vegetables with the rest of Little Kowloon. She was determined to make the very most of her enforced holiday. In comparison, I'd been playing games and watching TV all day, every day. The closest I'd gotten to being productive was starting an augmented reality course in learning Cantonese.

I was stuck in a loop, reliving the worst year of my childhood. I hated having no control over my life, hated not knowing what would happen tomorrow. I was a planner and now nothing could be planned. Rationally, I knew H1N3 wasn't COVID-19 again, but the lockdown felt the same.

"It won't be in VR," I said. "I saw Reuben's name on the festival organizing committee. They wouldn't bring him on board for something completely digital." As I jogged backward, my glasses gave off a low warning buzz to remind me there was a runner approaching.

Cindy slung an easy pitch at me, the augmented reality ball catching fire moments before I switched to a catcher's mitt. I peered down the line in my glasses and flung the ball back.

"No one gets around the lockdown, not even the festival," shouted Cindy. "I'm calling Reuben."

I sighed as I saw Reuben Leung's avatar appear between us. I'd never gotten along with posh kids, especially ones educated at boarding schools like Fettes. Rumor was that he was close with Scotland's "first daughter." That would've been before he was suspended for vandalism and sent to Cindy's school in Kowloon as punishment, before they both became involved in the Umbrella Movement.

Cindy demanded, "Is it true?"

"Yes, it's true," replied Reuben. "Some of us have to work for a living."

"About the festival," I snapped.

"The big announcement is tomorrow, so I trust you two will keep this to yourselves." I rolled my eyes. "But yes. We just agreed it with the government. The festival will go ahead in augmented reality. Nothing to touch, nothing for the virus to be transmitted on."

"Sounds boring. And they don't know anything about AR," said Cindy.

"We don't have to. We're setting up marquees for the most important theaters and troupes and groups, and they can stage whatever they want, as long as they do it safely. There'll be one here, a few in the Meadows, a couple in Inverleith, one each in the Botanics and Princess Street gardens, the usual places. Six weeks to prepare, four weeks open to the public."

"PR bullshit!" said Cindy. "As if people will buy tickets to walk through an empty tent."

Reuben laughed. "We got the Treasury to pay for everything, through the business continuity scheme. All the tickets will be free. Yes, it's PR. What's wrong with that? This country is built on tourism, and we're putting on a show so people will remember to come back next year."

"Spoken like a true politician. Who decides which groups get to use which marquees?" I asked.

"Oh, I can guess," said Cindy.

"It'll all be announced tomorrow," replied Reuben. "But I made sure there'll be a Hong Kong marquee. Cindy, Elaine, you should volunteer."

"Mmm hmm," Cindy said, skeptically.

"They'll need people who know AR, not a bunch of old folk with too much time. I don't need to tell you how important this could be for Little Kowloon. For the whole diaspora, actually. We need to show we're fitting in," he said, before vanishing.

THREE YEARS BEFORE H1N3, MILLIONS OF HONGKONGERS LEFT THEIR HOMES forever. Having lost their struggle for self-governance, having being spurned by an America in turmoil, they'd been granted a pathway to citizenship in Australia, New Zealand, Canada, the UK—and in the newly independent Scotland.

I was at the airport to meet the first arrivals, press drones buzzing about in agitation. Of course, there were bagpipers. I explained over and over, no, I wasn't from Hong Kong, I was born in Inverness, but yes, my parents are from Hong Kong. Thank you, my accent is lovely, isn't it?

Then the gates opened, a stream of tired and elated and anxious and scared faces coming without end, as if a portal between our cities had opened rather than a 787 touching down every thirty minutes.

They bunched up in the arrivals hall, accepting their welcome boxes, posing for photos, registering with volunteers, taking interviews, waiting for their trams and buses. I spotted Cindy's family, friends of my mum from high school, and threw thick coats around their shoulders. It's colder than you think, I laughed. You're staying in Leith? That's near me, we'll be neighbors! We teetered between mania and trepidation. I wondered when someone would start crying. No one could tell if this was too much, too soon.

The bagpipers paused, catching their breath. The energy seemed to evaporate into the dry, cold air. Maybe this was a mistake. Maybe it was all too little, too late.

"Heung gong yan, ga yau!" shouted a young man.

"'Su ge lan yan, ga yau!' Hongkongers, add oil! Scots, add oil!" I explained to the confused Scottish staff. Add oil—it means "go for it!" Or maybe, keep going.

So maybe it would work after all. It'd better, with a quarter of a million more Hongkongers on their way.

I WAS A LITTLE NERVOUS WHEN WE VOLUNTEERED FOR THE HONG KONG TEAM. Technically, it was the "Little Kowloon Cultural Delegation," but everyone called them Hong Kong, much to the Chinese ambassador's irritation. When I confessed this to Cindy, she told me to stop being ridiculous and no one cared where I was born. We were hoping our gaming experience would earn us accordingly important positions, but we were firmly told those roles were filled. We were welcome to apply for the logistics crew, though. I was about to send an indignant reply when I saw who'd sent the email: Celia Chan.

I spotted her the next day, when the thirty-strong Hong Kong team gathered in their marquee in the Meadows, erected overnight by PPE-swathed builders directing a fleet of construction drones. The technical specifications showed every marquee as identical: ten meters wide, thirty meters long, and a generous three meters tall. Festival teams were permitted to modify the interiors as they wished, within a set budget and adhering to strict health and safety guidelines.

The festival's level playing field, an artefact of funding and pandemic regulations, led to unsavory talk of an "Arts Olympics." Most teams publicly rejected the comparison, but Cindy wasn't alone in joining the social media smack talk about who would get the biggest audiences and best reviews. The fact that audience numbers were being reported in real-time, as per health regulations, heightened the sense of competition.

Awaiting Celia Chan, we shuffled into a circle in the center of the marquee, gingerly testing how closely the social distancing software in our glasses would let us get to each other. Light streamed in through transparent panels in the ceiling, with a brisk breeze flowing through vents. Someone had set up high-resolution atmospheric sensors inside, feeding data to the physical distancing protocols on our glasses. As the wind dipped and rose, our circle expanded and contracted, a living, breathing diagram of viral transmission risk.

Scotland had been spared the worst of H1N3. After COVID-19, the public backed a swift and complete lockdown: security cordons across the border at Berwick, rapid antibody testing at the airports, overwatch and intervention drones to enforce physical distancing in Edinburgh, Glasgow, Inverness, and Aberdeen.

The Hongkongers, some of whom had landed only weeks earlier, handled the pandemic with grim determination. What were a few months of wearing face shields after years of struggle? They ignored the Scots grumbling about hospital beds being taken up, about the virus breeding in the cramped temporary accommodations of Little Kowloon. They shrugged off the rumors and leapt into the fight with the gusto of the newly converted, volunteering in their thousands as doctors and nurses and social workers. One group of students even helped set up the country's biggest mask-producing factory.

But there was a worry in Little Kowloon that they were being a little too exceptional. The problem with being a model minority is that you're still a minority. How, then, to be more normal, they wondered? How to become Scots as well as Hongkongers?

The Edinburgh Festival was the opportunity: the jewel in Scotland's cultural crown, the world's biggest arts event, somewhere Little Kowloon could contribute and distinguish itself. Among us, I spotted Doug Yau, an acerbic standup comedian with millions of followers; Tricia Lee, the hotshot architect named as the next Hadid; Chen Xi, darling of the Venice Biennale for his living sculptures; and Angela Cheng, whose latest play had been booked for Broadway. I was surprised to see them here rather than in the warmer diaspora destinations like Australia. Someone had twisted a lot of arms to assemble this artistic dream team.

Celia Chan finally arrived and clapped her hands. "Thank you all for volunteering your time for Team Hong Kong. I realize you all have other priorities in combatting H1N3 and helping our community become established in Scotland, but we shouldn't treat this opportunity lightly."

She turned slowly as she spoke. "We cannot be complacent just because we've been welcomed here in Scotland. We aren't citizens yet"—I looked away, feeling out of place—"so we need to prove our worth, and remind our hosts and the whole world who we are." Chan was an odd choice to be kicking off proceedings. She was one of Hong Kong's most famous names and a programming genius, but not the type to be working at the festival.

I wasn't used to this kind of tub-thumping speech from her, and neither was anyone else, judging by their rapt attention. "Let me cut to the chase. I'm not an artist. I can't claim the faintest experience in staging a play or doing standup or, I don't know, anything to do with dance. What I do know is how to develop technology that can give others an advantage." Everyone knew what she was talking about: Chan was the technical lead for the Diaspora Project that helped millions of Hongkongers emigrate safely with their physical, digital, and financial assets intact.

Tricia Lee stepped forward, an unmissable presence in her trademark black jumpsuit. "After I first learned about the new festival format, I reached out to Celia. We've been working together on a new dynamic distancing protocol, developed with the Public Health group at the university. We're going to adapt it so we can host the largest audience in the festival, but still give them more intimate experiences than any other team."

"What's dynamic distancing?" Cindy asked, messaging through her glasses.

I sent her a video I'd unearthed. The idea was that you could reduce the safe distancing requirements for respiratory diseases to a fraction of the usual two meters by predicting the exact movements of respiratory droplets that might carry the H1N3 virus. We were already using a crude form in the marquee by accounting for wind, but true dynamic distancing would allow people to get within centimeters of each other—especially if it adjusted for masks and face shields, speech patterns, sneezes, and everything and anything else that could affect droplet spread. The concept had been floating around ever since COVID-19, more as a thought experiment than a practical technique. The sensors weren't good enough back then, and even now, the computational requirements were scarily expensive.

As Chan described the technical details, my mind wandered. I didn't need glasses to imagine how she could fill the marquee. Dynamic distancing coupled with augmented reality would let us route audience members right next to each other. There'd be no flashing alerts or social distancing walls—if one person ventured too near another, the performance they were watching could adapt to pull their attention and control their movements, but otherwise they'd have the freedom to walk wherever they liked. The new protocol promised a lockdown experience like no other.

"Other teams will use the same old social distancing protocols that make it feel like you're queuing at a theme park," said Chan, summing up.

"But here, you won't have to. Here, our artists won't have to compromise. Here, it will be as if there were no virus."

"The audience won't forget that," Tricia added. "We talk about how the Hong Kong diaspora needs soft power to survive. This is what we're talking about."

Fierce nods and proud smiles all around. I raised my hand gingerly. Tricia frowned at me, her glasses no doubt itemizing my insignificance. "Um, as I understand it, the computational expense required for dynamic distancing rises exponentially with every additional agent. At least, that's what Disney's research group found."

Chan nodded briskly. "I've read Mathy's paper. It's good. But there's a way to scale the expense linearly. You can simplify the problem using moving cells, so you don't need to model the particulate spread across the entire space. It only works in smaller controlled environments like this one, which is why it doesn't work in a theme park. It's not impossible, but it's very, very hard."

"We can do 'very, very hard,'" said Tricia.

"I'm told China is sponsoring a venue," said Chen Xi, the elderly living sculpture artist. "Ours will be better."

CINDY JUMPED BACKWARD AS BOULDERS ABRUPTLY TUMBLED DOWN THE ESCARPMENT toward her, almost losing her balance. "Whoa!" she laughed, taking off her glasses.

"You don't think it's too sudden?" I asked.

"I thought that was the point?"

I sighed. To make dynamic distancing work, we needed the ability to trigger the audience to move at a moment's notice, but not at the risk of injury. Cindy flopped onto the marquee floor, grinning. One of the logistics volunteers looked down from his ladder and shook his head in mock disgust. They'd been working for days on end painstakingly stitching AR localizers and laser arrays into the ceiling, and Cindy had gotten the day off to help me test the system. I was glad she was enjoying herself, but I'd already logged a dozen bugs and was dreading what the afternoon would bring.

As amazing as Chan's technology was, wrangling the artists' work into a format that would play nicely with it was proving almost impossible. Half hadn't worked in AR before and the other half didn't welcome being dictated to by me, a mere technician whose mysterious elevation they'd witnessed just a month ago. Barely a day after I'd questioned Chan's approach, she'd taken me aside, peppered me with probing questions on my games programming experience, and unceremoniously announced my promotion to "Technical Liaison" between the artists and her tech team.

I was exhausted. My throat ached from explaining why they needed to design triggers that the dynamic distancing protocol could invoke to move audiences around, and my head ached from doing this as diplomatically as I could manage.

"Your land sculpture is sensational, it's so evocative of the chaotic climate that our old and new homes share," I'd said to an impassive Chen Xi. "I realize it's inconvenient to add trigger elements for the marquee, but I think they could complement or even enhance your work."

"What would you suggest?" he asked.

"We could add weather effects. Rain clouds and thunderstorms could steer people along a path."

He nodded. "My granddaughter told me about such a thing she'd seen in Hong Kong. She enjoyed it greatly." I smiled encouragingly. "It was at Disneyland."

"Well . . . that's just one example. We could try something else. Perhaps a wave of—"

"I understand what you need," he said. "You need to move people. Leave it with me."

The escarpment with its falling boulders was what Xi's team sent. On first glance, it was perfect, an organic part of his land sculpture, its programming fully synced with Chan's dynamic distancing protocol.

But it was all too dramatic. After a few of these surprises, the audience would figure out how they were being herded between artworks. Doug Yau's standup set had Cindy and me in stitches but the dynamic distancing trigger was literally him yelling at us to get out. Not the most subtle of transitions.

As I tweaked the parameters on the escarpment and ran Cindy through another simulated AR crowd, Chan's avatar appeared. "These things you're filing aren't blockers for opening," she said.

Despite having worked with Chan for a month now, her interruptions still flustered me. "I understand that, but Xi's team don't understand how triggers are meant to—"

"Fine. Harden the barrier around Xi for now. You need to start testing the other artists." Her avatar blinked away before I could even nod. When we couldn't figure out how to smoothly move audiences from one area to another, we'd resorted to creating virtual barriers around artists. It was a hack that eliminated agency, but it was better than having no art at all. When the barriers were turned on, we'd give people a tasteful but unmistakable AR icon to move on every few minutes rather than expecting them to follow a confusing AR butterfly from Angela Cheng's play.

I pulled Cindy up from the floor and led her to Anna Hui's area. I hadn't spotted her at our team meetings, but her short festival bio said she'd performed in the Hong Kong Ballet for a few years, after which she started her own private artistic practice. Cindy slipped on her glasses, joining me back in the marquee's AR testing layer. Two motionless wireframe humans appeared next to the two of us.

"Is this it?" said Cindy.

I swiped through the testing interface to see if I'd missed a startup command. "It's meant to launch automatically. I guess Anna forgot to set that flag," I said.

"Look!" Cindy pointed at the wireframe next to me, which was mimicking my swipes. Her own wireframe raised its arm toward me a second later.

We waved our arms and shuffled about, watching the wireframes as they followed us. They weren't echoing our movements perfectly—that would be boring, I realised. I started walking around, trying to figure out the trick. My wireframe kept up, drifting ever closer until it settled over me like a second skin.

As I paused, the wireframe subtly pulled from me, its mesh drifting a few centimeters away from my right side. I unconsciously followed it, not precisely—I wasn't a dancer—and caught myself. Did I really want to be a puppet? I stopped, and it stopped with me. I slowly pivoted on my left foot, an inelegant turn, and the mesh came with me, but in a cleaner swoop with a graceful follow-through. I was in control.

I glanced at Cindy, who was circling toward me. I couldn't see her wireframe anymore, but I followed mine, or it followed me, as I circled toward her. I flushed as we spiraled together, approaching two meters, beyond two meters, almost at one meter.

And in an almost-frozen moment, invisible planes of laser light intersected between us, scattering across thousands of droplets hanging in the air, the femtosecond pulses so fleeting they petrified us in stone, our exhalations as spun clouds. Trajectories weighed, temperature gradients observed, our heartbeats counted as closely as a lover. Then, as a stray breeze lofted a hundred tiny, deadly carriers of disease a touch closer toward our mouths, we were nudged another millimeter to the left by our wireframes.

Time resumed. As we spun around wide-eyed, our feet crossing over in turn, there was barely a breath between us. I waited for my glasses to buzz their physical distancing warning, but nothing happened. We drew back, bowed, straightened up, and then burst out laughing.

"That was way more fun than the land sculpture!" said Cindy. The whole experience had been barely two minutes from start to end, but it felt more intense than anything else I'd done since the lockdown.

"So that's what real dynamic distancing feels like!" I said. I was about to message the team about our discovery when I saw the alert in my glasses. It was from the Edinburgh Festival's computing cluster: in the 109 seconds we'd danced, we'd blown through an entire hour of Little Kowloon's precious festival computing budget.

"Whoa, what the hell?" I exclaimed, showing Cindy. She peered at the graphs and pursed her lips.

"That figures. Our glasses aren't powerful enough to choreograph a dance like that. But Anna must've realized she could use something else," said Cindy, nodding at the AR localizers.

I shook my head in admiration. "Her code's piggybacking off whatever resources it can find in the local network," I said. Anna's artwork had used the marquee's sensors and high-resolution laser scanners to weigh every breath and map every droplet to steer us around each other, closer than I'd have thought possible. Celia Chan's code was doing the heavy lifting; Anna married it with her wireframe dancing instructors.

"She's the best," said Cindy, beaming.

"She was the best." I shared a pending update to Anna's festival bio I'd just found. Cindy's shoulders slumped. Anna had died from H1N3 last week. Apparently the Hong Kong festival team hadn't made their minds up on whether they should still exhibit her work. But our testing results would settle the argument: there was no way we could spend so much processor time on a single artist's performance. There was no way to increase our computing budget, any more than we could extend the walls of our marquee. Another "competition" rule.

"We need to get onto the rest of the artists," I said, shutting down Anna's area.

Two standups, three plays, and one band later, I was getting a headache from being in AR too long. Worse, none of the artists had gotten the point of dynamic distancing, their works lacking any but the most basic triggers. We could build triggers for them, but the whole concept of throwing audience members out of one area and into another at a moment's notice was feeling like a fool's errand. It wasn't that it was impossible, it just wasn't compatible with how these artists thought about their work. I couldn't blame them, everyone was working under such tight deadlines.

I knew what Chan would say: harden the barriers. No more headaches. No more arguing with artists. Our marquee would still be impressive simply by using dynamic distancing to pack bigger audiences in closer together. But we'd have given away a dose of freedom in exchange for convenience. I snorted at the obvious parallel.

Cindy was lying on the marquee floor next to a heater, taking a horizontal break to scroll the news. I flicked into our private shared AR layer. Nothing too exciting. The Melbourne vaccine had been held up in its stage 3 trials, and two astronauts on the Alto Firenze space station had tested positive. In Scotland, the Yellow-Green coalition was at loggerheads on fast-tracking Hong Kong citizenship, hardly surprising given the recent polls showing which way the new immigrants would vote.

I sat down, glumly gazing at our vast, empty space. I wondered if the Traverse or Assembly teams were facing the same problems we were. Probably not. Reuben had forwarded me a video from one of the Assembly crew setting up raked seating in their marquee. They were giving audiences what they wanted, an hour of AR theatre.

"I could be enjoying my furlough right now instead of dealing with . . ." I waved around at the piles of tracking equipment and sensors and high-bandwidth networking points, ". . . all this."

"Yup," said Cindy.

"Wow, what a pep talk!" I flicked her an eyeroll emoji.

Cindy propped herself up on an elbow and gave me a look. "You hated furlough! Every time we were at the crags you complained about it. That's why I got Reuben to ask us to volunteer."

"What?! Why?"

"I guess I thought you'd enjoy the challenge. And I had this spidey-sense that Celia Chan would take you on." I raised my eyebrows. "But I had nothing to do with that," she said hurriedly. "And neither did Reuben. No way would she give either of us the time of day."

"Yeah, but . . . why here? I mean, I was thinking about volunteering at the library, not the festival."

"Oh, come on," said Cindy. "This is Little Kowloon. You want to be here but you couldn't ask. And this lockdown . . . I know it's lonely. I thought this could take your mind off things."

"Huh." I wasn't sure if I was offended at the subterfuge. I didn't like being manipulated, but she was right. The last few weeks had been so busy that I hadn't had time to get stuck in my loop. And it was nice to have a reason to be with people who looked like me. Who came from the same place my parents were from.

I'd never felt comfortable around the Hongkongers. I'd barely been there. How could you miss a place you'd never lived? I hadn't suffered as they had, and I couldn't be proud as they were. For most of my life, I'd wanted to be accepted as a Scot, but lately I'd wanted to be accepted as a Hongkonger. Or both. I wasn't sure.

"Don't overthink it," said Cindy. "I can tell what you're doing. We need your help, and this is it, you're helping. Yeah, you're having to handle all the shit, but that's because Celia trusts you. Myself, I'm only good for stitching sensors."

"To be fair, you're good at falling on your arse," I said. She flicked her hand at me, grinning. "And pep talks."

CRITICS LOVED OUR PREVIEW PERFORMANCES, DELIGHTED BY THE SENSE OF BUSTLE and movement. A reporter from the *Evening Journal* remarked on the "illicit thrill" of being so close to others during a lockdown and praised the "Hong Kong dynamism," hilariously unaware of how we'd fallen short of our ambition. In any case, our marquee was declared unmissable.

It took a little longer to get the public beyond their understandable apprehension of being close to strangers. Most still remembered COVID-19, and H1N3 had rammed home the message of physical distancing. Few trusted our technology enough to be comfortable navigating crowds without the clear physical or AR markers telling them where they could move, despite the government's imprimatur.

"It's hard being the first," said Celia, as we listened to a family bicker about their supposedly buggy glasses. She had to restrain me from marching over and explaining how our dynamic distancing protocol was safer than a normal two-meter separation. "Let them figure it out." Which they did. Eventually. Celia and I commiserated over plenty more incidents like this until we stopped fighting each other and united against a common enemy: the audience.

Confusion aside, the public loved our show, chuckling at Doug Yau's acerbic comedy, rapt by Chen Xi's beautiful, rugged landscape sculptures, reminiscent of the highlands. "Authentically Hong Kong, distinctly

Scottish," wrote one visitor in a survey. Mission accomplished, said Tricia Lee in an email to our festival team.

Celia tweaked her code in the following days to accommodate the growing crowds, introducing a new timing system to reduce bottlenecks. I designed a way to nest performances inside each other, so that Katie Cheung's AR violinist and her audience could sit within a larger dance performance. The result was that people could linger at Chen Xi's landscapes or Tricia Lee's miniature city if they were enjoying them and we'd route other audience members around or even through them.

During an operational review at the halfway point of the festival, Tricia hinted Little Kowloon was considering commercializing the dynamic distancing technology for use around the world, and that I would be welcome to join the team on a permanent basis. Rumor was that the tech could be worth hundreds of millions, a shot in the arm for the community and the wider diaspora.

I spoke to Celia again that evening about my misgivings. "I know why we made the decisions we did. The dynamic distancing triggers barely worked and Anna Hui's work would've burned through our entire budget in the first week. But still, I wonder . . ."

"You were expecting something more unconventional? Or . . . logistically impossible?" she said, with a slight smile.

I shrugged helplessly. "I don't know. I wish we could give people a more special experience, something worthy of what we've achieved here. Anna's dance, it was so enchanting."

"Enchanting? I think mesmerizing is closer. Don't look so surprised! You and Cindy aren't the only ones who think it's special. But special isn't enough by itself."

"I suppose it feels like we're only trying to get as many bodies through the door as possible, so we can be the best, whatever that means. I know this is only a festival, but these things matter. I never see anyone talking about the art, just the numbers."

"But that's where you're wrong. There can be romance in numbers. Those numbers are people, and it's not for us to say what they gain from our art." She sighed. "They're talking about making a TV show about me. About the Diaspora Project. A symbol of a glorious struggle. But it wasn't romantic. It was awful. I had to fight for every dollar in donations, every boat, every plane, every person we could get out safely. The only way I got through it is by focusing on the numbers alone."

"I get it. Everything is for the greater good, and what is it worth two people dancing if a hundred can see a show?" I instantly regretted it, and quickly added, "I'm not the one who's lost their home. I don't know what that feels like and I can't blame you for doing whatever you feel it takes to protect your new home. But I am a friend. And it doesn't feel right." I said.

She was quiet for a long beat. "Yes, the CCP said the same thing against our demands for self-governance. I am not blind to the irony of the situation. You've done a lot for us." Celia looked to her side, swiping through an invisible interface. "You can have the last day for Anna. Make the most of it." Her avatar vanished.

I MISSED REUBEN'S EMAIL AMID THE RUSH OF PREPARATION FOR THE DANCE. CELIA hadn't left me a single extra penny of computing time, so I was determined to wring every bit of efficiency out of Anna's code. Cindy received a field promotion to cover my technical liaison role, and I hunkered down for two weeks, puzzling over sensor interfaces and plugging in the latest H1N3 models.

The night before the performance, Cindy ordered me to get a proper sleep and had the network admins bar my access to the festival's servers. That's how I finally ended up reading his email, buried under a mountain of unread newsletters.

"Elaine," he wrote. "I'm afraid I can't make it to the performance. I tested positive, and because I have certain complications, I'm staying at Western General. I'm sure I'll be fine, but if I'm not, let me take this opportunity to be candid." Only Reuben could view contracting a deadly disease as an opportunity, I thought. "I respect your foresight in taking dynamic distancing to the next level with Anna's dance. It's what she'd have wanted, and it'll make the technology that much more valuable. If you need help handling Celia in the future, just let me know. Heung gong yan, ga yau!"

I took my glasses off and closed my eyes.

AFTER A FITFUL NIGHT, I ARRIVED AT THE MARQUEE AT DAWN. THERE WERE ONLY A few people waiting in line. Some had brought thermos flasks with tea and coffee, and were sitting on folding stools and reading the news. I frowned, ducking inside.

The marquee was deserted. The tech crew had cleared the few bits of equipment needed for the past month of AR performances, leaving the maximum space for the dance. I began the startup process, dozens of fans in the walls and ceilings whirring to life.

With some creative programming, I'd figured out that a specific atmospheric profile would make it easier to predict the movement of respiratory droplets. And since I had the entire floor, I could run multiple dances at once. In fact, the more the better, because it was cheaper to run our servers hot rather than stop and start them, so I needed a constant flow of audience members, entry and exit as choreographed as a ceilidh, but everything in between as free as possible. More contradictions.

I popped my head out the door an hour later. The line had lengthened considerably, and oddly, I recognized a lot of the people from Little Kowloon. Surprisingly, the Hongkongers hadn't shown much interest in their own marquee, perhaps thinking they'd seen it all before, or wanting to give locals more space to explore. But today was different. I spotted Cindy further back in the line, chatting to Tricia. They both gave me a thumbs up.

Everything was ready. I just needed to flick a switch and Anna's dance would begin. I returned inside and imagined the space full of people spinning so close to one another, ribbons of lasers sparking in between them, orchestrated by a technology that anticipated but didn't lead. The dancers became children and teachers, screaming and laughing and running but never colliding. Then a packed hall with voices raised, an angry debate, circles and spaces forming and collapsing, then a raucous marketplace, then a factory, then an emergency ward.

Then an empty marquee.

I pulled back the fabric doors, and nodded to the first in line. "Come on in."

3 PATRIOTIC CANADIANS WILL NOT HOARD FOOD!

Madeline Ashby

IT WAS JUST AFTER THREE IN THE AFTERNOON ON THE DAY BEFORE HALLOWEEN when the man from Toronto showed up for the third time.

"Again?" Dionisia asked. "Seriously?"

Erin chewed some of the skin flaking away from her lower lip. A dry fall was better for the wheat, but it was murder on the skin. Erin watched the man jump down out of his rented black truck. He was trying to dress like a local, this time: all-season boots, jeans, a collared shirt under some kind of tactical outdoor jacket that seemingly couldn't decide whether it wanted to be green or gray. She watched him amble up the drive, boots crunching in the gravel, as he squinted at all the pumpkins dotting the path. Most of them had already been carved, and he was clearly trying to identify some of the faces.

"He probably thinks the third time's a charm," Erin said.

"Is it?" Dionisia asked.

Erin twisted the linen tea towel in her hands into a rope and playfully snapped Dionisia with it. "Fuck off. Of course not. I don't even know why he keeps showing up."

Dionisia arched her pierced eyebrow. "Oh, you don't, eh? Well, I do."

Erin rolled her eyes. "You say that about everyone."

"You're the last single woman under forty in Dowling who doesn't already have children of her own."

"So I'm a withered old crone, is what you're saying."

"I'm saying you live in a house with seven bedrooms and you could be filling them up."

"But then where would you and Ruthie live?"

Erin always asked this question whenever this conversation came up. But this time, Dionisia had an answer: "We'd take the place over the garage! There's a whole finished apartment up there that you could be renting!"

Erin held up a finger. "This is because I've made molletes too often this week, isn't it?"

"Yes. You're going to get scurvy."

"Beans and cheese on toast is a perfectly reasonable—"

The doorbell rang. Erin sighed deeply. She rolled her head back and closed her eyes. Her neck crunched audibly. She wasn't sure if the tension in her tendons was due to the man outside, or the offer he kept making, or how much harder it became to refuse each time. Whatever it was, it was playing hell with her jaw. "If we ignore him, do you think he'll go away?"

"Did he go away the other two times?"

The doorbell rang again. Erin growled in the back of her throat, and made for the door. Callum Carruthers—he sounded like a bad guy on an old Hollywood Sunday night prestige series, like Don Draper or Walter White—stood on the screen porch with his finger hovering over the button.

"Hi, Miss Landry, I'm here to—"

"Yeah, yeah, I know," Erin muttered. She pushed out the front door and onto the screen porch. There were still a couple of pumpkins out there in need of carving, and she took one of the Muskoka chairs and hauled a pumpkin into her lap. She picked up the Sharpie marker she'd left on the pulp-strewn towels, and started absently drumming with it on what would eventually become the jack o'lantern's face. As she did, a white pickup truck drove past the farm, blaring music. She had to pause and let its noise doppler away before speaking.

"Okay, let's get this over with," she said.

Carruthers took the Muskoka chair opposite hers. He was too big for it, just like he was too big for everything in the house: his knees seemed almost level with his chest even sitting down. The first time he'd come inside he kept shifting uncomfortably on the antique chairs around the dining table, as though he were terrified of breaking them. It made the whole process torturously slow, and the second time he came around, Erin moved him to the living room, and that was somehow worse, because he kept staring at all of Ruthie's paintings and Erin had the weird feeling he wanted to make some absurd grand gesture of buying them all, just to prove he wasn't a total monster or something.

Now they looked out from the screen porch and onto the winding gravel drive and the scarecrows guarding the raised vegetable beds in the front garden. The first hard frost was still a few weeks away; after that, she could take in the Brussels sprouts and other brassicas.

"It'll look nice when they're all lit up like that," he said. "The pumpkins. There are more, now."

"They're supposed to keep away evil spirits, you know."

"And yet, I still keep showing up. Is that what you're getting at?"

Erin shrugged. "It's a free country. So if you really like Dowling all that much, I can't stop you from hanging around."

"It is actually growing on me. I have a thing for the croque madame at Tweed's."

The white pickup truck with the music passed by again. She frowned. To make that turn, they must have either sped way up to hit the nearest intersection, or pulled a U-turn in the middle of the road. Not that there was a lot of traffic, but the OPP drones were getting better at identifying offenders all the time.

"It's better with mustard than jam," she heard herself say.

"I know. I asked them to skip the jam after the first time."

Erin eyed him. "I'm not going to sell you the land just because we have the same taste in breakfast sandwiches, you know."

"I could tell you my latté order," he said, without missing a beat. "Would that help?"

"I'm a tea person."

He rolled his eyes. "Of course you are."

"So, show me the goods."

He blinked. "Excuse me?"

"Your tablet. Your pitch. All your fancy concept art and mockups and storyboards and whatnot. I want to see the drone footage of my farm that I never authorized anyone to shoot."

He snorted. "I left the tablet in the truck. There's no point."

"Finally, we agree." She scowled. "If you know I'm going to decline the offer a third time, what are you doing here?"

With difficulty, Carruthers twisted a little in his Muskoka chair to face her more directly. "I want to hear, in detail, why you're refusing me."

"*Refusing you?* This isn't an Austen novel, Mr. Carruthers—"

"It's Callum. And that's good, because Georgette Heyer is better." Before she could tell him she had no room for blasphemers in her home, he added: "I want to hear why you're saying no, so I can tell the people I'm representing. I want them to know exactly why they won't be bonusing me this year."

Erin rubbed the thumb and index finger of her left hand together. "Hold on, let me string up the tiniest violin in the world for this song."

"I'm serious! I want to know." He held up his open hands. "Think of it this way. You're providing me with on-the-job training. If you explain your . . ." She watched him struggle for the right word. By now she knew his little tics and tells. He wasn't as good at this whole real estate development thing as he thought he was. For a moment he'd gotten perilously close to the word *feelings*, but that would make her sound like an over-emotional feminine stereotype. And *line of reasoning* would have made her sound like her intellect was somehow compromised. He'd boxed himself in. "Your perspective," he said, finally. "If you share your perspective with me, one more time, I'll be able to consider other situations like this one from that perspective. I can learn how other prospective clients might be approaching a sale like this one. So I can be, you know, more sensitive. To their needs."

Erin cleared her throat. She sat up a little taller in her Muskoska chair. "I don't know why a simple *no* shouldn't suffice. It sounds to me like your firm has issues around consent."

"That's probably true." When she looked at him in surprise, he shrugged. "What? I'm not trying to snow you, here. You know bullshit when you smell it. I respect that. But my wanting to know more about why you're declining our offer isn't bullshit. I think our offer could fundamentally transform—"

"Here it comes—"

"*Fundamentally transform* not just your life, but the lives of countless children and young adults. Building a fully air-gapped, quarantine-safe boarding school on 190 acres, with room for an agricultural and veterinary program, and trails for horse therapy, could enrich the lives of children whose parents can't afford tutors and nannies, whose parents have made the heartbreaking decision to send them away for their own safety—"

Erin uncapped her Sharpie as though unsheathing a sword, and made a show of very deliberately ignoring him. She focused narrowly on drawing a face across the warty, dimpled flesh of the pumpkin. She considered how complicated it might be just to draw a big dollar sign, and whether it would get her point across.

"Can you guarantee the school won't be private?"

"Well, no, it's a public-private partnership. You know that; we've gone over that. There are several sponsors from the Toronto-Waterloo tech corridor—"

"So this theoretical school would have all kinds of smart-building sensor technology—"

"Yes—"

"Which means it's spying on the kids, and there's probably spyware in all their tablets, and there's probably corporate propaganda from the sponsors, everywhere from the restaurants on campus to the infirmary. And that's another thing: can you guarantee that the students who need it will get access to birth control? The virus isn't the only thing those kids have to worry about. Are we talking a dusty little dish of free condoms, or IUDs on demand? What happens when one of those kids needs the morning after pill? It's a boarding school, after all, things happen—"

"We haven't gotten that far, yet, but—"

"I'm not selling." Erin made her voice as flat as possible. "I know that a small farm that grows government grain for the ration—"

"Is that truck lost?" The music from the white pickup truck had returned. Carruthers was sitting up in his chair. His whole body pointed forward like a dog who'd nosed a rabbit. On the wood armrests of his chair, his knuckles had gone white. "Why are they slowing down?"

"Get down," Erin said, and rolled smoothly out of her seat to the floor. *"GET DOWN!"*

But he wasn't getting down. He was standing up. His mouth hung slack and his head tilted, like he was trying to make out the image on a buffering video signal, and he turned to look at her stretched flat across the floorboards. Erin knew that her sense of time was dilating, stretching, that only a single agonizing second had passed, but it felt like he was standing there in the open for hours. For some reason, the music seemed so much louder. So much closer. "What are you—"

And then the dry pops started.

It took a seeming eternity for him to realize what was happening. And then he was covering her, his chest to her back and his fingers curled over her head, covering her eyes.

"Jesus *Christ*," he muttered through gritted teeth.

The pops stopped. The music remained. Erin wondered if she would hear their boots on the gravel, over all that music. Probably not. Especially not with this huge wall of man covering her. She would not have time to push him off and go for the deer rifle inside the house. She would not have time to find the hatchet duct-taped to the bottom of the coffee table. She would not have time to pick up the high-intensity water gun, propped innocently beside the front door, and shoot them with the industrial-grade bleach hidden in its modified glass tanks.

But then she heard laughter, and the truck revving its engine, and the music retreating. And then nothing but Carruthers's breath, fast and light across her neck, and his heart hammering at her back like it wanted inside.

"Dowling still growing on you?" She squirmed and twisted until she was facing him. "Or are you reconsidering the property values in this area?"

He blinked at her and she realized his eyes were bright and wet. "What?" he asked, and his voice was thick.

"I was just asking—"

"This isn't fucking funny. How can you fucking *joke* about this, Jesus God, we just got fucking *shot at*—"

The front door creaked open and they turned to see Dionisia army-crawling her way out the threshold. "You're okay," she said, and smiled.

Erin threaded her arm through a gap in the cage of Carruthers's body and reached for the other woman. "Are you?"

Dionisia snorted. "I was in the bathroom. When I heard what was happening I hid in the shower."

"Ruthie?"

"She was in the studio in the back. Headphones on; she didn't hear a thing." Dionisia jingled the watch on her wrist. "I had to text her for an answer."

As if on cue, Ruthie burst into the screen porch. Her hands were covered in red. For a moment Erin's heart entered her throat, until she realized the crimson streaks down Ruthie's arms and tank top and shorts were paint. It was the same deep vermilion as her dyed hair. She'd been working on some kind of epic self-portrait this month. "Oh my God," Ruthie was saying. "Oh my God, I'm so sorry, I'm so sorry I wasn't here . . ." She took a series of delicate steps around Carruthers and Erin. "Oh, hi, nice to see you again, mister real estate developer guy. Some fun, eh?"

Carruthers said nothing. He didn't move. For once he seemed incapable of making a witty retort or mocking remark. He just kept looking from Ruthie to Dionisia to Erin and back again, as though he were waiting for something. Screaming, maybe. Hysterical tears. Anything but Erin's jokes and the wives kissing each other in between nervous laughter.

"We should . . ." His mouth seemed to have trouble forming words. "We have to call the police, we have to do something—"

"You have to get off me, first," Erin said, and tried wriggling free of him.

His attention snapped back to her, and she watched him look her over and realize the awkwardness of their position. "Oh. Shit." He sat up on his haunches. "Sorry. Fuck. Sorry."

"No worries," Erin said, and wriggled the rest of the way. She sat up and stood carefully. There were no holes in the screen. No holes in the windows. They'd aimed squarely at the scarecrows, then, the same as last year. Only this time, they'd attacked in broad daylight. "You should check your truck," she said. "The tires, I mean. It's probably just BBs, or buckshot, or rock salt, but—"

"*Just* buckshot?" Carruthers hopped to his feet. He loomed over her, six feet four inches of ginger Viking sunburn and spanking new gentleman farmer cosplay from Mountain Equipment Co-op. "What the hell are you saying, *just buckshot*? Jesus Christ, Erin—"

"There's a jack in my truck, if you need it, but I don't think—"

"Erin!" His voice was ground glass. When she looked at him, his breath was still fast and his fists clenched and unclenched. He was rigid, trembling, a wire about to snap. He swallowed. He pointed out the screen porch, at the fallen scarecrows. "What the fuck just happened?"

Erin followed the line of his finger to the lengthening shadows outside. Abruptly she realized that whatever had transpired for her, something else entirely had transpired for him, and it had revived something in him that he'd likely worked very hard to bury. A phobia, or worse, a memory. "Maybe we should take this inside," she said.

RUTHIE HAD LIT A SWEETGRASS BRAID AND WAS METHODICALLY CLEANSING THE house, all the doors and windows top to bottom, while Dionisia fussed in the washroom for a CBD nerve tonic.

"I've got a nice rhubarb gin from Niagara, if you're interested," Erin said, with her head in the freezer.

"What?"

"I'll take that as a yes," she said, and pulled out the bottle and some ice. She found her grandmother's nice lustre carnival glass tumblers, and topped the gin with club soda and the brandied cherries she usually reserved for Manhattans. The more sugar the better, after moments like this. She remembered that much. After a moment's digging she found a purple Quality Street tin at the back of the pantry, shook it to determine there were still some chocolates inside, and emerged with their drinks and the candy on a tray. She set the tray on a table between the armchair where Carruthers sat, a quilt haphazardly thrown over him, and the sofa. She found a place on the sofa, picked up her glass, and gently tapped the bottom of it against the top of his. "Your health."

He picked up the glass shakily, but didn't drink from it. Erin made sure to slurp hers noisily, and this seemed to clue him in that he should do the same.

"What," he croaked, "the fuck."

"The neighborhood kids don't really like me," Erin said. "Well. I take that back. Some of them don't like me. Mostly their parents don't like me, I think, for a lot of reasons. One of them is that I put little disposable masks on my scarecrows."

She made the universal gesture for masking up.

"That's just a visual reminder, though. Of my politics. Of how I'm different. How this farm is different."

He frowned. "What's so different about it? Aside from the fact that it happens to be situated on prime land for educating young people."

His voice was still hollow, but he was coming back to himself a little. That was good.

"Because, we still farm for the ration card program." Erin gestured at the vintage wartime propaganda poster hanging on one wall. It read PATRIOTIC CANADIANS WILL NOT HOARD FOOD and it depicted a couple hiding their sacks of flour from a constable outside.

"We still blockchain every part of our process to guarantee we know where potential contamination and outbreaks happen, and give our vendors chain of custody. E. coli? Listeria? Salmonella? An outbreak among the workers? With the ledgers we know exactly where it happened. End-to-end, full transparency. We started doing that because it was a requirement of the ration program. Anyone participating had to meet the food security regulations. But we still do it. That's why my buyers are loyal. My product is guaranteed. But everyone else in this area . . ."

She drew a circle in the air. "Everyone else in this area, the moment the ration exchange switched to a voluntary program, they quit so they could try selling at higher prices and get by with fewer regulations. But I still get subsidized labor and equipment, and as a participant I'm still legally allowed to sell my excess at lower prices, so everyone comes to me first. Meanwhile they started growing these designer American grains with their own goddamn end user license agreement, and those designer grains couldn't handle our winters, and, well . . ." She shrugged. "You know the Salem witch trials were actually about real estate? The accused had properties everyone else wanted. All the finger-pointing about devil worship was really just a roundabout way toward asset forfeiture."

She watched him watching Ruthie sweep the air with her smudging braid. "I did not know that."

"It's true. You can look it up." She wrestled open the tin of chocolates. "Eat something."

"I can't." He shook his head. "I don't eat refined—"

"Don't be an asshole. Eat the fucking candy."

Meekly, he picked out a single candy and began twisting it open. "I could be diabetic, you know."

"If you were diabetic you wouldn't be eating breakfast sandwiches at Tweed's."

He snorted. Then he popped the chocolate in his mouth. It was like watching someone hit a reset button on him. He went fully still for a moment, then relaxed utterly, while a groan issued from behind his closed lips.

"I forgot," he said, finally. "I forgot how good these were."

"Sucralose is Satan's sweetener," Erin said.

He laughed, short and sharp, like he didn't really mean to. And then he reached for another. Erin reached for her own.

"So that's it, huh?"

"That's the long and the short of it," Erin answered. "I'm still a part of the Ministry of Agriculture and Food Security's rationing program, and my neighbours don't like it. I sell product at lower prices than they do, and I pay less for parts and labor than they do, and my demand is more predictable than theirs, and apparently that pisses them off. Of course what *really* pisses them off, deep down, is that I'm *helping the government give handouts*, or whatever, and it burns them up that some refugee kids from Yemen might, like, actually get to enjoy some French toast made from my grain."

Carruthers drained his drink. "Don't hold back. Tell me how you really feel."

Erin gave him a very halfhearted version of the finger and sipped more of her drink. "This program is the closest thing Canada has ever had to food stamps, or SNAP or EBT or whatever it's called, and it's been good for my bottom line. Did you know that Canada raised half of England's grain during the Second World War? There's absolutely no excuse for us not to feed our own people. It's total and complete bullshit that we never had something like this before, and I for one am not going to abandon it just because the crisis is allegedly over."

Carruthers remained uncharacteristically silent and she caught herself missing the friction. Ranting was easier than processing. Anger was easier than vulnerability. Not that she felt any particular need to justify her decisions, but explaining them in detail filled the silence that would otherwise be filled with the realization that yes, they'd attacked her farm, just like last year and the year before, and that they were growing bolder with each passing autumn.

"I was a card holder, once," he said, as though there had been no break in the conversation. "In university. The ration card, I mean. The points. I mean I know everyone technically has one, they technically have a number for everybody, but I was a regular user. For a while it seemed like the only way to get groceries in Toronto, because of the railway blockades and the tariffs and the meatpacking shutdown. It was the only guaranteed system. Unless you had a good relationship with the guy at your corner store."

Erin drained what was left of her drink and stood to make her way to the kitchen. "And I'm guessing you didn't have one of those?"

"Well, no." He stood to follow her. She reached into the freezer and brought out the bottle, plus a tray of ice. Then she moved into the dining room and found the carnival glass pitcher that matched the tumblers on her grandmother's sideboard. When she turned around Carruthers was in the threshold between the kitchen and dining room, filling the door so effectively that she couldn't weave around him.

"Everything here seems so delicate," he said, out of nowhere. "All this glass. The plates on the rail up there. The lace on the table. It's all so . . . breakable. Everything in here. It just seems really tiny and fragile."

Erin craned her neck back to look him in the face. "What are you trying to say?"

"Nothing," he said, swallowing, and he moved aside to let her through. Erin snapped the ice tray and poured ice cubes halfway into the pitcher, then wedged the bottle of gin inside. "Where are the others?"

"Dio and Ruthie?" Erin listened carefully. She heard the sound of the shower running. "Probably blowing off steam."

Carruthers went red to the roots of his hair. "Oh."

"Everyone decompresses differently." She carried the gin and the club soda into the living room, set them on the tray, and started pouring. "Do you still want to call the police?"

He watched her pouring and held up two fingers when she'd poured enough for him. "Yeah. I should look at the truck, first. Check the tires, like you said. It's a company car; it has front and rear cameras. They might have caught something. A face, a plate number. Worth a look, anyway."

Erin hadn't thought of this as a possibility. But it was one of the advantages, if there could be such a thing, of having been attacked in the afternoon. There was enough light for a camera to pick up something. "Yeah," she said. "That's a good idea."

Carruthers fussed with his device. Erin suspected he was downloading the footage from the car. "Have you ever pressed charges?" he asked.

"The first year, I tried to," she said. "But the investigation didn't go anywhere. Every year I take pictures, and we have a camera rigged up at the front door, but they've never come close enough."

"The *first* year?"

"Probably the year before the ration program went voluntary," she said. "I made my opinion pretty clear, and, well, so did they."

Carruthers put his device down and massaged his temples. "That's like five years, Erin."

Erin wasn't sure when exactly she had switched from *Miss Landry* to *Erin*, but it seemed like a permanent shift. "Well, there was a break, the second year. I think one of them must have been sick. Or on probation for something else, maybe. I don't know. I didn't expect it to continue."

"And you report it? Every year?"

"If only to establish a paper trail," she said. "Much good that it's done me."

"Well, this time, if you don't mind, I'd like to be the one who makes the call." He flipped his device around to show her the image of a license plate slowly resolving into clarity.

TALKING TO THE POLICE WAS VERY DIFFERENT WHEN YOU WERE A MAN, APPARENTLY.

"You see, my company," Carruthers flashed the logo on his tablet, "is looking to make significant investment in this property, but I have to say I find this history of violence and vandalism extremely concerning."

It was evening by the time an officer of the Greater Sudbury Police Service arrived, a Sikh man whose bracelet glittered in the growing dark when Erin opened the door. They received him in the dining room amidst all the fragile things Carruthers was so nervous about, and they served him warm apple cider from their own orchards, and he was deliberate and attentive and he took notes on a big chunky tablet whose case seemed designed to survive an explosion.

"And you've reported this activity before," Officer Singh said.

"Yes," Erin and Carruthers said, in unison.

Officer Singh frowned. "One at a time, please."

Erin nodded. "Yes. I've reported it. I've uploaded all my photos and video to your website, every year."

"And I can do the same," Carruthers added.

"Thank you. Ma'am, if you could forward me your confirmation numbers from those uploads, that would help." Erin nodded, and Officer Singh used his stylus to point between the two of them. "And you, sir, were here to discuss the purchase of the land?"

"Yes. I'm the manager of this account, and I like to take a very hands-on approach," Carruthers ignored the sudden snort from Dionisia, but the officer didn't, "and that's why I was here. And thank God, because now we have this video, and now something can finally be done. Right?"

His voice invited no argument. Erin felt him looming in the chair beside her like a warm shadow, not touching but not distant either, and for a moment she remembered the sudden darkness of his hand over her eyes, as though he too had expected her windows to shatter all around them. She shuddered for just a second, and instantly felt him put his hand on the table beside hers, not touching but within reach. Officer Singh noticed the movement, and his nostrils flared slightly.

"And, ma'am, regarding the sale of this land, for how long have you been in negotiations with this man? With his company?"

"Um," Erin looked at Carruthers. Suddenly it was difficult to remember that afternoon, much less the past year. "It's been—"

"I sent my first letter to you in February," Carruthers said. "And then I called you every month after that, to update you on plans for the boarding school."

"Right." Erin nodded at the officer. "That's correct."

"So these incidents started *before* there was any offer made to purchase the land?"

"What are you implying?" Carruthers asked.

"Sir, I'm not implying anything, I simply want to know if—"

"If you think I would *ever* hire some fucking goons to intimidate one of my accounts—"

"Sir, there's no need for that kind of language—"

"They fucking *shot* at us, Officer Singh. They *pointed guns* at this farm. A farm, by the way, which has queer women of color living on it, which might technically make this a *hate crime*, which means they have every right to bring the full force of the Ontario Provincial Police down on these kids if your department won't—"

"Callum," Erin said, and when he turned to her his face was white with high spots of red spattered across his cheekbones, and his chest was rising and falling as it had on the screen porch after the shooting. "It sounds like Officer Singh really does want to help. I think we should give him the benefit of the doubt."

"I assure you that something will be done," Officer Singh said. "This is really troubling. For all the reasons you mentioned. Now, ma'am, I have to ask: do you feel safe, here? Incidents of vandalism do go up a little around Halloween, usually just kids smashing pumpkins, but with your particular history, you might have more cause for concern."

"Thank you," Erin said. "For asking. Dionisia? Ruthie? How do you feel?"

The two women glanced at each other. "Well, there are three of us here," Dionisia said. "And you have the deer rifle—"

"I'm staying," Carruthers said. When everyone frowned at him, he hastily added: "In the area, I mean. I'm staying in the area. Until we finalize our negotiations."

"For the land," Officer Singh said.

"Yes. For the land."

Officer Singh raised his eyebrows, but nodded. "Okay. Sure. Well, let me get to work on this, and I'll be in touch."

They saw him out, and when Erin wandered back into the kitchen Callum was washing her grandmother's teacups by hand, very carefully, as though still afraid of breaking them. "You don't have to do that," she said.

He stared out the window over the sink. "I needed something to do with my hands."

"Well I have a couple of acres' worth of corn that needs shucking, if you're into that kind of thing," Erin said.

He shook his head ruefully. "I have . . ." He cleared his throat. "I was downtown. During the Canada Day attack. I was in the subway."

The hairs on Erin's arms rose. "I'm sorry. No wonder today was—"

"Yeah." He wiped something from his face with the sleeve of his upper arm. "Yeah, it was. You're a lot better at this kind of thing than I am. You're a lot tougher than I am."

"I'm not sure that's true." Erin tried to smile. "I mean, most other people find me pretty prickly and awful to deal with, but not you. You just seem to take it in stride."

He snorted, but said nothing.

"You extended your stay? At your rental?"

He shook his head. "No. I mean I will, but I haven't. Yet. But the officer has a point: I don't know if Devil's Night is a thing out here, but—"

"Have you even checked your tires?" Erin asked, suddenly catching on.

"No." He set the last teacup upside down on its drying mat, aligning it with the others just so, and turned to face her. "No, I have not."

"So you don't even know if you can get out of here."

"I'm pretty sure I can't, actually," he said. "In fact I'm pretty sure I'm . . ." He licked his lips. "I think the technical term is *ensnared*. I'm pretty sure I'm ensnared, Erin."

She swallowed in a dry throat. "Oh. It's . . . like that?"

"It's like that." His eyes widened. "I mean, not that I'm asking for anything specific, I can sleep in my car—"

"Don't be an asshole," she said, lifting the back of her hand to whack his arm. But he caught her hand before she could make contact, and he held onto it, running his thumb over her wrist. She stared at their linked hands. "I hope you know I'm still not going to sell," she said. "If I haven't sold this land after five years of having my scarecrows shot up, I sure as hell am not going to sell because you happen to be very—"

"Very?" He was grinning.

Erin looked at the teacups all in a row. "Detail-oriented."

"Erin," he said, "you have no idea."

4 INTERVIEWS OF IMPORTANCE

Malka Older

THEN THE NOTIFICATION WENT OFF, A SHORT MINOR-KEY MELODY, AND CHELA FELT the usual pang of surprise and sorrow, although she was fairly sure she knew who it would be.

She picked up her phone and checked. Yes, the ninety-eight-year-old, the registered nurse and great-grandmother, had died. Not unexpected, but still sad.

Elder Resources talked a good game about recognizing the necessary emotional complexities of the work, and they were allowed to—really allowed to, and not discouraged—wait a few days before opening a new client relationship, but Chela preferred to set one up right away and then take a little time before the first interaction to psych herself up. She pulled up the app and spun the simulated wheel.

Chela thought, as she did every time she fired up the app, about how much they must have spent on user experience. It was just a randomizer; there was no need for a pretty colored wheel that clicked so satisfyingly as it turned. Compensation, she imagined, for the rest of the process being distinctly low tech. Everyone wanted a fancy solution, something new, and so even when the obvious answer was *just talk to people* they tacked on technological frills and furbelows to get you to do it.

Regardless of the reasoning behind it, there was a sensual pleasure in the design, the spin of the randomizer, the palette, the pacing. And then she had been assigned an elder to refill her portfolio.

A man. Chela wished they would let her filter by gender, but no. Eighty-seven, no major health issues but some recent cardiovascular concerns that would have moved him up the list. He had lived in Boston his entire life. Chela usually loved listening to people who had moved around, but there was a certain interest in the view of a single place over a long stretch of changing times.

Bueno. No point in delaying it. She pinged with an appointment request. A few seconds later he called. *Of course.*

"Hello? Hello?"

"Hello, this is your Elder Resources interviewer. I was hoping to set up a time to talk."

"Sure, now's fine, nothing else to do."

"I'm afraid I can't do it right now." Chela didn't have another appointment, but she needed to prepare herself. She needed to know when it was going to happen, build up to it, settle herself first with her routine. And she needed to set the tone from the start, control access to herself. She was so grateful that the interactions were anonymized both ways.

"Then why did you call me?"

"To set up an appointment." Practice had made Chela smoother at this, no longer inclined to argue the fact that she hadn't, in fact, called, only sent a message. She knew her irritation was unfair. Who knew how she would manage with newer technologies when she was eighty-seven?

The man was still grumbling. "An interview, as if anyone cared what I thought."

"We care," Chela said, with a fixed stare to get herself through it. *We*, a kind of we that might not include her individual *I*.

No, that wasn't true. She did care. Or, at least, she found it mildly interesting. "And it's not just what you think. It's what you remember. What you've seen. What you want to contribute that maybe no one is listening to."

"You're only asking me because I might die." There was an extra querulousness in his voice for that, and his fear opened up a welcome path to sympathy.

"*I* might die, and nobody's interviewing me. Anyone might. That's not why we're requesting an interview with you. It's because your long memories are rare and useful." She didn't know yet whether he in fact had long memories. She had interviewed some people who couldn't tell her much of anything about their childhood or young adulthood, others who'd recalled movies as their own history. And she didn't know if the memories would be useful. But there was no reliable way to find out without trying.

"Not so rare as all that," he mumbled, but he agreed to a time two days hence.

Why did some people not want to be interviewed? Yes, there was the whole reminder-of-mortality thing—would have been very fashionable in the Middle Ages or whenever those skull paperweights had been trendy—but it seemed more than that. An ingrained reticence about seeming to demand attention? Some old-fashioned notion of privacy? The recordings were fully anonymized if people asked, but most didn't.

The interviews were what everyone thought of when they thought about Elder Resources, this new agency in every local government and at the federal level. It wasn't supposed to be the most important part of their mandate, at least not when the program had been designed, shortly after the pandemic. The goal had been to create a network connecting elders with working-age people, both to reduce loneliness and isolation (supposedly among the elders, although Chela thought that was also what some of her colleagues got out of the job) and to have some early warning and support for vulnerable people in any kind of future disaster. Then there had been the additional consideration of technological competence for the elderly: the new measures for digital democracy required people to feel comfortable conversing, debating, and ultimately voting virtually, and the user interface for the network had mimicked the one used for civic participation.

It had been a grand idea, one of the sweeping policy innovations that had come out after the crisis, ticking off the objectives of valuing the elderly and creating jobs and community preparedness and democracy. And then the misinformation had hit. Suddenly everyone was asking why the government wanted to track old people (as if that weren't thoroughly answered in the policy paper and legislative documents!). People posted indignant comments about other people letting themselves be controlled by government agendas. The phrase *death panels* resurfaced. There were suggestions that anyone who let their parents enroll in the program didn't care enough about them to take care of their elders themselves. Predictably enough, participation plummeted, as did the energy of the employees. Even Chela's mother had asked her—cautiously, because they were having a lot of fights about politics at that time—whether she was *sure* she wanted to work for Elder Resources.

Somehow, though, the interview component had escaped most of the opprobrium. Maybe because the interviews were a one- or two-time thing, instead of an ongoing relationship. Maybe people liked talking about themselves more than they liked the idea of someone keeping tabs on them. In any case, at this point, seven years later, Elder Resources was almost exclusively associated in the public's mind with the interview portion of the program; the networks still existed, but the agency focused its public communications on the interviews and how they "preserved knowledge for the future."

Chela had been trying to persuade her own mother to do an interview for months, and the vieja always put her off. She wasn't on the roster yet, since Chela's mother was (thankfully), at sixty-two, not considered remotely urgent, but anyone could request an interview.

"Mmm, I don't know, I don't really see the point," her mother said, and Chela felt like kicking her.

"It's only my *entire thankless underpaid job* that is predicated on there being a point to this, Mami."

"Claro, claro, that's not what I meant. It's a lovely thing you're doing, you know I think that."

Chela did not know that. Even after she had (more or less) convinced her mother that Elder Resources was not an evil, exploitative conspiratorial government surveillance operation, she still reliably made a face whenever Chela mentioned it.

"Es que I just don't know what I have to say that should be recorded for posterity. Lots of people lived like me."

"Not all of them are getting their stories told, Mami." Chela had explained it to her so many times: how the priority was given to the oldest and the chronically ill. A lot of people got missed, their stories lost until it was too late, which was exactly what the network was supposed to mitigate . . . but no use crying over that at this point. "They do adjust somewhat for different life expectancies for historically oppressed groups." That was the usual term these days; Chela had expounded often on how the oppression was *not just historical.* "But not enough, and definitely not a granular enough level to account for—"

Her mother usually interrupted her before she could list some of the conditions that could exacerbate standardized categories—displacement by violent national upheaval, poverty-wage work, poverty-wage nutrition, child-bearing and -rearing—and eventually Chela had twigged to the fact that her mother didn't enjoy being reminded of her own diminished life expectancy.

Which was reasonable enough.

Still, though.

"Your perspective is so important. We don't hear from enough people like you—"

"I know, I know, because we fall apart before you can get to us."

"—precisely *because* you've all been taught to believe your voice is unimportant! None of you want to talk about it because you think your lives are boring or trivial, but—" and Chela had to stop before blurting out how much she wished she could better understand her mother's life, how frightened she was of losing her before she could.

"I just think they should be paying you more," her mother said with classic tangentiality.

"They should, but nobody else is going to, so why should they?" Chela responded almost automatically. She didn't know what strand of disinformation was making her mother so resistant to being interviewed, and she didn't have the strength to attempt a debunking right now, so they might as well rehash her salary expectations again.

THE INTERVIEW WITH THE EIGHTY-SEVEN-YEAR-OLD MAN WENT ABOUT AS EXPECTED. Chela's avatar was designed to be noticeably not video—a slightly stylized line drawing, like a filter set over the video—but it still showed her reactions and expressions in real time, allowing for nonverbal encouragement. She couldn't see her own avatar, though, because it would always match the respondent's in race; ergo, if she saw it, she would know the race of the person she was talking to. Not that it was hard to figure out, if she cared to. She probably could make a statistically certain guess if she bothered to track the demographics of the various neighborhoods he had moved into and out of throughout his eighty-seven years in the Greater Boston area. But she had a pretty good idea already and it didn't matter enough to her to confirm it.

He started about as antagonistic as she had expected from their earlier conversation. "I hope this is worth my time. And my tax dollars!"

Chela did not say that the last time they spoke he had said he had nothing else to do, did not point out that as a retiree he was on the benefitting side of taxes. "Sir, do you participate in ElderWheel?" She already knew he did, so she didn't have to wait for his affirmative grunt. "Have you benefitted from the Supporting Aged Independent Life Act? Both of those initiatives came directly from ideas and information collected during interviews like these, and they might not have become reality without the accumulated data we collected about the needs and preferences of the elderly."

"Well, I suppose . . ."

"Did *you* talk to elders when you were younger?"

"Well . . . my parents and other relatives, I suppose. Never really had much call to barge in on other old people."

I made an appointment! Chela screamed internally. "This program gives younger people like me the opportunity to connect with and learn from our elders, even without a family relationship and in perfect anonymity."

She had said this so often that she didn't even have to think about it—and this was the extra, extra pitch. People really did hate being interviewed.

"I guess. What is it you want to know about, anyway?" the old man asked, suspicious.

So predictable. If it weren't for the fact that most of them loved it once they got into it, that so many of them showed her explicitly or implicitly how much they appreciated the conversation, Chela probably would have quit by now. "We want to hear about the conditions of your life, the context, what was going on in your neighborhoods and city when you were younger, as well as anything you want to share with the future." She phrased it as soothingly as she could (not saying, for example, *tell us what you would want to tell your grandkids if they cared to listen to you*), although that last bit was always dicey. Hard to refer to posterity without reminding people of death.

The old man was silent for a moment, and Chela spoke again. "If you have a story or impression you want to start with, we can do that." Some people were primed to share, stuff they had told their grandkids a million times or maybe didn't have any grandkids to tell. And then there were the other ones, who for one reason or another—dominance, the opposite of dominance—had been trained not to talk about themselves with any type of interiority, anything that might spark emotions. "But otherwise I have plenty of questions."

"Oh, yeah," he said. "I'll answer whatever you've got."

So she got them started. There was a backbone (that was Elder Resources' term, not Chela's) of questions they had to ask everyone, but from there Chela had the latitude, or responsibility, to explore different avenues.

It had started out as latitude, when Chela was still excited about the job and the way it dovetailed with her grad school research, when she found everything interesting, when she believed in the whole Elder Resources concept, hoped it might fulfill itself like a fucking prophecy. Now she told herself it was a responsibility, that she had to do her job as well as she could, for professionalism if nothing else. Not that she didn't still occasionally get interested enough in what some elder was telling her to want to explore more, but a lot of the time she had to remind herself not to rush through it.

She was trying not to get so calloused that she would forget about anything but the backbone.

"What's the point of this, anyway?" The old man sounded restless, and Chela realized she probably hadn't been giving the right cues (*I'm interested, I care, this is fascinating and useful, tell me more*) for the last few answers.

What *was* the point? Chela took a fortifying gulp of her now-cold espresso and a deep breath.

The old man, probably not realizing that she was about to speak, went on. "I mean, I understand the *principle*. People think that maybe what some old people knew, if we'd paid attention to it, could have prevented a lot of the stuff we're dealing with now, or fixed things sooner, back when—but I mean, do you really think *I* hold the answer to any of the world's problems?"

No, I don't. But that self-deprecating note reminded Chela inescapably of her mother. "That's not really what this organization is about."

"It isn't? But everyone says—"

"There's a lot of misrepresentation." That understatement explained their entire century. "Yes, it would be gratifying if these interviews were to result in some breakthrough—and it would certainly help with our budget. But our agency was founded by people who lost parents, or other elders, and wished they had spent more time with them, learned more from them. There's value in your stories even if there's no monetary value in them."

The old man's voice was gruff. "My kids don't want to spend any more time with me than they have to."

And probably had good reason for that. "Maybe they will someday." Or maybe they will just want to learn about you without *having* to spend time with you. "Or maybe it will be nephews or nieces, or kids from the neighborhood. Or, maybe a historian studying the time of your youth, or a novelist writing a story set there. Who knows? But I'll tell you something." Chela lowered her voice to indicate truth, or rather, a secret, which most people believed was like truth. "I think your first idea was right too. We don't know what the next threat is going to be or what might help, but based on the last few, it seems prudent to collect as much knowledge as we can."

"All right, all right." And by the end of the interview Chela had that tired but satisfied feeling of difficult work well done. The old comemierda even thanked her at the end, sort of. "Nice to talk to you. Nice conversation. Brought up some things I'd forgotten."

Then she settled down to the solitary part of her job, the paperwork and coding of the topics he'd mentioned, so that future researchers could dig information out of the transcripts. She set an alarm to check in on the old man in a week, see if he was still ornery or if he was ready for the idea of joining the Elder Resources network and getting regular pings from her. She didn't have any other calls that day, but she messaged some of the other elders in her portfolio, and got satisfying replies: all well, all well, talk next week. And she thought about her mother.

Chela wasn't even sure why she was so insistent on getting her mother's story. Surely not because of some commitment to her organization and its principles. Nor was it some emotional existential question like *Who is my father?* (she had heard plenty about that man from her mother, none of it good.)

There weren't gaps, exactly. But there was a difference between knowing the outline and understanding why things had happened and what they felt like. Why had her mother left the island and taken the huge and dangerous step of immigrating? What had it been like when she arrived? What had she thought when her new country convulsed around her? Had she ever imagined going back? She had asked these questions a few times, but her mother always changed the subject or plain ignored her.

Chela had trawled through traces of her mother on the Internet, in search of this elusive understanding of the woman who knew her better than anyone. But the pickings had been sparse. Her mother's Facebook account was mainly postings picked up from other people (including several very debunked viral bits about what to post on your wall to prevent Facebook from invading your privacy in whatever sneaky new way, with comments below from a younger Chela explaining that they were both false and useless) and a few back-and-forths with childhood friends from the island that never went beyond "Cómo estás, amiga?," "Bien y tú?," "Todo bien, cuídate," "Que Dios te bendiga." She had a Twitter account briefly but had used it only to retweet Chela and her sisters before letting it trail off into disuse. No, although her mother was theoretically a member of the social media generation, she had never entrusted the Internet with her thoughts and feelings and the record of her selfhood.

Good, thought Chela. But also bad. There were no diaries, no journals, no baby books; some photos, yes, but not very many, and fewer still once cameras had gone digital and phones had been successively lost or broken.

Where was her mother's life? Where were her memories?

Only in her mother's brain and body.

Where no technology in the world could get to them.

ON TUESDAY CHELA GOT AN EMAIL STATING THAT BUDGETS, DIFFICULT TIMES, high demand, and so on meant that all Elder Liaisons would need to add one person their portfolios. She could almost hear all of her colleagues groaning in near-simultaneity. Except she couldn't hear them because she'd only ever met five of them, and those only virtually. For all she knew, the email was a lie and not everyone's workload would increase; maybe it applied only to her.

But either way, Chela wasn't planning to quit her job over one more relationship; might as well get on with it. She spun her randomizer, watched the colors trickle by (technological frills for non-technological solutions, etc., etc.).

A woman. Sixty-two years old.

It was like a thump to the stomach, the surprise and burst of excitement, and Chela tried to calm herself. So unlikely. So unlikely. There were thousands, tens of thousands of interviewers. The *great re-employment scheme*, some senator had called it, as if that were a bad thing. (Chela did wonder how many of the interviewers had any research training or experience at all, but maybe she was wrong; there were an awful lot of out-of-work postgraduates out there).

She checked the location: Maryland. Her heart beat faster.

Nothing else in the data, nothing about how long she had lived there or where she had moved from, or her profession.

It was possible.

She sent a ping for an appointment, wondering if it would be her mother's voice calling her back to ask if they could start right away (surely her mother, after delaying so long, would be eager to get started?). Did they distort the voices? She had never thought to ask.

But the response was a laconic text message suggesting a date and time, and Chela accepted with a feeling of unreality.

She called her mother, as usual, during her lunch break and had to hold her tongue gently between her teeth a couple of times as a reminder not to bring up interviews.

"How is everything?" her mother asked.

"Fine." Chela peered at the bottom of the screen, trying to make out what her mother was eating. "Is that a salad?"

"Chicken salad." Her mother waved the fork. "Fake chicken, ya tú sabes, this new stuff they say is so much better for you, with all the vitamins and no sé qué added."

Chela fought down a burst of panic. If her mother had decided to eat healthy *and* suddenly given in to doing the interview, that suggested something about her state of mind. Or her body. "Everything okay with you?"

"Oh sure. Busy."

"Nothing new, um . . ." How to ask? "Any reason you're eating so sensibly?"

Her mother laughed. "No, hija, this was the special of the day, I figured I'd try it." She made a face. "Fake meat. I can try it once."

"And?"

Another mueca. "Fine." In the not-fine sense, clearly. Chela sighed. One more technological solution failing in the face of personal preference and habitual behavior. She searched for another topic. *Don't ask her about doing an interview, you talked about it last week, it would be weird to bring it up again so soon, don't mention interviews . . .*

"How's work?" her mother asked, and Chela jumped, but her mother's eyes were on something else—another app? A telenovela playing in the back room of her shop where she ate?—and it was almost certainly a ritual question requiring only a ritual answer.

"Fine." Not-fine. Her mother didn't seem to notice.

MOST PEOPLE WHO ACCESSED THE INTERVIEW ARCHIVES WERE LOOKING FOR someone specific: a parent, grandparent, another relative. If they could prove the relationship, they could access the file by name. With other search criteria—a location and a place, for example—they could get detailed but anonymized accounts. There was also a function allowing for randomized snippets, an attempt to make the whole thing a bit more fun and social-media palatable.

Maybe some researcher would extract some life-changing, otherwise missed bit of knowledge from the archive someday, but Chela kept thinking about the people who went in trying to find their relatives. Did they feel satisfied after listening to their family stories told to someone else? Did they feel loved? Loving? Guilty? Wronged?

How would she feel if her mother was only willing to tell her story when she thought she was telling it to someone else?

Maybe she already had? Chela checked the archives, but there was nothing under her mother's name.

SHE WAS FLUTTERY BEFORE HER INTERVIEW WITH THE SIXTY-TWO-YEAR-OLD WOMAN from Maryland. Surely she would know immediately whether it was her mother, even if her voice was distorted? There had to be enough details in the early part of the interview for her to figure it out? On the other hand, how many sixty-two-year-old immigrant women lived in Maryland? A lot. How much did their experiences overlap? Probably quite a bit. Would there be enough specifics in the backbone questions for her to be sure? Would it be latitude or responsible professionalism if she asked the questions that would confirm it?

Chela initiated the call and waited for the response. It was the first time she had ever really wanted to see her avatar; she didn't want to be wasting all this time stressing over some white woman who had nothing to do with her.

No answer. Chela panicked, called her mother, then realized what she was doing and hung up.

Her mother called her back ten minutes later. "¿Qué pasó? I was busy but then I saw your call."

"Nothing," Chela said. "Butt dial." A desperately anachronistic concept, but her mother had loved the idiom when she discovered it, back when Chela was a teenager, and they still used it for that reason.

The (other?) sixty-two-year-old woman called her back two hours later. "I'm so sorry, I forgot, is now okay?" Would Chela's mother be so flustered about missing something? Maybe for a stranger. Was it her mother's voice, distorted? She wasn't sure.

Normally Chela would have said no and insisted on rescheduling, but she was so worked up she thought it better to get it over with. "No problem, these things happen." Soothing, that was her interviewing persona. Her mother would never recognize her in it.

There was a silence. It was time for Chela to do her intro talk. Instead she blurted out: "Why did you request an interview?"

She held her breath, waiting for the woman to say *my silly daughter works with you and she kept bugging me until I decided to just get it done* and then maybe *won't she get a surprise when I tell her triumphantly I did it.* But the woman sighed and said, "I don't know. I have some things to say. Sometimes it's easier to tell these things to a stranger."

Yes, that could be the reason, Chela thought, even as she made a note to offer this woman who might or might not be her mother the list of therapists provided by the organization, with a special note on those who practiced the talk therapy. *That could be why Mami wouldn't tell me.* Meanwhile, the sixty-two-year-old was off, talking about her life and her difficulties and her long-ago childhood. She was an excellent subject, verbose but clear, with interesting stories from an interesting if unremarkable life, and she wasn't Chela's mother.

EVEN SO, WHEN SHE CALLED HER MOTHER THE NEXT DAY AT LUNCH TIME, SHE FOUND herself expecting at every conversational turn for her mother to come out and say *Guess what? I did the interview you've always been wanting me to do.*

"Mami," she said when she couldn't take it anymore. "Why don't you want to do the interview?"

Her mother, who had been telling her some story about her prima Graciela and her kids, stopped and looked at her. "Hija, if it means that much to you, I'll do it."

Inside her head, Chela screamed. *Of course it means that much to me, I've been asking you to do it for months, how could you not notice?* "I don't want you to do it if you don't want to," she said, calmly. At least, she hoped she sounded calm. "But I don't understand why you won't. All those things you've been through . . ." Chela paused, searching for examples, for the right examples. "When we were kids, and you had to deal with the pandemic, all by yourself. Or when you came to this country, and found a job, and what that was like. Or when there was that riot here, and you were working the whole day and couldn't get home, had to sleep at the shop at night . . . Those things are important. Don't you want us to know about them?"

"Ay, hija," her mother said on a long sigh. "Don't you know, these things, they are not so easy for me to talk about?"

Chela didn't know. Of all the reasons she had imagined for her mother not talking to her, the idea that it was difficult, painful even, had never occurred to her.

"I didn't think you needed to know those things. I thought you just wanted me to do this thing for your work."

"No, Mami!" Chela almost yelled it. "I don't need you to do that for my work, I wanted to know for *myself!* So I could understand."

Her mother dabbed at her eyes, and fussed, peering at the screen to check her mascara. "Look now, I can't cry here, I have to go back out to work."

"I'm sorry, Mami," Chela said. "I just want to understand you, and—"

"And you want me to tell all this to some stranger who will record it in a machine, so that other people can listen to it whenever they want to, for *posterity* you say?"

"You don't have to," Chela said, forlorn, and also a tiny bit resentful that she had been put in the wrong so effectively.

But her mother went on: "If you want to know about those things, of course I'll tell you. If you want you can even record us talking or qualquier cosa que haces. But I don't want to talk about all of this to strangers."

"Of course, Mami, of course I'll do it with you." Chela was sniffing now too, and thinking about how she would show her mami the way the app worked for her, the spinning colors of the randomization, so unnecessary and so pleasurable; the mystery of the avatar; the coding, even. But probably her mother wouldn't care enough to pay attention to all those minutiae, probably she was exaggerating what it would be like, as usual, pinning her hopes up too high. "When's a good time? We—we can even do it in sections if you like, if you don't have time to get through it all at once. Should I come over?"

"Oh, I don't know. Maybe we could do it like this, on a call, instead? It might be easier."

Chela swallowed her disappointment. Her mother needed the distance. Since she was making the effort to talk about things she didn't want to talk about, it seemed only fair.

"But tell me, hija, why do you care so much? You know all these things that happened."

Chela held back *it's my job* because that was only partly true and because she wanted to meet her mother's willingness to talk about herself at least halfway. "I might not know all the things, and anyway I'm sure we remember them differently," she said, aiming for a reasonable tone. "Also . . ." This was harder. "I guess . . . I listen to old people's stories all the time. I want to hear yours."

"It's not going to be so exciting," her mother grumbled. "You are imagining me much more important than I am."

And Chela told her mother what she would have liked to be able to say to every elder as she interviewed them. "No one is more important than you are."

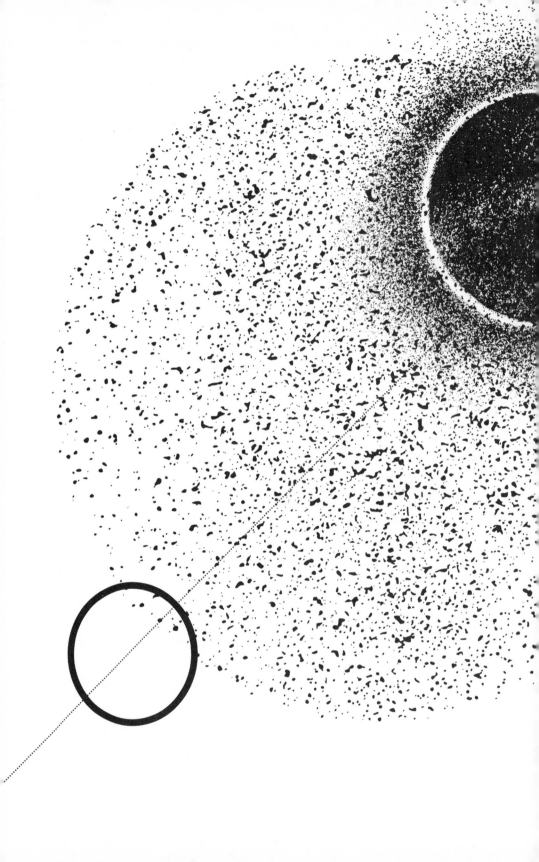

5 JAUNT

Ken Liu

Archival VNN footage of Ruutuutuu Protests at the Port of Seattle, Pier 91, July 10, 202X

[A MAGNIFICENT CRUISE SHIP, *PACIFIC UNICORN*, IS DOCKED AT THE PIER, READY TO begin its seven-day tour of the Inside Passage. Luggage is being loaded; passengers in long lines are embarking; everything seems perfect: a normality that everyone has been craving for many months during the pandemic.

Except . . . a swarm of small boats—dinghies, speedboats, kayaks, even a few fishing trawlers—numbering in the high hundreds have congregated in front of the cruise ship, filling much of Elliott Bay and blocking its course. Protesters throng the pier, holding up signs with the mustachioed cartoon rutabaga that has become the symbol of the movement and shouting "Shut it down!"]

Interviewer: Unicorn Cruises say that they've implemented every precaution for the safety and health of the crew and the passengers. All their ships have obtained the STERLING-20 certification—

Protester: STERLING-20 is a worthless piece of marketing spin. The certification process was created by the cruise industry, for crying out loud. The truth is, there is no way to run cruises safely. None! Have you forgotten what happened barely two years ago? My parents were stuck on that ship wandering the Pacific with no port to take them in, and they both got infected. My mother died. Do you understand? Died. How can you pack thousands of people into close quarters like cattle, feed them at trough-buffets, recirculate the same air in every room . . . and believe this can ever be *safe*? It's a goddamned lie.

Interviewer: There's been no evidence of another pandemic—

Protester: [mimics] "There's been no evidence . . ." Where have I heard that before? The virus hasn't gone away. We've got to live with this thing for the foreseeable future. And the next pandemic *will* come—it's not *if*, but *when*. No more cruises. No more tour groups. No more jumbo jets stuffed full of sweaty bodies breathing on one another for twenty-plus hours. No more tourism. Shut it all down!

"See the World Like You've Never Seen it Before"—video advertisement for Unicorn Travel Enterprises, produced by TIDE=/=AL Partners, September 202X

[THE GREAT PYRAMID OF GIZA LOOMS IN OUR VIEW LIKE A MOUNTAIN.

The camera holds still as time speeds up. The sun rises and sets; the stars spin overhead; shadowy figures flit in and out of frame like mayflies dancing with eternity; the pyramid's shadow sweeps across the sand like the gnomon of a world-pacing sundial. New Age music plays.

Then, just as the sun is low in the west once more, the music stops, time returns to normal, and the camera begins to move forward, swaying slightly from side to side.]

Woman (O.S.): They tell me the record for climbing to the top is six minutes twenty-nine seconds.

[We're running toward the base of the pyramid. Faster and faster. Despite the optical stabilization, the swaying becomes more pronounced.]

Woman (O.S.): (*Panting*) I signed up to be first in line today so I wouldn't have to slow down for anyone else.

[We reach the bottom of the pyramid. The camera tilts up. The jagged blocks seem to scrape heaven.

We climb. Although the action cam is clearly streaming the POV of the climber, we don't see her hands or feet. In fact, for viewers who are used to consuming such footage, there's something distinctly odd about the camera angel and movement—too close to the surface, perhaps?]

Woman (O.S.): Talk to you again at the top.

[Up-tempo, pulse-pounding music plays. We hear the sounds of her exertion over sped-up footage of the ascent. Most of the time, the unsteady camera is focused on the limestone block or blocks right in front of the climber. But from time to time, it swerves for a peek at the apex. Closer. Closer. It's frantic, thrilling, exhilarating.

Finally, we reach the top.]

Woman (O.S): Oh . . . Wow . . .

[The camera swings around to give us a dizzying view: the Pyramid of Khafre nearby, which appears even taller than our summit; the sprawl of Cairo in the distance, reminding you that almost five millennia of history have been compressed under your feet; the hazy horizon all around you, promising unknown, arcane knowledge; the vertiginous sensation that you're about to plunge hundreds of feet to your death . . .

Only then do you notice the unusual scene on the slanting face of the pyramid below you: dozens of robots scrambling up the limestone blocks after you. Each robot is about the size of a large dog, with four padded feet that grip tightly onto the limestone blocks, a camera in front, and a screen that shows the face of a climber-teleoperator. A quick scan of the screens reveals that the climbers come from all over the world.

A robot hand rises into the camera's view, waving.

The screen splits to show a woman in climbing gear strapped into a full-motion harness waving. Her movements have been mapped into the movements of the robot. She lifts off her full-immersion goggles, wipes the sweat from her face, and proudly holds out her watch for the viewer.]

Woman: Six minutes and twenty-six seconds. Not too bad.

[The Unicorn Travel logo swerves onto the screen, followed by a link to their web site.]

Woman: And I've still got enough time to shower before work.

[Text on screen: A NEW WAY TO TRAVEL: EVEN BETTER THAN BEING THERE.]

"Opinion: It's Time to Admit It: We Were Wrong to Oppose the Ruutuutuu Movement," by Johanna Tung, *Boston Globe*, July 10, 203X

LIKE MANY OF YOU, I WAS DISMAYED WHEN THE RUUTUUTUU PROTESTS ESSENTIALLY shut down the global tourism industry shortly after the annus horribilis that was 2020. As the owner of a company specializing in curating and creating unique experiences for tourists from all over the world interested in sampling Xhong culture, my life's work would be destroyed by the movement to abolish global tourism.

The protesters' immediate concerns were to prevent COVID-19 from flaring up again, or, even worse, the emergence of another pandemic, but over time, their mission evolved to saving the planet from our relentless drive to consume experiences without regard to the future.

I found myself in a hard place. Having devoted much of my career to the intersection of economic development and sustainability, I understood the math behind their protest signs better than most.

The people who bought my tour packages came from Europe, the United States, Japan, Australia, the biggest cities in China and South America.

They were the kind of individuals who recycled, drove electric vehicles or even biked, tried to be good to Mother Earth. They thought of themselves as good people, with expensive educations, the right opinions, virtuous intentions. That was why they wanted to spend a week living in a Xhong village and attempt to understand a way of life different from their own.

But all their efforts at conservation were wiped out and more the moment they decided to get on that plane. A jet flight to carry a family and all the luggage needed to sustain their Western comforts across an ocean or a continent is among the most wasteful activities ever invented by the human race. And that's without even accounting for the environmental cost of transporting them from the airport over new highways, across new bridges, through mountain tunnels and flattened forests until they reached their vacation destination.

The mountainous regions of Southeast Asia, where the Xhong people live, contain some of the most vulnerable ecosystems in the world. Droughts, storms, mudslides, and other consequences of climate change have already wrought havoc with their lives. Each new airport, road, bridge, tunnel, and tourist meant more cement—perhaps the most destructive, poisonous, and unsustainable construction material ever invented by humans—more fossil fuels, more wrecking of forest, soil, aquifers. It meant another step closer toward the day when the area would become uninhabitable by the very people the tourists came to visit.

Moreover, I was acutely aware that my tours were perpetuating a colonialist legacy of violence and exploitation. Though I tried to design my tours with input from Xhong elders and artists and strove to make the villages who hosted my guests equal partners in the business, activists had for years argued that my cultural-immersion tours differed only in degree, not kind, from the exploitative vacation resorts and "cultural showcases" operated by mega corporations and centralized governments, which had little interest in preserving Xhong culture. My customers were of course not overtly exploitative, unlike those who went on sex tours or hunted for exotic animals in Southeast Asia. But they wanted to play at living another culture, to consume a way of life, to find "spiritual meaning" by reducing the traditions and practices of the Xhong into processed trinkets and pseudo-New Age pap that reaffirmed their own choices and sense of superiority. The very notion of tourism in the modern sense is an act of voyeuristic pleasure experienced by the Western (and would-be Western) colonizer subject gazing upon indigenous populations, an act of vicarious subjugation; the global tourism industry is rotten at its foundation.

And yet. And yet.

Without airplanes bringing tourists from across the globe, how was I supposed to keep paying my tour guides and drivers? Without the dollars and euros and WeChat balances, how would the Xhong families who had planned their entire lives around housing and feeding tourists make a living? Without their cameras and phones and excited chatter, who was going to buy all the handicrafts made specifically for them? The Xhong had become dependent on tourism, even as it further eroded their world. Entire villages, which had already suffered enormously through the tourism drought of the pandemic, would now tip over into ruin. While many villagers remained terrified of tourists bearing another wave of infections, many more clamored for the economic life raft they represented. I had no room to think about the planet's future or the ramifications of colonialist structural inequality when I needed to figure out an immediate way to save the families who were my employees and partners.

Many independent tour providers, including myself, tried to band together to push back against the Ruutuutuu Protests. But like many movements of the era, the Ruutuutuu protesters were a loose coalition with divergent, even contradictory demands. Some were concerned about the cultural and environmental externalities of global tourism, which I sympathized with. But others were motivated by less noble concerns. Some were convinced that tourists from Asia had caused the pandemic in Europe and the United States. Some were isolationists who wanted to seize the opportunity and reverse globalization. Still others believed in conspiracy theories that argued cruise ships and jumbo jets were UN-sanctioned experimental vehicles for Chinese and North Korean spies working under the direction of Russian scientists funded by Bill Gates. Our advertisements and calls for a dialogue made little impact.

There was a cultural shift. Celebrities posting photos of getaways to faraway tropical paradises were now shamed as though they had posted pictures of hunting trophies. People looked at those who flew around in jets the way we used to look at smokers.

Dire warnings were issued about the collapse of tourism-driven developing economies and the hollowing out of indigenous communities. Many of us experienced a sense of helpless rage at the protesters who seemed too blinded by their own zeal to have compassion for those who depended on the cruise ships and jumbo jets. But gradually, as the protests raged on and global tourism numbers remained depressed, we learned to adapt.

The first to try something new were the giant cruise lines and resort owners. As their ships remained docked and their hotels empty, they started to sell "remote tours," which tapped into VR and telepresence, two technologies that saw unprecedented adoption during the long pause forcefully imposed on much of the world by COVID-19. Many of these packages relied on gimmicks that allowed teletourists to do things they couldn't have done even in person. Governments, desperate for tourism revenue, readily relaxed various restrictions for these teletourists.

For example, Unicorn Travel, one of the largest cruise lines, ran a program that gave customers the chance to climb the Great Pyramid of Giza when embodied in a telepresence robot, an act that was (and still is) illegal to perform in person. Supposedly, the telepresence robots, being light, electric, and well-padded, posed little risk of damaging the pyramid (and could be programmed to prevent the operator from carving graffiti into the limestone). Similar programs allowed teletourists to stroll through the Taj Mahal at night, to "climb" glaciers in Alaska, to watch tortoises in the Galápagos Islands, to scramble over the ruins of Tulum and Chichen Itza, and numerous similar feats.

But these packages were aimed at the luxury-travel market. They didn't help the rest of us: the independent tour providers, the cultural experience curators, the local guides who relied on one-on-one tips.

The game changer was the Nene Be, an open-source specification for a small telepresence robotic platform built around single-board computers like the Raspberry Pi. The Nene Be (and its successors) relied on cheap cameras, cheap screens, cheap processors, cheap manipulators and batteries, cheap (but fast) wireless networking, and open-source software. They were easy to make and even easier to operate. They gave the teleoperator the ability to talk to people on the other end, to control their view, and to move around and manipulate objects (with severe limits). They didn't give one VR-like immersion, but they were just good enough to make you feel like you were doing more than chatting through a webcam. You were *there*.

The Xhong, like people dependent on the tourism economy around the world, soon built new business models based on the Nene Be. Instead of serving xoi ngai ngai noodles to tourists in person, the stall owners now gave cooking tutorials to paying students from around the world, hosted competitions among teleoperators to see who made the best noodles, and partnered with Southeast Asian grocery stores in the home cities of the teletourists to sell them the ingredients needed to create the dishes at home. Instead of catering to the needs of a tourist family who wanted to pretend to be rice farmers for a week, now Xhong families could simply set up a few Nene Bes near the paddy (fenced in so they didn't accidentally fall into the water—though telepresent "paddy races" were also a thing for some) and charge people who wanted to drop in from time to time to do some telepresent farming or help chase off vermin as a way to unwind. Instead of selling tourist-pleasing wax-dyed prints, Xhong artisans now could teach workshops, take on teletourist apprentices, or license their unique designs for 3D printing or one-off dyeing in the tourists' own countries. The possibilities were endless.

Involving no jets traversing oceans, no SUVs bouncing over winding mountain roads, no giant staff to tend to the passengers' every whim, even accounting for the investment in network infrastructure, a visit through a Nene Be requires less energy than it takes to keep the lights on in an average American house for an hour. Because a teletour can be booked with so little friction, the average visit lasts only twenty-eight minutes. In the trade, we call them "telejaunts" or just "jaunts."

Critics initially feared that jaunts would cheapen the experience of travel and, by being too easy to fit into our increasingly attention-starved modernity, remove leisure travel as one of the only ways left for us to depart from the everyday and reflect on our inner lives. But experience has proven these fears unfounded. Travelers take jaunts far more frequently than physical trips, often returning to the same place multiple times over a period of weeks or months (we all probably know of a friend who goes to the same noodle stall in Taipei every day for ten minutes just to watch the owner pull the noodles by hand). They form deep, sustained connections with a place and the individuals in that place, gaining insights into the human condition deeper and more authentic than could ever be obtained during a week-long physical vacation in a tourist trap overrun with crowds.

Jaunts have completely transformed the landscape of global tourism. Gone are the days when global tours were both too expensive to be truly accessible to the less-than-affluent and too cheap to prevent ecological disaster and cultural commodification. Nowadays, more people are touring distant places than at any point in history, but their impact on the environment, both physical and cultural, is also much lighter and less destructive. Instead of flocking to the same places that everyone else does, tourists can go to places far off the beaten path—the Nene Be has essentially opened up the tourist economy to entrepreneurial residents and communities in remote hamlets and rural sanctuaries without the requirement for costly infrastructure or putting their fragile way of life at risk. By transporting presences instead of atoms, teletourism is a magical spell that has given us the best of all outcomes.

To be sure, not everyone is convinced of the benefits of jaunts. So-called populist political parties in the West as well as repressive regimes elsewhere have taken advantage of the rise of teletourism to further restrict the movements of refugees, journalists, and migrants seeking a better life elsewhere. We must remain ever vigilant against the virulent possibilities when good ideas are twisted to serve dark purposes.

To that end, I also believe that jaunts offer the potential to subvert the traditional power imbalances between outbound tourist source regions— which tend to be more economically developed and Western—and inbound tourist destination regions—many of which are less developed and suffer from a legacy of colonial oppression. While many tourists from Boston, for example, visit Xhong villages in Vietnam and Laos, very few Xhong tourists can afford to visit this city. This is why my company has formed a partnership with anti-colonialist and anti-racist activists to develop programs to help more teletourists from the Xhong and other indigenous peoples to come visit places like Boston. As the United States has grown ever more hostile to immigration and voices from around the world, teletour jaunts, which require no visas and no border searches, may be the best way to challenge this trend.

Joanna Tung is the founder of Teletourists Without Borders, a nonprofit dedicated to developing sustainable models of cultural exchange that reverse the legacy of colonial exploitation. She also hosts jaunts to her office in Vietnam on JauntsNow at the following BnB code: DXHHWU-TCU.

Excerpt from *Be My Guest*, a documentary series focusing on the lives of JauntsNow hosts and guests, first shown May 203X

[THE CAMERA IS ON AL BURTON, SEVENTIES, STROLLING THROUGH BOSTON COMMON. From time to time, he stops to examine a flowerbed or a birdfeeder by the side of the path.]

I never traveled much back then. In twenty years my wife and I took the kids on two trips, one to Thailand, another to Mexico. After she died, I didn't go anywhere at all except to fish on the Cape once a year. Running a dry cleaning shop is a lot of work. Too much.

But I had no work for those months during the pandemic. Even after the lockdown ended, business was terrible. The virus moved in and made itself comfortable. People didn't go to the office; they didn't get dressed up;

they didn't need to have their clothes dry-cleaned. I had no choice but to shut it down. My life's work. Gone.

[Ken Burns-style panning over photos Burton took of his shop before he shuttered it. The place had been meticulously and lovingly cleaned.]

I was sitting at home when I got this coupon by email, telling me that I could go on trips to China, Vietnam, Mexico, Costa Rica . . . wherever I wanted for just fifteen bucks. I thought it was a scam—or maybe the airlines were so desperate to get people to fly again that they were willing to sell tickets at a loss. I knew they were having trouble with the protesters at the airports and the cruise ship docks.

So I took them up on the offer. Put in my credit card info to lock up a spot.

And only then did I find out that they weren't talking about real trips, but trips where they put you in control of a robot already there.

[Shots of surviving specimens of the first generation of crude Nene Be teletour robots, most of them about the size of a domestic cat. Even controlling them can be a chore. We see Al miming his clumsy attempts to use a phone as a physical gesture control device for the faraway robot, tapping the screen to make the robot move and shifting the phone itself about like a tiny portal to get a look at his remote surroundings.]

At first I thought about backing out and asking for my money back. I didn't even like the idea of chatting on a webcam with the kids, much less with strangers. It felt like something for young people, not me. But then I thought: why not? If I really hated it I could just hit the "disconnect" button. Not like I would be stuck overseas, right?

Because I paid so little for my ticket, they couldn't get me into Tokyo or Bangkok or Dubai; instead, I ended up in northern Japan, a tiny town called Bifuka, in Hokkaido. The robot was located at the rail station, which hardly got any passengers, a handful every week, maybe. When I arrived, it was deserted. But I liked how clean and neat it was. Made me feel at ease right away. I could tell it was a place that people loved.

[The camera shows the lone, single-room station next to the train track. The deep blue sky is dotted with sheep-like clouds. Inside, we see a table, a few stools, posters, maps, the floor swept free of all dust, a tiny skittering robot, its single-board computer guts exposed, roaming about.]

I learned to move myself about with my phone until I could climb the wall like a spider and read the Japanese posters with machine translation overlays. I bumbled my way out of the door and rolled along next to the tracks until I reached the limit of the wireless signal at the station. The view went on and on all the way to the horizon, a vastness that soothed my heart. I couldn't believe how fun it was. I giggled like a kid. I never even thought about going to Japan, and here I was.

I don't know how to explain it. After months and months of being locked up inside my house, seeing my business crumble, not being able to go anywhere, worrying about friends and neighbors dying—being there, under the sky in Japan, looking at Japanese mountains and grass and trains, that gave me hope. That did.

On the way rolling back to the station, I met a man who was about my age, just out walking. I was never the type to talk with strangers, but it felt odd to say nothing when we were the only two humans—well, human and human-in-a-bot—for miles. I didn't want to use the machine translation—didn't trust it. So I just waved an arm and said "Hello" in English. He understood that, at least, and nodded at me through the camera, saying a greeting in Japanese. We stood in the road like that, me looking up at him, him looking down at me in the screen on the robot, not knowing what else to do except smiling and waving. But it didn't feel awkward, you know? After maybe twenty seconds, he nodded and I nodded, and we parted ways.

After that, I took many jaunts, practically one every day.

[Footage of various teletours taken by Al: a busy kitchen in Yangzhou, China, where teletourists are perched on a shelf above the cooks, skittering from side to side as they watch the complicated, hours-long process for making the famous shizitou meatballs; somewhere in the Great Barrier Reef, where submersible teletour robots on fiber-optic cables can dive and observe the ecosystem with minimal impact or damage; a village in Indonesia, where a traveling shadow-puppet troupe is putting on a show not for Western tourists, but for an audience that is in sync with the story, with just a few teletour robots in the back perched on a tree, no translation, no explanation, no intervening guide; Chobe National Park in Botswana, where teletourists dangle from helium mini-airships and watch a pride of lions going about their business . . .

Over time, the control rig used by Al has been upgraded, allowing him to be more immersive with the teletour robots.]

I got to visit just about every country in the world, and I've met so many, many people. Teletours are different from the physical trips I took as a tourist back in the past. When I was in Thailand and Mexico, I could never feel comfortable: people were catering to me, and everything I did I couldn't stop this nagging voice in the back of my mind telling me that it was a transaction, and I needed to get my money's worth, even if that meant being petty, demanding . . . an ass.

With a teletour, it didn't feel like that at all. Precisely because the stakes were so much lower, it also felt, oddly, as if my host and I were more like equals, not two sides of an unbalanced coin. I'm sure that sounds naive and wishful, but it's how I feel.

I felt so good about the tours that I started hosting visitors myself.

[Footage of Al hosting jaunts at home: Al chatting with one of the cooks from the restaurant in Yangzhou as he attempts to recreate the shizitou, with the cook laughing and offering critiques; Al taking a group of teletourists fishing on a pier, the old man walking behind the row of robots and their fishing poles, advising, bantering, encouraging; Al showing two Xhong visitors how to eat a steamed lobster the New England way, struggling to describe the taste while the teletourists dined on a platter of crayfish to approximate the experience . . .]

Some of my hosts and guests have become my friends. I know it always seems odd to say that you can become friends with someone you've never met, but it's not just chatting through a webcam, you know? You actually *do* things together. That, to me, makes all the difference. Maybe if the president went and did things with other people he wouldn't sound so angry all the time.

[The camera pulls back to show that a teletour robot has been gliding along next to him this whole time. It's squat, cylindrical, about the size of a small lobster pot so that it could be easily transported by one person when necessary; it has wheels as well as segmented feet for all-terrain operation; a camera is perched atop, along with two manipulators; a high-resolution screen shows the face of the visitor.

Al turns to speak to the visitor in Japanese, subtitled for our benefit.]

Takahashi-san, would you like to visit the Swan Boats next?

[The visitor assents.]

Are there swans in Hokkaido? You must show me next time . . .

[Together, Al and his teletour guest stroll away toward the Public Garden lagoon in the distance.]

Statement by President Bombeo, September 3, 203X

MY FELLOW AMERICANS, TODAY OUR GREAT REPUBLIC FACES AN UNPRECEDENTED challenge to its preeminence in the world. Hostile foreign powers are emboldened while feckless allies cower and dither. However, if there's anything that history teaches us, it's that the great American nation can defeat all enemies and overcome all challenges when we are decisive and take bold action.

My administration has been distinguished from the very start by a robust, potent foreign policy. In contrast to the previous administration, I made it clear from the day I took office that no one can defy, defraud, or deceive the United States without paying a heavy price.

To secure American borders, protect American jobs, and free the American people from unwanted foreign influence, my administration closed loopholes in the immigration and visa laws, voided suspicious naturalizations, rationalized birthright citizenship, and deported numerous foreign nationals who may harbor dual loyalties. We attempted to get Congress to reenact and expand the scope of U.S. Code Title 8, Chapter 7, though the effort was contemptibly blocked by the quisling opposition. We also drastically reduced the number of foreign students allowed to come to our great universities to study advanced technology and science—research funded by American taxpayers—only to take the knowledge back to their home countries. I specifically made it impossible for students from hostile or untrustworthy nations such as Iran, Russia, China, and many others to study in our country unless they first take an oath of loyalty to the United States. Despite the outcry from radical-left academic elites, these steps have unquestionably made America safer and stronger.

However, many of these prestigious universities, instead of faithfully carrying out my executive orders, have sought to bypass or subvert them, to the detriment of the American people. As Vice President Gossy's investigative report shows, top universities such as Harvard, MIT, and Yale all attempted to route around the restrictions. Many created so-called remote-residency programs that make heavy use of advanced telepresence robots. Taking advantage of the mobility, dexterity, and advanced sensors enabled by these machines, students in foreign countries can attend classes alongside American classmates, make use of expensive laboratory equipment, and even experience much of the joys of campus life. Although these foreign students are, for all intents and purposes, here on American soil, the universities argue disingenuously that visa requirements don't apply because they are simply engaged in "web-based remote learning."

But the universities are hardly the only scoundrels.

Life in America has been fundamentally transformed by ubiquitous telepresence. In the aftermath of the great pandemics of the last decade, telepresence robots helped many Americans return to work and saved our economy. A general-purpose household robot, for example, allowed nervous homeowners to receive services from cleaners, electricians, plumbers, hairdressers, piano teachers, and so on without having to let strangers enter the house. Moreover, the robots could be programmed to limit their operators' movements inside the house via geofencing and audit trails of actions performed. The social distancing enabled by telepresence saved many American workers from economic ruin.

But today, many of the remote operators you permit to inhabit your household robots are not Americans at all, but foreigners stealing American jobs without even leaving their own houses. Companies, greedy for profit, have shirked their patriotic duty. The gains we've made by reducing and regulating immigration have been lost through telepresence, with real Americans suffering the consequences.

Moreover, teletourists from abroad, without having to pass through comprehensive vetting at ports of entry or during the visa process, now visit America in greater numbers every year. Although teletour bots open to operation by foreign visitors are in principle subject to strict regulation that prevents their operators from wandering outside of specific designated tourist zones, enforcement is spotty, and many teletour bots owned by small consumer-providers are exempt.

Thus, our streets today are clogged with foreigners embodied in robots, subject to little surveillance or control. It defies common sense to think that these foreign operatives in disguise would not poison our public discourse with unfiltered foreign propaganda. After repeated demands from me and Vice President Gossy, our intelligence services have uncovered vast and sophisticated attempts by foreign states to influence American policy and elections. For example, the PNA sent waves of teletourists to describe alleged conditions in Palestine to the American people in February this year, in advance of the planned peace summit, and Chinese trolls disguised as ordinary tourists flooded the District of Columbia in June to participate in the "Million-Bot March" against our deployment of advanced tactical nuclear weapons in the Pacific. Indeed, the recent waves of demonstrations by anti-war radicals in California and New York appear to have been directed and amplified by Russian intelligence using hired teletourists from around the world.

Despite this clear and present danger to our democracy, my attempts at regulating the speech of teletourists have consistently been rebuffed by the courts. My order that all teletour robots be equipped with a filter that automatically refused to translate or silenced utterances of ideas and phrases not compatible with American interests has been voided by extremist left-wing judges defying my constitutional authority. They appear to hold the mistaken notion that foreigners, present in the United States only by remotely operating a robot, somehow enjoy the same God-given constitutional rights as real Americans. The very idea is absurd. This is especially so when regimes like China have erected virtual walls that make it extremely difficult for American citizens to take jaunts into China. We cannot remain open when our enemies do not extend us the same courtesy.

We cannot allow telemigration to undo all the gains we've made in regulating immigration. Thus, in order to protect American jobs from unfair foreign competition, to defend our technological secrets from foreign spies, to ensure that our citizens are not subjected to foreign propaganda delivered in the guise of teletourism, I am issuing an executive order that immediately bans all attempts to connect to telepresence robots within the United States from abroad. Secretary Narro will have the details.

Don't tread on us.

God Bless America.

Factchecking Notes on President Bombeo's Statement by Teletourists Without Borders, September 3, 203X

. . . (39) "THUS, OUR STREETS ARE CLOGGED WITH FOREIGNERS EMBODIED IN ROBOTS."

According to the Association of Teletourism Providers, the largest US-based trade organization for the industry, foreign-based teletourists were only 3.4 percent of the total number of teletourists in the United States. According to JauntsNow, less than 5 percent of the jaunts booked on US-based teletour robots were from addresses abroad. In any event, it seems clear that the vast majority of jaunts in the United States are taken by other Americans.

. . . (43) "Our intelligence services have uncovered vast and sophisticated attempts by foreign states to influence American policy and elections."

The President's examples of bot-swarms by foreign nations attempting to influence American politics have been well publicized, but there is considerable skepticism among security experts because the reports were produced by the spy agencies under intense political pressure and thus considered not entirely reliable. The President also failed to note some other instances of foreign-sponsored bot-swarms that may have been more in line with his preferred policies (see below). Thus, the picture he presented is misleading.

- The bot-swarm in support of Myanmar's government when Congress contemplated sanctions against officials in Nay Pyi Taw for persecuting ethnic minorities. The officials in question enjoy a close relationship with President Bombeo, and multiple researchers have concluded that the demonstration involved protesters-for-hire purchased in the Philippines.
- The bot-swarm in support of President Bombeo's decision to reject the findings of the United Nations Human Rights Council against Saudi Arabia. Multiple researchers have concluded that the demonstrators were using a semi-open relay known to be closely associated with ascendant members of the ruling family.

. . . (45) "Indeed, the recent waves of demonstrations by anti-war radicals in California and New York appear to have been directed and amplified by Russian intelligence using hired teletourists from around the world."

The report from a privately funded Washington, D.C. think tank that a large number of demonstrators were Russian operatives controlling multiple bots has been dismissed by most security researchers as based on flawed metrics and over-aggressive machine-classification algorithms. The lead authors of that report are also known for arguing that the Black Lives Matter protests from the last decade were instigated by Chinese and Russian trolls, a position that has been comprehensively debunked.

. . . (47) "My order that all teletour robots be equipped with a filter . . ."

The President failed to make it clear that his order not only applied to foreign teletourists, but also could potentially be applied to American citizens and permanent residents using telepresence robots as well.

README.txt

NENE HUDDLE IS A HIGH-PERFORMANCE, PRIVACY-FIRST, ADAPTIVELY STRUCTURED, peer-to-peer network to facilitate anonymous, hard-to-trace connections between telepresence robots and operators.

Running the Nene Huddle software turns your machine into a node (called a "pylon") on the Huddle network. The pylons communicate with one another through encrypted channels that are constantly multiplexed and switched to defeat attempts at tracing metadata. The ultimate goal of the network is to enable operators anywhere in the world to connect to telepresence endpoints without leaving a traceable record linking any individual operator with any individual endpoint.

It is primarily useful for getting around the restrictions various states have imposed on inbound and outbound telepresence connections. For instance, if you don't live in the United States or one of its four "Deep Trust Allies," then currently the only way to take a jaunt into the US without going through the onerous and Orwellian televisa process is routing yourself through the Nene Huddle network. It is also one of the only avenues left to enter China without giving up all your data at the border.

Note, however, that the Nene Huddle network doesn't directly provide any consumer-oriented functionality such as searching for open telepresence endpoints, advertising to jaunt customers, paying to use open endpoints, disguising yourself as a domestic teletourist on JauntsNow, and so on. You'll have to use other applications built on top of Nene Huddle.

It is already confirmed or at least very likely that running the Nene Huddle software is considered illegal by authorities in countries such as the United States, Russia, India, China, Saudi Arabia, and the United Kingdom (the list of such states is growing). Before installing and joining the movement, weigh your risks carefully. It is simply a fact of life that freedom requires you to be ready to pay a price, to have skin in the game.

Frequently Asked Questions

Who makes Nene Huddle?   Volunteers who have made it a point to not know one another's identities.

Why do you make it?   There is no way to answer this question for everyone who has contributed to the project. By design, we don't know one another's real names, real jobs, real nationalities, real motivations, anything at all, really.

Based on posts in the project forum, the most popular (self-reported) reasons for people to contribute to this project are:

- Dislike of the actions or policies of the United States / China / Russia / India / Saudi Arabia / the UK / some other country
- That freedom of movement, including telepresence, is a fundamental human right
- The world is a better place when people can move around and get to know one another and teach one another—telepresence is the best way to do that without polluting and ruining the planet
- The world is a better place when people stay where they are and stop crossing borders and trying to change how other people live—telepresence is

the best way to do that without turning everyone into a prisoner or forcing them to starve for lack of economic opportunities

- It's fun to mess with governments and see politicians' heads explode

How can I trust the software? By reading the source code. That's it.

As you can see from the answers to the last question, the self-reported reasons for why volunteers contribute code here are often mutually contradictory, as is the case with all leaderless, distributed movements.

Is it possible that there is code in here from PLA hackers in Beijing? Of course.

Is it possible that the CIA has contributed? Yep.

Is it possible that— Let me just stop you there. Yes, yes, and yes.

Every state thinks there's a way it can turn Nene Huddle to its own advantage; spies, like everyone else, want to jaunt. Nation-states' self-interest and mutual suspicion redound to our benefit: no other open-source project has received as much adversarial code review and scrutiny. Out of swords, secure telepresence tunnels.

Still, you can't trust people's motivations, only the result. Read the code, verify for yourself that it's safe to run. You have the freedom, which means you have the responsibility.

Doesn't your software facilitate crime/enable money laundering/hurt democracy/ perpetuate imperialism/etc.? You're asking the wrong question.

All right, maybe this is worth elaborating a little more.

Is it true that people can use the network to do terrible things? Without a doubt. But that's true of any technology. (However, every single instance where the United States claimed that our network facilitated terrorism—so far at least—has turned out to be a lie.)

What do *you* want to do with Nene Huddle?

In a world where borders are increasingly impenetrable, Nene Huddle is often the only way for us to remain together. Those with skills but no markets at home use it to secure for themselves and their loved ones a better life. Students, scholars, and researchers use it to find the collegiality and inspiration that feeds invention and free thought. Journalists use it to tunnel into oppressive countries to get the facts and shoot footage that can't be obtained any other way. Activists from across the world use it to bot-swarm protests in the United States because American policies have a disproportionate impact on the rest of the world even though most of us don't get to vote in your elections. Religious leaders who have been forbidden to speak at home can preach abroad through telepresence. Individuals who are not free to date, love, express their own identities at home can live the lives they wish to live remotely through a long-jaunt tether, a literal lifeline.

Every technology that begins in the hope for freedom eventually risks being co-opted by centralized power. Telepresence was originally a way to allow people to move more freely without the costs associated with transporting physical bodies. It has also, over time, turned out to be a great way for those in power to regulate and control the exchange of ideas and peoples.

The only way to oppose centralized power is to become its very opposite: distributed, leaderless, inventive, formless. If you want your freedoms back, don't count on a wise leader to save you. Join us.

Download. Encrypt. Jaunt.

6 KORONAPÁRTY

Rich Larson

IT'S LOCKDOWN AGAIN, SO I'VE GOT THE TRAM MOSTLY TO MYSELF ON THE WAY HOME, grocery bags penned between my feet. The tram's nice when it's empty. No nerve-shredding sounds of snuffling or coughing, nobody talking on their phones. I can relax.

I look out the window and see Prague sliding past in the dark. Sometimes I see my reflection, which always looks gaunter and wrinklier in the tram window. I listen to the whalesong groan of the tram following its track, curving with the river. In the old days I sometimes put my head up against the glass to feel the vibration, but of course I don't touch public surfaces anymore.

The tram is peaceful until Vltavská, when two teenagers get on, chattering in Czech as they scan their phones on the ticket reader. Both of them are wearing those stupid holomasks, and when the big cartoony mouths aren't fluttering open and shut to match their speech, they project eerie grins. Always make me feel like they know something I don't.

I glare at them as they surf handbars down the rattling tram and pick a seat two in front of me. Socially distanced, so I can't even resent them for that. People are good at following bug policy here.

Not like in Paris. In Paris, every time there's a wave they have to 3D-print these knobbly pads to glue onto every other metro seat, and then have to chase away the people hawking 3D-printed cushions that fit right over them. That was the last trip me and Jan took together, Paris and then Nantes. Lots of laughs.

Anyways. Here, people play by the rules. I remember visiting Prague once before the Big One, and even back then everybody was painfully polite on the tram. Hardly ever talking, always ready to spring up out of their seats when anybody old got on. Happened to me a couple times, and that was when my hair was only halfway gray.

But these two in their glow-up masks are excited, and it makes them loud, and that makes them annoying. The stream of Czech is punctuated by whoops and laughter. I've been here a decade, but I catch hardly anything. It's rare I speak Czech now that Jan's passed, and I was shit even before the rust set in—I took lessons for his sake, but I've got no aptitude for language.

Especially not ones with seven cases, free-for-all word order, and the ř sound, which basically requires turning one's mouth into an electric drill. If I ever have to differentiate between *třicet*, which is thirty, and *čtyřicet*, which is forty, I go straight to showing fingers. Better than scaring people who might think I'm having a stroke.

But then, from behind the taller teen's grinning mask, I hear a word I can suss out: *koronapárty*. We all know that prefix, and "party" has invaded an awful lot of lexicons, Czech included. But we're on lockdown again, which means curfew's in effect and partying with over ten people is prohibited.

Maybe they're discussing a nine-person party, or maybe they're using the term ironically. Kids do love their irony. Or maybe they're planning a massive, illegal, underground infection vector fest. It's not really my business.

Until I hear another intelligible word: Dělnická. Which is the name of *my* fucking street.

I link my hearing imp to my phone, one of the few things I know how to do with it, and crank the volume up. Then, feeling like a bit of a sneak, I thumb my translator app, the one that helps get me through Czech ministry visits. Inside my left ear, the teens' conversation turns into electronic English.

"Mate, it's all set up. It'll be great."

"So many people, though. It makes me nervous."

And I think, yeah, no shit, as it should. We're on lockdown for a reason. The latest coronavirus isn't as deadly as the Big One, but it spreads fast and parties are like petri dishes. These little twerps are endangering themselves and their neighbors and the grandmothers who probably make *knedlíky* for them.

The taller of the two teens just shrugs. "Wait until you see the place, mate. It's perfect."

"Next stop: working class."

That last bit comes from the tram itself, which is pulling away from the Pražská tržnice stop where nobody ever gets on, seeing as it's an open-air market and those are all closed during a spike. The translator app got overzealous. It meant to say next stop: Dělnická, a street that hasn't been industrial or working class for a very long time but still bears the name.

The teens are still chattering about their party, but I've got my own concerns now. Getting out of a seat is a lot slower than it used to be.

THE TRAM BANKS ONTO KOMUNARDŮ, PAST THE NEW DRONE-PAINTED GRAFFITI installation. That means I've got about ninety seconds to prepare myself. I scoot all the way to the edge of the molded plastic, hinge myself over to grab the straps of the grocery bags, then brace the better of my two shoulders against the seat in front of me.

When the tram slides to a halt just outside the Vietnamese restaurant, I use the rock-back momentum to heave up onto my feet. It's smooth, which makes me feel proud, and then feeling proud of getting smoothly out of a seat makes me feel vaguely ashamed—that old cycle. The tram doors whisk open and I stump down the steps.

The teens spill off too, which means I heard them right about Dělnická, and start ambling toward the zebra crossing. Even the way they walk is obnoxious. All free and flappy and gangly. Their vertebral columns are still stretching skyward, talking back to gravity. Every bit of them's still on the way up instead of on the way down—which makes it even more infuriating that they're planning a corona party. They have no idea what it's like to be on the way down. To be fragile.

One of them elbows the button for the zebra crossing. They're heading the same way as me, down my very street, so I speed up a little and follow them across the tram track. I used to have a bad knee and a good knee; now I've got a bad knee and a worse knee. Both of them click. One's just a bit more sore.

Fortunately, the kids are in no rush. They're both buried in their phones again, meandering along, and they don't notice me tailing them. Tailing them. Ha. Like I'm some sort of spy. Some sort of arthritic James Bond. It's stupid, but I sort of like imagining it. I keep my chin tucked to my chest, breathing my own hot breath inside my mask, as we move down Dělnická.

My hearing imp picks up bits and pieces of the conversation, but the translator app doesn't have much to go on. They might be talking about farts. Actual farts, not boring old farts who go around spying on illicit party planners.

"Mine are always silent. That's my gift."

"They're not always silent. I've heard them."

"Maybe hearing them is *your* gift."

We pass the Žabka, where an employee on break is tugging her mask down to vape. I know she recognizes me—I go to her convenience store every third day or so—but her eyes slide right off. People aren't big on eye contact in Prague, or smiling, or waving. It used to drive Jan mad. He grew up in Brno, and always swore it's much friendlier.

We pass Vnitroblock, which is all shut down for the wave, all its little studios and shoe shops put into stasis. Then the pizza place, which has shrunk to a single delivery window. Then the boarded-up pub that didn't make it through the last big spike and had to close for good. We're getting close to my apartment, so close for a wild second I think that's where they're headed.

Then the teens look both ways, dart across the road, and head into the abandoned building across the street. I can't exactly dart these days, so I just watch them go. Construction crawls in this city—Jan said it was like that even before the Big One. That building's been half-finished since we moved here, and people mostly ignore it, although one night I remember some musicians from Cape Verde shot a music video there.

But that was during a lull, not a lockdown. I should hobble over there and wait, and when they come back out I should tell them to get their act together, tell them there's no way I'm letting them throw an infectious party right across the street from me. I can't remember the Czech word for irresponsible, but I can app it. Or probably just talk English, since they're young.

That would mean getting right up close to them, though. All that breathing, all that misted saliva. And if they're irresponsible enough to break basic bug policy, they might be carriers already. Plus, I hate confrontations. Just raising my voice at someone makes my heart beat double-time for the next three hours or so.

Somebody else can shut down their stupid *koronapárty*. I head the opposite way, toward my apartment building, and start fishing out my key.

BACK WHEN JAN AND I FIRST MOVED IN, WE HAD THIS SILLY GAME WHERE IF THE LIFT was on an odd-numbered floor, we had to take the stairs. Jan was always in unfairly good shape for his age—jogged along the river every morning—and I only had one bad knee back then. Now walking up six flights of stairs sounds unrealistic and frankly unneighborly, since someone would end up finding my carcass and scaring themselves.

So I take the lift. I use my key to push the button, and then me and my groceries rattle on up to the top floor. There's a film of smart plastic on the metal wall, playing some reminder tutorials, pixelated people washing their hands and handling their masks correctly. I puzzle out a few of the accompanying Czech words.

The lift doors slide open. I brace myself, haul my grocery bags up off the floor again, and stump down the short hall to apartment 21A. They put a little yellow sticker on my door, to indicate I'm at increased risk during a spike. It's a good thing for them to indicate, but it still feels a bit like they're rubbing my face in how old I'm getting.

I key the door, shoulder it open, and walk inside. It feels good to be back inside. Safe. I won't have to get groceries for another three days.

"Hello, Ivan!" the housebot calls, aggravatingly genial—I can tone down its enthusiasm, but it always resets during updates. "Remember to wash your hands, you asshole!"

At least the vocabulary modifications stuck. I don't get a lot of laughs lately, but hearing the housebot cussing like a very chipper, electronic sailor is good for at least a couple smiles per day. It was a gift from my sister, same as the VR goggles she gave me for facecalls that I hardly ever use.

"I always do, dumbshit," I say back, unhooking my mask and dropping it straight into the laundry.

After Jan died, my sister floated the idea of me moving to Seattle to live nearer her and her family, maybe even live with them for a while—she has a heart two sizes too big. And it's true Seattle has bounced back better than most cities over in the USA. But moving felt like running away, so I told her I was staying.

And a week later a little yellow Amazombie dropped the housebot off at my door, machines delivering machines, very Escher. My sister programmed it herself, and the two of us generally get along okay. I just hate it when it starts trying to run therapy routines.

"There were only twelve new cases in Czechia today," the housebot chirps as I lug the groceries to the kitchen. "Lockdown is expected to end Wednesday."

Its body pads into view, a little white machine about the size of a cat, equipped with simple manipulators. Mostly it's just there to put an emoji-projecting face to the basic AI synced into the apartment's retrofit network. Its manipulator telescopes to start putting the groceries into the fridge. Meanwhile I wash my hands, thoroughly, fingertip to elbow with a coconut scented soap Jan got me into the habit of buying.

"Wednesday," I echo. "Huh. Kids couldn't wait four fucking days to have their party."

"Are you going to a party, Ivan?" the housebot asks. "Remember that groups larger than ten . . ."

"I don't even know ten people in this whole city," I say, scrubbing my hands, jigsawing my fingers to get the soap in all the cracks and creases. "It was just some kids on the tram. They're planning a big bug fest. Because, you know, kids are invincible and never think shit through."

"Kids can be either children or young goats," the housebot says. "Both are capricious. Ha!"

I turn the water off and stare. The housebot's screen is projecting the crying-with-laughter emoji. Maybe the last update included some kind of humor patch, or maybe it's just glitching.

"Right," I say. "Capricious. Hey, what's the Czech word for irresponsible?"

"*Nezodpovědný*," the housebot says, and it seems unfair that its pronunciation is so much better than mine when it's put in none of the time. "Would you like to play some word games this evening to help improve your vocabulary?"

"Already got plans," I say.

"That's great, you asshole," the housebot says, reaching for the last grocery bag. "What are you planning to do?"

"Off," I say.

The housebot freezes with its manipulator halfway inside the bag, and there's a little downscale chime to let me know the AI's in sleep mode. I pull the bag away and pull the beer out. The Czech Republic has so many wonderful beers. You can pretend you're on some sort of cultural mission to sample them all for a very long time before you realize you're just a lonely old man with nothing better to do in the evening than drink.

Eventually you just do what I do, and grab a big plastic bottle of whatever's eye-level. This time it's Krušovice, which I remember Jan always hated. One and a half liters, perfect for pouring you and your friends a pint each, and also perfect for sending me out of my head for the rest of the evening and making sure I fall right asleep.

The housebot's not programmed to be judgmental, but somehow I always end up turning it off when I drink, and recycling the bottles on my own. I pour myself the first glass, raise it in the housebot's general direction, and begin. It's a party of one, which is very responsible. Very *odpovědný*.

THE HANGOVER IS PART OF THE RITUAL, AT THIS POINT. IT HITS A LOT HARDER THAN IT used to: I wake up feeling it in my whole body, not just my aching cranium and mummified mouth. Luckily I've got nowhere to be. The bed's twice as big now, but I always end up on the same side of it by muscle memory. I sort of resent Jan for that—it took me ages to get used to sharing a bed, and now that I've got the whole thing to myself I can't take advantage.

I look at the big empty beer bottle on my nightstand, feel faintly sick, then haul myself out of bed one lead-dipped body part at a time. I always wake up needing to piss these days, so that's the first step. Afterward I clump into the kitchen and find the housebot still frozen where I left it.

"On," I say.

"Good morning, shit-head!" it chirps, but it doesn't seem funny today. "How did you sleep?"

"Like a drunken baby," I say. "Thanks."

I pour myself a glass of water, gulp down half then give the rest to the plant on the tabletop. Now that the weather's warming up I have to keep a closer eye on it. Last week I walked past and found it all drooped over, leaves hanging off the stalks like they'd had their necks snapped. I won't lie; it panicked me.

All the plants were Jan's. He brought them home the way kids in books bring stray dogs home, and now it's on me to keep them alive. I've been thinking about buying smart pots for them, the kind with little white legs that let them follow the sun and tap impatiently when the soil gets too dry. But repotting would mean getting rid of the pots Jan picked, and it sounds like a lot of work, besides.

Everything sounds like a lot of work lately. Especially now that I don't actually work—I've lived here long enough to qualify for UBI, one of the reforms that got pushed through after the Big One. Right after Jan passed I went through a stretch where I worked like mad, took every commission and client I could, but eventually it didn't help anymore, so I stopped. I tell myself it's because I've earned the right to relax for a bit.

"What are you thinking about, Ivan?" the housebot asks.

"Not a thing," I say.

"Lockdown is expected to end Wednesday," it says. "Three days until freedom!"

That's the thing, though, isn't it. For other people, it's freedom. For me, nothing really changes. I'm always on lockdown.

THE DAY GOES AT A TRICKLE, LIKE MOST DAYS. I'VE GOT MY ROUTINES, OF COURSE. Lunch is half an avocado and fried egg on toast, and while I do the washing up I listen to a certain astronomy podcast. It's not quite the same without Jan complaining how boring it is. After soaping and rinsing the handful of dishes, I leave the housebot to scrub the floor and I go sleep on the foam couch.

I used to set an alarm, have the housebot get me up after a half-hour. But that was when I was working. Now I find being unconscious is my preferred state: no aches, no pains, no memories. So I sleep off the rest of the hangover and wake up groggy two hours later, at which point I read for a while, an old stain-covered book of Pablo Neruda in translation. My fingers are stiffer than usual turning the pages and I can't really focus on it.

Eventually I give up and go to the balcony. It's the best part of the apartment, I think. South-facing, so there's always plenty of sunlight. Big enough for two chairs and a slightly wobbly tripod table. We used to drink gin and tonics out here in the summer, and curse at the pair of pigeons who always shit on the railing.

We tried all sorts of things to get rid of them. I remember we found an audio track of falcon noises, and tried blasting that through a speaker. It spooked the blackbirds roosting on the roof, but these two insolent pigeons just waddled right up to the Bluetooth to investigate.

And now they flutter in, right on cue, to perch on the railing and eyeball me.

"Fuck off, birds," I tell them.

"Sorry, I didn't catch that!" the housebot sings from inside. "Can you repeat yourself, Ivan?"

"Nothing," I say, but the housebot's body comes padding out onto the balcony anyway. One of the pigeons startles, flurrying its wings, then recovers.

"It's a beautiful day to sit on the balcony," the housebot says. "It's twenty-four degrees Celsius with a mix of sun and cloud."

I lean back in my chair and put my feet up on the wobbly table. Past the pigeons, across the street, I see the abandoned building and remember the kids from the tram. I can see why they picked it: it's partially rubble, and slathered in graffiti, and partying there would give them that real grungy rebellious feel.

"Would you like to facecall your sister?" the housebot asks.

I bristle. "Quit asking me that," I say. "I'll call her when . . ." It's absurd, but I say it anyways. "When I have time."

"Okay, Ivan," the housebot says. "I'll quit asking you that."

"Good."

I slump back in the chair. The housebot starts scrubbing a white blot of pigeon shit off the edge of the balcony. Makes me feel guilty when it cleans in front of me—even though it's a machine, I always feel I ought to be helping. To distract myself I look across the street again.

I don't know how the scamps are planning to get away with it. Maybe they have a sound damper to hide their voices, or maybe they're all going to be listening to the same music in their earpods. I picture them all sneaking in, two or three at a time, grinning smug little grins to each other.

I picture the party, picture all the aerosol saliva, all the droplet clouds misting through the air carrying virus, and it makes me furious all over again.

Then and there, I decide: there's not going to be any *koronapárty* tonight. Not on my street. Yesterday I did the arthritic James Bond thing, with the tailing and the eavesdropping, and now I'm going to do a good old-fashioned private eye stakeout.

Right after I use the toilet again.

I SETTLE IN TO WATCH FROM THE BALCONY, ME AND MY COHORT OF PIGEONS. PRAGUE is quiet during lockdown. Hardly any traffic noises. A few delivery drones zip up and down Dělnická carrying take-out in insulated bags, and a few people hurry past in masks, keeping their one point five meters distance from each other.

The light fades, turning the sky a cold blue, and it gets cold enough that I pack in. The housebot badgers me, so I eat something, but I don't really get hungry anymore. Food is mostly just something to take with medications. The housebot helps me drag an armchair right up to the window, so I can still watch the building.

I've got the book of poems in my lap but never manage to focus on it for more than a few stanzas. It's fully possible the kids will never show up. Maybe they came to their senses, or maybe they picked somewhere better-concealed for their little party. It's fully possible I'm doing this for nothing, but at least for once I'm doing something besides drinking cheap beer and trawling old message threads for new memories.

I drift off re-reading the poem where death is a hungry broom, and an admiral, and it gives me a weird little dream where Jan and I are chasing the pigeons off the balcony with brooms while a woman in a big admiral's hat supervises. Fortunately, I instructed the housebot to wake me if it spotted any activity across the street.

"Sorry to disturb your nap, asshole!"

I blink my eyes open.

"I think the party you mentioned is starting," the housebot says.

I sit up; my spine cracks and pops. The housebot's right: across the way I can see lights, holoshow-type stuff flashing up into the sky over the block. They're not even trying to be subtle about it. I send the alert to the lockdown-breach app, all righteous anger and savage triumph. I'm sure mine must be one of a dozen already.

"Idiot kids," I say, leaning my elbows on the windowsill. "Hope they get a fine."

I wasn't expecting the housebot to do much more than blandly agree, but its emoji display turns into a thoughtful frowny face. "Why do idiot kids make you feel angry?" it asks.

My ears go hot. "Not angry," I say. "Just looking out for the greater good. Even if this bug's not as bad as the last few, we're still in lockdown for a reason."

"Some types of party are more risky than others," the housebot says, then pops up a health display. "I am worried by your increased blood pressure, asshole."

I grit my teeth. "I've got increased blood pressure because I don't like watching people be selfish," I say. "People not giving a shit about anybody but themselves. If they cared at all about the people around them, they'd be indoors."

The housebot got me: I *am* angry. And now that I'm talking I can't stop.

"They'd be doing what I do," I say. "They'd be living in a little box all alone with a fucking housebot, where they can't hurt anybody, where they can't be vectors, and where they can't get sick and turn into another burden on the healthcare system. That's how people are meant to be living during lockdown." I swallow. "I'm living this shitty-ass little life for the greater good, not because I like it. And I'm calling the police on those kids for the greater good, too."

I can feel a whine in the back of my throat, which makes me feel even more pathetic. My pulse is squeezing fast, thudding in my wrists and neck. If my blood pressure wasn't up before, it's skyrocketing by now.

"I think most adolescents live with their families, Ivan," the housebot says. "Not all alone."

"Exactly my point," I say, no longer sure what my point was. "They're putting people at risk just so they can have a laugh. And they deserve to get in shit for it."

"Maybe you should communicate your feelings to them directly," the housebot says. "Have you considered attending their party?"

I've obviously taken the basic AI to its limit, so I fold my arms and stare across the street at the flickering lights. The minutes tick by. I wait for the police drone to come swooping in, loudspeakers on full, to scatter the little shits like how pigeons ought to scatter when confronted by the looped calls of predatory birds.

The minutes keep ticking by. I check my phone, and see that my alert has been processed and filed, whatever that means. But there's no police drone, and nobody shouting off their balconies to tell the kids off. Everybody's just looking the other way, how they look the other way in the street, too polite to start any sort of confrontation. Everybody's minding their own business with no thought to the delayed consequences.

I rock once, twice, and heave myself out of the chair.

"Where are you going, Ivan?" the housebot asks. "Curfew begins in twenty-two minutes."

"I'm going to a party," I say. "Briefly."

"I'm glad to hear that, asshole," the housebot says. "Have fun!"

MY FINGER TREMBLES WHEN I JAB THE BUTTON FOR THE LIFT. I'M THAT WORKED up—mostly anger, with a decent helping of anxiety over what I'm about to do, too. But it's got to be done, and in a weird way it feels good to be worked up over something again. For so long I've just been monotone. Just drifting.

On the way to the ground floor, watching the little animation of the scrubbing hands, I rehearse what I'm going to say. I've got it all floating around in my head: how I'm risking my life to come over and tell them off, how utterly selfish they are, how ashamed their parents must be. My phone is along as a simultaneous interpreter; it can echo the whole thing in loud electronic Czech.

Night's fully fallen when I hobble out of the apartment. For a moment the blurry orange of the streetlamps and the warm breeze on my face takes me back to when I loved this neighborhood. I used to be so fascinated by the Communist-era architecture and the little *potraviny* shops, used to adore Letna Park—limping up the hill was always worth it to look out over the city.

The neighborhood was bigger back then. Now it's just my apartment and a grocery store every three days. Sometimes I feel like I barely live here at all.

But I do, and I've got the right to stay living here, which I can't do with little idiots endangering my health and that of the public at large. I stump across the deserted street, checking the seals on my mask one last time. I brought the good one for this, full face coverage. No telling how many spit clouds I'll have to walk through.

Like a moth to fluorescent, I follow the lights. There's still no sounds of conversation or laughter, which boosts my theory about the sound damper. If the kids are really committed, they might be subvocalizing to each other and letting their fancy masks synthesize speech into text—read an article about that.

I walk through the crumbling entrance and start hauling myself up the concrete stairs. Jan would be proud—first stairs I've walked in ages. It's only two flights but I'm gasping by the time I reach the top, so I take a moment to catch my breath, and to steady my nerves, too.

I can hear the sounds of humming equipment, whatever they're using to project the lights, but still no footsteps. Czechs aren't much for dancing. Maybe they're all just sitting in a circle with their beers.

Hopefully everybody turns around and sees me at the same time, instantly startled and ashamed. More likely I'll have to wave my arms around to get their attention. That doesn't seem dignified, but I'm in too deep now to worry about dignity, so I round the corner and step inside the party.

The room is empty.

I blink, then blink again. Lighting equipment is set up, strobing electric lime and purple across the bare concrete walls, and there are a couple little pocket drones circling the room, cams rotating for a full view. But there are no irresponsible kids coughing in each other's faces. The only human is me, a confused old fart with all the righteous pent-up anger leaking out of him.

There's a freshly stenciled message on the wall, and I don't need my phone to understand it: *Koronapárty ve VR*—Corona Party in VR. The words are accompanied by an old-school QR code.

I stare at the message in disbelief, then dig out my phone and scan the code. My screen fills instantly with a mob of avatars, dancing cartoons superimposed over the grungy concrete room, all grinning because they know something I don't. I walk in a dazed circle, holding my phone out in front of me. The avatars can't see me. I walk through them like a ghost.

I disconnect from the feed, feeling a lump of hard plastic in my throat. I'm in an empty half-built building, pissed off at people who aren't here. Nobody to rage at. Nobody breaking lockdown rules or curfew, except for me in about ten minutes. Just a bunch of kids throwing an online party and using a slummy old building as their backdrop.

And of course I didn't storm over here for the greater good. I did it to unload some of the anger that's been curling around me tighter and tighter for months now. Anger at Jan for leaving me all alone. Anger at myself for keeping it that way, for turning down my sister's facecalls and backing out of visits, for giving up on work. Lockdown's the perfect excuse to shrink the world down to a cage and not let anybody inside.

Since nobody's around, I finally let a few tears out. It hurts. Feeling mad's always been so much easier than feeling sad for me. But I let the tears come, and after a while it feels okay, even if it's fogging up my mask something awful.

There's another message stenciled under the QR code, and this one I feel I should know—the words sort of prick at my memory. *Každý je vítán*, it says. I blink and frown at it, then finally hover my phone over it.

Everyone is welcome.

I think of the VR goggles gathering dust at the top of my closet, the ones I promised my sister I would start using. I really doubt the kids meant me, but it would be kind of a laugh, wouldn't it, just to pop in. Maybe just long enough to tell my sister I attended a localized virtual reality corona party when I finally facecall her.

The housebot can probably help me calibrate everything. It's cleverer than it lets on.

7 MAKING HAY

Cory Doctorow

ALL OF WILMAR'S FRIENDS AT THE FACTORY HAD WATCHED THE STORM HEADING toward the Mojave for a week, watched it gathering force, watched as it defied the best predictions as it failed to veer off toward the ocean, carving a line from Portland, through Sacramento, sparing Vegas, arrowing for their concrete plant.

Wilmar had a feeling about this one. It was going to squat over the factory for a long, long time. Long enough that he could go home to Burbank, see his family, his old school buds. He hadn't been home in the fall for a long time, but the weather kept getting weirder and the spring rains were now fall rains, he guessed.

But after five days back home, Wilmar was ready to get back to work. It wasn't that he missed his work friends. Truth be told, he wasn't that tight with anyone in Mojave yet. He'd been at the factory for most of a year, ever since graduation, and he'd made only weak friendships there. But he missed the work.

HIS FIFTH MORNING BACK HOME, WILMAR COULDN'T EVEN BE BOTHERED TO GET OUT of bed. His internal weather matched it, grayness clouding his personal sun, and he recognized the signs of his brain doing its bad thing again.

Hiding under the covers, he started pull-refreshing Friendster and swiping.

It offered many people for Wilmar to hang out with—old high school friends, people who loved the same board games as him, people who liked hiking the same trails as him, people who liked the same kinds of clubs as him. There were dinner parties and dance parties and people who needed help moving or with community projects like digging out empty lots contaminated by old Lockheed fuel leaks. Burbank didn't have a lot of heavy industry anymore, but the construction sites and even some of the productions at the studios shut down when the sun stopped shining, and there were lots of people with time on their hands. But he swiped past all of them.

He knew himself well enough to recognize the signs of depression, and he knew that the best thing for it was to socialize, but he just couldn't bear the thought of it. Somewhere, the sun was shining or the wind was blowing or the tides were crashing on the shore, and there was energy to spare, and so in those places, workers who'd been enjoying a break had been liberated from parties and family and lying in hammocks and had been sent back to work in factories just like his, sintering prefab concrete and craning it onto long, slow-moving electric trains for shipment to the inland newtowns.

"Wilmar, are you still in bed?"

His mom had surprised him by seeming *much* older than she had just a few months before, but now he'd gotten used to it and was mostly surprised by how hard she found it to knock before entering his room. She said it wasn't his room anymore, it was her "office."

"Yes, Mom."

She scowled. "I have work to do, kiddo. Papers to mark. Up and at 'em."

Mom had always marked papers at the kitchen table, and as far as Wilmar knew, that was fine with her. Apparently it wasn't fine with her and had never been fine with her and she wasn't going back to it any time soon. How much concentration and peace and quiet did she to need to review eighth graders' essays about Shakespeare anyway?

He pulled himself out of bed and dressed and even made the bed and gave his mom a kiss on the cheek when she pushed past him to sit at her desk with her tablet.

After a late breakfast, he sat on the front lawn on a folding chair, amid the late zucchini and the *very* late sunflowers—in September, seriously?—and nodded at the people going past. A dozen kids blocked off most of Verdugo and set up a street-hockey game, letting the odd car squeeze past at a crawl in the single lane they'd left clear, calling a time out and making more space if two cars needed to pass in opposite directions, though the drivers got dagger-stares for not timing their crossing better.

In Wilmar's boyhood, every day had been known and knowable far in advance—if you asked him what he'd be doing on a specific Tuesday two years from then, he could tell you that—barring illness or maybe a wildfire—he'd be in school, and then maybe at band practice, and then home gaming.

Then the first pandemic had broken that rhythm, and the second pandemic had killed it. The idea that what was going on in the world would have nothing to do with what you did in the world had seemed totally natural until he was twelve. Six years later, it was such an obviously stupid idea that he couldn't believe that whole civilizations had fallen for it for, like, *centuries*.

All of the panels he made at the factory had been headed for San Juan Capistrano, a city he'd visited in elementary school when they'd done a unit on the eighteenth-century Missions of the Spanish conquistadors. The Surfliner was still running then, and his class had taken over a whole car. Now most of the Surfliner tracks had been dangerously undermined by years of storm swells. The last train had run five years before.

Suddenly, Wilmar stood bolt upright, the chair tipping backward into his mother's succulents. He should go to San Juan Capistrano!

HIS MOM MADE A FUSS BUT HE COULD TELL SHE WAS GLAD TO SEE HIM GO. HE FOUND a bike and rode it to the Burbank Airport station just in time to hop a train to Union Station, and used the short trip to swipe through a lot more Friendster profiles, these ones all for SJC. The system found him a ton of friends-of-a-friend, and by the time he got to Union Station, he'd found a FOAF sofa for two nights and had a FOAF dinner date. He changed trains and an hour later, he was pulling into SJC and the dinner date had turned into a dinner party in a new park in the New SJC.

He found a bike and clipped his phone to the handlebars and let it map him to the park.

It was getting on rush hour and there were tons of bikes in the bike lanes, and full buses passed him in the bus lane. Even this far inland, SJC's air smelled of sea salt, and lots of the apartment balconies had wetsuits and surfboards on them. The route to the new park was uphill all the way, of course. Everything in new SJC was uphill, because going inland was good, but high ground was better.

The park was in the shadow of a grid of huge turbines that thrummed overhead and creaked as they tuned themselves so that each one fed its slipstream to the one behind it, maximizing efficiency. He ditched the bike against a rack and flipped Friendster into friendfinder mode and let it guide him to a group of people his age with blankets and frisbees and deep tans and scratched knuckles.

"Hey," he said. "I'm Wilmar?"

They shouted a flurry of hellos and someone handed him a beer and someone else gave him a tamale from a thermos steamer. He tossed it from hand to hand until it cooled off, then unwrapped it and accepted a dollop of habanero sauce.

There were a dozen people when he arrived, but more trickled in, and he was given a fresh orange, half an avocado (and a compostable spoon), hard kombucha, and a cup of gazpacho. He played frisbee, talked Burbank politics, talked national politics, collected tips on the best coffee and baked goods in newtown and old SJC, and even saw a swallow.

"We're putting nesting cavities in every building," Treesa said. She looked younger than Wilmar but she said she was working on the new-town buildout so he figured she had to be older than she looked—the Jobs Guarantee wouldn't give heavy industry gigs to people until they were eighteen. She had gone to summer surfing camp with a guy who'd been on Wilmar's swim team and had a first cousin who worked at the gym where Wilmar's dad went for physio. These connections didn't make for much conversation beyond the openers, but the openers were all they needed. She was funny and smart, and she knew every single thing about the newtown.

"No one knows where their migration patterns'll be in a decade or two, but there's a prof at UC Riverside who thinks that if we provide them with habitats and food there's a good chance that they'll keep this as their terminus."

"Are you studying zoology?" Wilmar asked.

"Maybe," she said. "I got my AP biology, but I'm taking a couple years off for this—" She waved her arm at the mid-rises around them, the street-car and bus tracks, the park. "My family's been in San Juan Capistrano since the Mission days. My umpty-great grandpa was a bricklayer, and when I was a kid my dad used to point out all the buildings he helped with. Doing this—" another expansive gesture—"it feels right."

"That's incredible," he said. He cracked another hard kombucha. It was sour and tart, and someone told him it was 7 percent, which explained how lightheaded he was. "Working in Mojave, I'd watch the slabs pile up on the loading docks, watch them head out on the freighters, and I'd wonder about the people on the other end."

"Did you ever put notes on them?"

"Notes?"

"In marker," she said. "That permanent greasepen? We get a lot of slabs with notes on 'em, I see them sometimes when I'm priming the slabs after they're in place. I've got a whole gallery of them." He leaned in close to see the screen she spread out, swiped through her pictures: "THIS SIDE UP" and "HELL OR HIGH WATER" and then political slogans "UWAYNI FOR A THIRD TERM" and "HART'S A TOOL."

"There was so much election stuff, it was crazy," she said, finding him more.

"I had no idea," he said. "Maybe we don't do that in Mojave—maybe it's just the other factories?" He knew of at least ten that served the San Juan Capistrano project, in an arc that went south to San Diego and north to Nevada. Mojave was the closest one to home, so he'd gone for it, thinking that he could shuttle back and forth. Why had he thought that would be good?

"Treesa!" They both looked around to see who was calling, and then Treesa's hands tightened on the screen, scrunching it. It was an older woman, hair under a kerchief and dirty clothes, heading their way across the park. She looked homeless, but did they really have homeless people in San Juan Capistrano? What about the housing guarantee?

"Hi, Auntie Lanelle," Treesa said, rising to intercept the woman before she could reach them. Wilmar tried not to stare as they started talking in low tones.

But then the woman started crying and Treesa hugged her and patted her back, and that only made her sob louder. Wilmar decided he should help.

"Can I do something?"

Treesa glared at him for a moment, then softened. "It's OK," she said. The woman loosened her grip on Treesa, dug a dirty face-scarf out of a pocket and wiped her eyes and blew her nose.

"Hello," she said. "Are you a friend of Treesa's? I'm her great aunt, Lanelle Carter." Her voice was thin and cracked. She held out her hand, and Wilmar made himself shake it, and immediately got that "need-hand-san" feeling on that hand, the subconscious need to keep from touching anything else. He noticed the feeling and was mildly ashamed: he could tell himself that it was just normal pathogen prudence, but he knew deep down that he was recoiling at her broken-ness, her living proof of social failure.

"It's nice to meet you, Ms Carter. I'm Wilmar Nazarian. I'm visiting from Burbank."

"Oh," she said, and got a faraway look. "We have people in Burbank. Did you know that, Treesa? My mother's baby brother Norbert took his family there. We used to visit them for Fourth of July. Such wonderful fireworks."

"How are you doing, Auntie?" Treesa asked. "Come and get a plate."

None of Treesa's friends wanted to hang out with her homeless great-aunt either, so they formed a little island on a picnic blanket, with a wide, empty space all around them. "Are we socially distancing again?" Treesa's auntie asked vaguely.

"No, Auntie," Treesa said, giving her a handful of freeze-dried apple chips.

They sat in awkward silence as she ate. Wilmar thought of watching *A Kung-Fu Panda Christmas Carol* with his brothers, thought of the Ghost of Christmas Past. After his glum days in Burbank, he'd felt like he'd found a better mood in SJC. But the darkness was creeping in around the edges again.

"These are wonderful," she said and daintily dabbed at her lips with her dirty scarf.

"Where are you sleeping, Auntie?" Treesa's voice was soft.

Her aunt got a suspicious look. "I'm fine, girl, don't worry about me."

"You can get an apartment here." Now Treesa's voice had gone hard. "You're entitled to one. Everyone whose place was flooded out—"

Her aunt cut her off with a sharp gesture and suddenly she was much more present. "I have made it very clear that I do not want to live here. I want to live in my home. Our family home. Your great-grandfather—"

"Built a home that is now *underwater*, Auntie. I loved that house, too. But we're not fish, Auntie."

She made a sour face. "I don't want to argue with you."

A glum silence descended again. Treesa avoided Wilmar's eye. He wondered if there was some graceful way to gtfo, but now that everyone else had distanced themselves, he'd be abandoning her. True, she was basically a stranger, but she'd come out for his Friendster call, so she was the kind of good person that he should be good to.

"I love you, Treesa. Best be on my way."

He watched her struggle with herself. "Stay at my place, Auntie. I'll take the sofa."

He aunt didn't even look back: "Told you I didn't need charity." She walked off, stooped and limping.

They didn't say anything for too long. He decided he should say something.

"I'm sorry about your aunt, Treesa."

A flash of anger, then sadness. "Me too."

Should he go? Could he? He could fake a message from his couch-surf for the night and slink off. But Treesa really looked like she was hurting.

"You remember Uwayni's first inauguration?"

"Sure," he said. He'd been nine and everyone in the house had gathered around the biggest tablet to watch it, playing the audio on every speaker. His parents' faces had shone and he'd caught some of their excitement. "For the first time in a century, we will raise—"

She picked up it: "A generation that is not afraid of the future." She smiled. Such a sad smile. "Musta heard that a thousand times in school." She pulled up a tuft of long, blue-green, drought-resistant grass, shook it like a pom-pom. "Our cheerleaders even had a cheer for it."

"Well, it's true," Wilmar said. "Isn't it?"

A silence so long that he wondered if she'd heard, then, "Yeah, it's true. Talk to my dad, he still doesn't believe it. Secretly he thinks we're all doomed, the planets' gonna roast and drown. And the generation before him—"

"Your aunt's generation."

"Them. For them, it's like they're refugees. We think we're building the promised land, they see it as a camp." She flopped on her back on the blanket and threw the clump of grass away. "Sometimes, I'll come around a corner here and there'll be a whole new building, a whole neighborhood even, and it doesn't matter how many times I do the city plan flythrough and how many AR walkthroughs I take, it always takes my breath away. For me, this isn't a refugee camp, it's salvation. Our city was drowning and we used our own hands and our own backs to move it a mile inland and 500 feet uphill. We even relocated the Mission, one brick at a time!"

Wilmar lay back too. "I watched that. We all did, in Mojave. The stream was amazing. So many cool things under the ground and in the walls. Those dirty drawings that nun did—"

She laughed "You know they bricked them back up in the wall when they put it back together?"

"No way."

She waved her hands in the air over them, seeming to grab at the stars appearing overhead. "Scanned them first, of course, but yeah. Every weird thing, down to the tin can full of old bottlecaps we found under the vegetable beds."

He laughed, and they got quiet again.

"I'm sorry about your aunt."

"I'm sorry you had to see her. It's hard."

"Don't be sorry for that."

"I am, though. My family business. My problem."

To his great surprise, Wilmar began to weep.

"Oh, shit, dude—" She was looming over him now, worried.

He armed tears off his cheeks and dug tears out of his ears and sat up. Why couldn't he stop crying? This was so stupid. He found his own face mask in a side pocket of his backpack and wiped ferociously at his face.

What he wanted, more than anything, was to stop crying, but that was not possible, it seemed.

"Wilmar? What is it? Can you talk about it?"

He pushed his breathing, slowed it, wiped his eyes and nose. "I'm sorry."

"You've got nothing to be sorry for and I forgive you anyways. Want to talk about it?"

"It's just my shit," he said. "Honestly, it'll be OK."

"I believe you. But also, if you want to talk—"

He did, but he didn't want to burden this stranger. "It's OK."

She got in his face. This close, he could see that she had a little zit on one cheek, see her dimples, see the dot where she'd taken out an old nose piercing. "Wilmar, dude, if it's OK, it's OK. But everyone's got some shit and everyone needs to talk about it from time to time. You don't know me and I don't know you and sometimes, that makes it easier. Just think about that before you bottle this all back up again."

His breathing and tears were under control, but the clouds that had closed in on him that morning and kept him in bed were back again. He thought about Treesa's great aunt, broken and alone, and wondered if that could be him in a few decades.

He thought about how she'd refused to even discuss the situation. He opened up.

"OK, the fact is that I live with depression. I mean, everyone does to some extent and it's not always on top of me but sometimes it just comes for a visit and sits on my chest and won't get up. It whispers in my ear, tells me things will be terrible, that I'm terrible, that I'm not doing any good."

He drew a shuddering breath. "Something about that Uwayni speech always seems to bring it on." What were the right words for this? He'd never said them. Could he find them now? "I am afraid. That's it. I'm supposed to be unafraid of the future, the first fear-free generation in a century but I'm so scared all the time. I watch the panels come off my line and

I think it's crazy, there's no way we're going to relocate every coastal city in the country—"

"In the world," she said.

"The world! No way. The storms are worse every year, the heat is crazy, none of the flowers bloom on time anymore, the bees are still dying—"

"Not as quickly."

"Not as quickly. Fine. Maybe we can save the bees. But I just can't make the math work in my head. There's so much to do. And then they send me home because there's clouds over the factory—"

"You can't save the world from runaway CO2 by producing trillions of tons of CO2. You know that, Wilmar. The job feels too big for you because it *is*. It's a team sport, dude. The best thing you can do for the planet is fix stuff. And when you can't fix stuff, the best thing you can do is stop breaking stuff. Hanging out in a park is just about the most benign thing you can do for the planet. The sun's out somewhere, and they're doing the work for us. You can stand down."

"I know you're right. But I feel like such a, such a fraud. Like everyone else is all 'we got this,' and I'm all 'holy shit, we're all going to fucking roast' and the only thing that keeps me going is working so hard I don't have room to think about it. Soon as work stops . . ." He flapped his arm at the world, at himself.

She stood up and stuck her hand out. "Come on," she said.

He took her hand. It was strong and calloused from building a new city. As the sun set, she took him on a tour of it.

IT WAS A BEAUTIFUL PLACE. THOUGH THE BUILDINGS WERE BUILT FROM STANDARD parts, there were so many ways to recombine them, and more were emerging every day, as modelers and designers and builders shared their inventions. Some neighborhoods were made from buildings that looked like scaled-up missions, others had a beachy, SoCal, mid-century feel, while others were like jumbled-together craftsman houses, hard to tell where one stopped and the next started. All had broad public spaces—interior courtyards, community gardens, playgrounds. He fell in love with a place that had the feel of a Moroccan town from an old movie, with tall pink stucco buildings whose round-shouldered doors echoed the archways that defined their alleys. They got delicious strong coffee from a self-serve cart and baklava from some kids with a card table and a hand-lettered sign, and two older women came and kissed Treesa on the cheek and made her promise to come for dinner that week. She seemed delighted to make the promise.

Everywhere they went, they saw people—cooking out, playing, jogging, strolling. It was a strolling city, with even the biggest structures pierced by walkways that led out to narrow streets or broad parks. Even carrying his backpack, even tired and emotionally wrung out, Wilmar kept pushing on, curious about what he'd find around the next corner, and the next.

"It's amazing," he said, as they reached a lookout that offered a clear vista out to sea, where the moonrise was staining the tips of the waves white.

"How are you holding up?" she asked.

He did his mental-health thing, actually cataloging the messages in his brain for signs of the inward-spiral of self-loathing. It wasn't so bad. In fact, it was absolutely better than it had been. "OK, I think." He dug a baggie of trailmix out of his bag and shook himself a handful, then offered some to her.

Now she led him to the old town, the original town. The drowned town. The outskirts were marshy, but soon they found their way to an interconnected set of pontoon walkways that floated in the shallow, brackish water over the old lawns and streets and sidewalks, the splash of the pontoons and the creak of the wooden sections mixing with the insect roar. It was a haunted place, soft and decaying, with houses down on their knees or reduced to just a few uprights. Fish splashed in the distance, and the old graffiti was still visible in the twilight: "2 INSIDE"—"DEAD INSIDE"— "TRESSPASSERS WILL." Rusted parking signs stuck up out of the water like Venetian gondola bricolas, and they heard the distant voices of canoers out for an evening's paddle. The storefronts' windows were long, long gone, and the stores themselves were dark caves blowing soft fungal smells.

But amid them were sprawling mangroves, planted early in the crisis and now grown to early maturity thanks to their hybrid genes, knucklebones piercing the Pacific Coast Highway where it stuck up out of the water.

"In a couple years this place will be all marshland," she said. "But there's plans to keep a surf beach a couple miles up the coast, somewhere that doesn't have quite so many buried snags."

The insect song rose with the moon. They watched as it silvered the ruins and turned the ripples of the water into light shows, thinking their thoughts, watching a city that had stood for a quarter of a millennium disintegrate before their eyes.

BY THE TIME WILMAR AROSE THE NEXT DAY, HIS COUCH-SURFING HOST WAS ALREADY at work, having left behind some breakfast stuff and a nice note with some tips for things to do and see in town. The list was great, especially the little museum of treasures they'd found when they dug out the old town, but Wilmar didn't want to do any of that stuff.

He DMed Treesa instead, and an hour later, he was on her job site, getting trained on fitting together the slabs that they craned off of the railcar on its spur. An hour after that, he finished his first stretch of wall, on the third story of a ten-unit low-rise that followed a ridgeline with good views inland, to the scrub and woods on the site of the old golf course.

When it was time for lunch, they sat together and ate tamales. "You're supposed to be on vacation, dude. Are you sure this is good self-care?" Her tone was light but she was serious.

"I'm fine. Better than fine. I think the problem was that working in Mojave, it was like this endless conveyor belt—make a slab, ship a slab, make a slab, do it forever, until the world is saved. But this—" he slapped the wall they were leaning against "—it's real. You can *see* it. You can *live in it*. I think maybe I wanna try working here for a while."

"If you say so." She gave him a half-joking side-eye. "But you're the one who says you work to get away from your anxieties."

He felt himself getting angry, caught the physical signs in his jaw and hands, then made himself calm down. She wasn't wrong. "I have a theory about you," he said.

Full side-eye now. "Go on."

"I think this work is how you cope, too. Like, if you can build the right kind of new city up here on the hill, your aunt and everyone else can stop mourning what they lost."

She looked away and was quiet for so long he got worried.

"Treesa, I'm sorry, that was out of line. I apologize sincerely."

She looked at him, eyes brimming, then swiped at them. "It's OK." Her voice was thick. "Really. Yeah, that's it all right. My mom went in the '28 pandemic, and at the end she was so scared. Not scared that she was gonna die. So many people had died then, we'd made our peace with that, all of us. She was scared of the world they were leaving me in." She thumped the wall. "When I do this, it's like I'm dealing with it for her.

"Truth is, I'm scared of the future. Sure, we can build a new city in the hills. Maybe we can do that for every coastal city. But it won't do us a damned bit of good against wildfires. It won't bring back the extinct species. It won't stop the plagues. When I get to thinking about it I am so scared.

"But when I'm working, I can pretend that we can fix this. And if I can fool myself into thinking it's fine, then maybe I can deal with whatever's coming."

She blew her nose on a face-scarf. "It's stupid, I know."

"No," Wilmar said. "No, that's not stupid at all."

Karl Schroeder

THE SPACE IS AN ABSTRACT GAME LEVEL, RENDERED IN LOW-RES CELL SHADING. Gray and beige; benign but not very informative. Remy slides his finger along the smooth arm of his glasses, and the scene becomes textured.

"—of interest is over here," somebody is saying. Remy looks for his usual cues to understand who it is, and spots the worn sneakers that Inspector Kraft insists on wearing with any suit. Kraft isn't looking his way, but Detective Sendak is frantically waving Remy over. He has no trouble recognizing her distinctive slouch. He turns around several times as he walks over, still taking in the overall shape of the location.

"—that the forensics consultant?" somebody else says. "He looks a little—?"

"Yes, this is Remy Reardon. Hsst, Remy, get over here! He's not part of my regular team, he usually works with architects. We hire him sometimes."

Despite his attempts to be inconspicuous, several heads turn Remy's way, including the inspector's, so he tweaks his detail levels. *Appear normal*, he tells himself. The blockiness of his surroundings dissolves, in its place brick and old wood beams, grimy industrial pebbled-glass windows. It's cold in here; he had already noticed the smell.

He's overtuned his glasses in his hurry, and they go flatly realist for a second, then color- and contrast-enhance everything. He can see every pore on Kraft's face, and every scuff on the floorboards. "Good morning," Remy says, walking over to the two ordinary chairs that sit facing each other in the center of the space. Bright pink ropes coil around the legs and back of one of them.

Kraft is standing behind that chair, and another man Remy recognizes as the medical examiner is kneeling in front.

Kraft is looking at him; does he expect something? Remy casts about for a helpful statement, and finally comes up with, "This placement is interesting."

"What placement?" Kraft stares at him.

Remy feels like he's made some kind of faux pas, and clears his throat. "The chairs are sitting in the acoustic center of the space." He sweeps his hand in a circle. "It's a fifty-foot cube, with a loft overhang fifteen feet wide on the entrance side." His glasses gave him all these measurements; it's so much easier to navigate using the numbers than to drown in the visual details of the actual place.

He walks past Sendak, who smiles at him, and over to one wall. There's a radiator and above that a half-open window of heavy wired glass. "Somebody climbed out there?" Remy asks. "I saw blood stains in the parking lot."

Sendak nods. "What about the placement?"

"A normal person would be more furtive. Whoever did this wasn't ashamed. He wanted his victim to hear his own screams reflected back . . . It's very deliberate."

Kraft laughs humorlessly. "Well, an amateur wouldn't have dissected this guy's forearm while he was still alive."

"Oh? And the victim still climbed out a window ten feet off the floor? Who is he?"

"Ralph Cawley," says Kraft crisply. "Computer programmer, lives on the east side. He's alive, and made it to a hospital before he collapsed. When he's awake enough to talk, he's refusing to do so. But the reason I called you is Cawley's family, his wife and daughters, they're missing. Looks like yesterday, just after he escaped. Seems to me whoever took him wants something, and didn't get it from him on their first try. Now they've got his wife and girls. Finding them is the most important thing right now." Kraft looks at Remy, who recognizes his frown.

"You called me because you're grasping at straws."

Kraft blows out a breath. "Sendak's boys have already been all over this place and Cawley's not cooperating. You're a genius at noticing little details that other people miss. I thought you could help, is all."

The examiner is on his feet now, dusting his hands. He eyes Remy. "Those smart glasses you wear. They have something to do with it?"

"I'm very sensitive to noise and light," he tells the examiner. "Nikola Tesla was the same way. These help me narrow in on important details. Tune out the background."

"A cousin of mine is on the spectrum. Maybe he could use a pair."

"They need to be custom designed. I know a guy who does the programming."

Remy notices that he's started tapping his belt in a repeating pattern, one-two-three-four, one-two-three-four. He searches himself for signs of agitation, finds faster breathing, that he's swaying a bit on his feet. He starts turning down the detail in the room. "As I was saying, whoever tortured Cawley arranged this setting for maximum effect. Probably a man, who clearly wanted something from him. Cawley . . . the name sounds familiar. What kind of programming does he do?"

Kraft pulls out his phone and flips through his notes. "Sez here . . . homomorphic encryption systems. Secure voting. Didn't you do some work on that?"

Remy nods once, has to do it three more times. He turns down the room's detail some more. "There could be a motive. He may have wanted Cawley to tell him how to hack the quadratic polling system. Even torture didn't work, though, so he decided to take the family hostage. For leverage. I say 'he' because if it was just one person, he had to leave Cawley alone to go after them. That's how Cawley escaped."

He turns up his glasses so he can see Kraft better. "You're right, we need to find the kidnapper right away, before he decides that what Cawley told him is true."

"Which would be . . . ?"

"That hacking the vote is impossible."

"I KNOW WHAT 'DOWN THE HALL' MEANS," REMY SAYS IN THE CAR, FIFTEEN MINUTES later.

"What do you mean?" He's memorized Sendak's broad, indigenous face and noted that she has a ready smile. Her squad car isn't one of the new self-driving models, but he's developing a theory that she likes driving, from the way she attentively steers them through complex downtown traffic.

"I heard Kraft say to the examiner, 'he's the responsibility of the boys down the hall.' I know what that means."

She shifts in her seat. "Do you mean he thinks of me as your babysitter?"

"No. Major Crimes is one of the few departments left over from the old police force. Kraft resents the replacements, like the Mental Health Emergency Task Force, Short-Term Housing, Domestic Abuse. The targeted initiatives. They're all down the hall from his office, along with your Forensics department."

"Don't rain all over Kraft. He's watched his whole way of life turn into a dumpster fire. The pandemic, the defunding, then the economic reset—you should be grateful he hasn't joined all the other old geezers in their bunkers, with their canned beans and ammunition."

"Where are we going again?" Remy tunes his glasses down to the point where they're gliding through a featureless blockworld.

"To the Cawley house. Kraft thought you might spot something there."

"Something that your team missed."

"Well I haven't been there yet either. You want to make a bet who'll find the first clue?"

Remy blinks at her.

He says, "Community Outreach is more likely to get you results. Maybe someone in the neighborhood saw something."

"Yeah, yeah. You're gonna tell me it's faster and more effective than looking under shoes. Everybody says that, lately."

"Maybe we should bet. Where is the Cawley house?" She tells him and he nods. "That's near where I live. I can make you lunch."

"Remy, we have three missing people to find. No lunch."

"Oh, of course."

"Argh, they're drowning us with those things!" She's glaring at something above street level; he fumbles with his detail levels and looks up to see some billboard screens. One is screening a referendum ad: Vote Early, Vote Often! A little up the avenue another is saying Buy Votes for Citizens' Panels. His glasses' preferences highlight a more distant one that says Testing Centers Get No Traffic in Ten Days, but Sendak's probably not talking about that one.

She says, "Back at the crime scene you said you thought they didn't like what Cawley told them. Something about the vote."

"It can't be a coincidence that he helped program the system. There is the referendum coming up."

"Yeah." She returns her attention to the traffic. "Not sure what to think about that, myself. Not that I'm feeling murderous, but potentially changing how our municipal democracy works is a pretty big deal. There's a lot of people just like Kraft, they want to keep the old city council even though it was totally corrupt. For them the referendum choices amount to another huge change after years of change—and nobody over fifty understands quadratic voting anyway. Five years ago I'd never heard of it."

"I remember Cawley a little now, though I never met him in person," says Remy. "Before I . . . moved into the city . . . I worked a bit with his team. That was at the tail end of the Third Wave. Even then he was getting huge push-back—people either wanted to crack his code so they could rig the vote, or they wanted to prove it could be hacked so they could derail the whole project." He watches the signs dwindle behind them. "I vote whenever I can, but a lot of people resent not being allowed to vote every time."

"Yeah, and why can't we? I keep hearing explanations, but they never add up. My cousin swears it's totally to control the electorate."

"No, it's the opposite." Remy remembers the fine-tuning that went into the system. In the quadratic system your first vote is free, but you can buy more. Each vote after the first one costs the square of its number times 10. So the second one costs $40, the third costs $90, the fourth $160, and if you want to buy a thousand you'll be paying $10 million. The system's designed so that people literally invest in the issues that matter the most to them. People with a lot of money might sway the vote, but only by putting a lot of cash into the public purse.

Early on some developers had tried paying off large swathes of the city's poorest to vote their way. The random lottery solves that problem, by making sure that most, possibly all of your vote-fixing money goes to people who won't end up being able to vote. Instead, a representative minority casts the actual ballots.

"Yeah, it probably feels wrong to people who are used to the old system. But a random lottery to select voters makes it way more expensive to buy votes. People just don't get the math."

"What?" says Sendak. "You think that somebody who *doesn't get the math* went after Cawley, thinking he could do something he couldn't to the voting system? What a waste."

Remy blinks. "Or maybe Cawley just had gambling debts. We'll see."

BUT IT WASN'T GAMBLING DEBTS. "THE BANK SAYS CAWLEY WAS GETTING SOME pretty big payouts from offshore accounts," Kraft tells Remy an hour later. "He wasn't losing money, he was making it. Tons of it."

Remy's taking the call outside the Cawley house, which is in one of the reconstructed neighborhoods near Downtown. This side street has been given over to bikeways and parkland, probably after the Second Wave. Many of the eyesore buildings and empty lots in the area, fought over for decades by developers, are now green space. After the contraction of the fossil fuel industries, the air is clean.

Sendak strolls up. After a cursory look through the house, which has already been thoroughly combed by her team, she's decided to speak to the neighbors. Community Outreach, like Remy suggested. She's wearing a mask, which she carefully stows as she comes up the walk. "Lot of locals still won't talk to you at the door unless you're wearing one," she explains.

"That's ridiculous. There hasn't been a case in the city in months."

"Once bitten, twice shy. Thrice bitten, thoroughly paranoid. Find anything?"

He shakes his head. "I'm sure your people saw that their suitcases are still here. Just to follow up, I compared the trash to what they had in the pantry. When people are getting ready to travel—or run—they tend to use up their perishables. That's not the case here. I don't think they left of their own accord."

She waits, then when he just stands there, she says, "This is the part where you say, 'What about you, Maureen? Did you find anything?' And where I say, 'Yes, why yes, I did.'"

Agreeably, he says, "What about you, Maureen? Did you find anything?"

She takes out her phone. "A couple of people saw a black SUV parked in front of the Cawley place two days ago. It wasn't there long."

"Did they get a license plate? Because there must be thousands of black SUVs in town."

"A lot of people 'round here have porch cams. So I asked around, just to see if anybody had footage that showed the street. Got a couple of hits."

She shows him the videos on her phone. There are three, none of which are good enough to read the license plate. One, though, shows a vague, pixelated profile of the driver through the side window.

"That might be a tattoo on his neck," says Remy, "but it's too dark to see the face. Maybe they can do signal processing on it. Wait, what's that?" He points.

"Hmm—wrist watch?"

"Mm, more like a tracker." After the first vaccines proved to be insufficient on their own, social isolation and contact tracing were rolled out nationwide. Companies making fitness trackers were happy to add the functionality to their devices, and suddenly they were no longer just for exercise buffs and 'quantified self' people. At one point he remembers every single person he met wearing a tracker of some kind—mostly on the wrist.

"So we got nothing," she admits. He stares out at the little urban gardens for a minute, and when he glances at Sendak he sees a pinched expression on her face. That must be what frustration looks like.

"Look, Remy, I'm on the clock," she says. "I've gotta get back to the lab, is there anything more you can do?"

Remy literally has no idea. He doesn't like this feeling of helplessness. "I live a few minutes from here. Could you drop me off before you go back?"

She sighs. "Okay. Maybe Kraft's got a new plan."

They drive into one of the former business areas, now converted into low-cost housing like much of Downtown. Sendak parks next to a glass-walled building that used to be part of an office park. It's across from a real park, with trees and grass and open space. This is Remy's essential source of peace and quiet if he's outside, but today it's overrun with people. Somebody's holding a political rally.

He starts to tune it out as he gets out of the car, then notices something. "There's a friend of mine," he says to Sendak.

She blinks. "How can you tell?" The nearest person is a hundred feet away.

"He's got a flag up in my glasses." Remy crosses the road and heads for the gates to the park. This is only possible because he tunes the detail levels right down to the minimum; even so he can feel the chaotic pressure of the crowd in his mind as he approaches it.

He expected Sendak would drive away but she gets out of the car and follows him up to a table by the entrance. Here, volunteers are handing out wrist bands. One jumps up, laughing, as Remy approaches. "Remy Reardon! How you doing, man? And who's your friend?" Remy belatedly remembers to introduce Sendak.

"Xander Reese, nice to meet you. So you know the great Remy Reardon."

"Yeah, we work together, sometimes. How do you know him?"

"I was the contact tracing expert at St. Mary's Hospital." There's just the faintest pause then, as he and Sendak exchange a look; St. Mary's is a psychiatric hospital. This shared look is one of those episodes of invisible communication that intensely frustrate Remy. When it happens, it's like the other people are talking behind an invisible pane of glass. "I also programmed his glasses," Xander finishes.

Sendak crosses her arms and stares into the crowded park. "Look at it! A mob. Who'd have thought ordinary folk would get that close again?"

"That's why we're here." Reese holds up one of the wrist bands. "Some people have been tossing their trackers. Privacy, you know? I get it. But if there's an outbreak, we need to trace each and every contact to squash it. So you gotta wear one to get in."

The sound of the crowd is creeping around the edges of Remy's mind, increasingly distracting. He stands still, head tilted, vaguely aware that

Reese is telling Sendak about the contact tracing app, about the cryptography it uses to perfectly preserve anonymity.

"Crypto!" Her voice rises in a way that means Remy should pay attention. "Like these clowns and their quadratic vote! It's all game theory and math. You can't turn something as sloppy as human nature into math."

Reese shrugs. "I guess you're in favor of citizens' panels?"

"Damn straight. Grab a bunch of people at random, just like you do for jury trials. Give 'em a minimal test to make sure they understand the issue they're gonna be dealing with, and then let 'em work the problem. But no, 'the quadratic way is the best!' Bend over backward to prevent voter fraud by draining away all the human elements, until all that's left is an algorithm. It solves your problem, but only by sucking the life out of politics." She takes a calming breath. "Okay," she says, "so here's a question: What could you do if you could hack ballot software?"

"Well . . . you'd be able to influence the vote, obviously."

"Influence? Not outright ballot-stuff?"

"It's pretty obvious when a hundred percent of the voters choose one candidate. Yeah, you can stuff digital ballot boxes, but man you gotta be subtle. Anyway, the whole point is that it *is* hack-proof. You can't cheat. Nobody can. I mean—you've been using it every day for years," Reese adds.

"When?" says Sendak. "I don't vote every day."

"You don't use it only for voting. Like I was saying, the first place they used it was for contact tracing, in the middle of the pandemic. So you could be part of the tracing network without ever giving away your personal details. You're being tracked anonymously every time you spend more than fifteen minutes near someone. So, weirdly enough, a lot of the same tech went into both the ballot system and the contact tracing software."

"I like quadratic voting," Remy tries to say, but the world's receding down a tunnel of sound and light. The glasses are only so good at blocking things out.

He vaguely hears Sendak say, "Um, Remy? Yeah, I think I'd better run you home."

"Yeah, he's gettin' overloaded, isn't he? Take it easy, Remy! Talk to you soon."

Remy doesn't answer as Sendak leads him away.

REMY PUSHES INTO HIS APARTMENT, SENDAK RIGHT BEHIND HIM. HE PAUSES TO lean on the kitchen counter and after a while, notices that she's stopped in the doorway, staring.

"Yeah, I painted everything black," he admits. Not just the walls, but the appliances, the chairs, the cutlery. "That way I can skin things however I want, you know, with the glasses." To him it's all its usual neutral shades of beige and mauve, with callout labels attached to various things that are out of sight—like in drawers or under other objects. All very convenient to him, but Sendak doesn't use Mixed Reality. To her his home must look like a vortex of darkness.

"Aw, Remy—"

"Go." He waves at her weakly. "Go. You have to win our bet. There's not much time."

"You're sure you'll be okay?"

"Yeah. I just get overwhelmed sometimes."

"Then why do you live here?"

"This place?"

"No. This city."

"Oh. I kind of . . . ended up here. After we sold the farm."

"We? You've got family?"

"My mother. She raised me in the country. Nice little farmhouse, been ours for generations. But she had to sell when the pandemic deepened and they reformed the property laws to try to kickstart the economy."

"Oh, I'm sorry."

"It was the right thing to do. Me and Mom argued. She said she had every right to hold onto the place." Almost the first thing the Liberal Radicals did when they got control of the state legislature was institute a new property regime. Under it you can put any value you want on your place, but you pay the tax at that rate, and you also have to sell to any buyer who makes an offer at the asking price. "Mom set the price higher than she thought anybody would buy at, but then she couldn't afford the taxes. And somebody bought. I told her it was logical; it got money and assets moving through the economy, which was what we needed right then. She didn't see it that way. We haven't spoken in a couple of years."

"Oh, Remy, I'm sorry."

"Don't be." He straightens up. "Thanks for dropping me off. I'll review my glasses' footage from today."

She nods curtly. "I'll check in later. If you want me, here's my number." She borrows his phone to enter it, then leaves.

He makes himself lunch. Normally he would nap after, but he's restless. A woman and her two daughters are missing, every second counts, yet here he is sitting in his black cave, helpless to do anything about it. It feels like a billion-fold amplification of all those times he's disappointed others who expected some normal human response from him. He wants to help, wants to say the right thing, think the right thing. He just doesn't know how.

Mother had been so angry. "You're helping them do this!" she'd kept saying, as the sheriffs threw them out of their generational home.

"Mom, it's just a different property algorithm. You don't fight the System. You fight the Algorithm." She didn't understand it, that algorithms were how you voted, how money got allocated; they weren't some nebulous Deep State that you could rail against but never change. They were the concrete steps you took to get things done. And they could be improved.

He ends up standing at the window, gazing down at the mass of people in the park. No way he can ever be part of that. He remembers when he first came here, the roar and tumult of the streets where he'd panhandled. There had been no escaping the noise, until the doctors at St. Mary's, and people like Xander Reese, helped him organize it all.

He needs his algorithms. Still, he touches the glass, marveling at the people bouncing around like atoms in a jar, impervious to being bruised by the Brownian motion of random social life.

They were so irrational. Like, who would expect people to wantonly tear off their contact tracing bracelets? If you were rational about it, if you organized your life properly, you wouldn't do that.

He thinks of the placement of the chairs where Cawley had been held: in the mathematical and acoustic center of the space. Not where a normal person would place them, but logically . . .

Remy almost fumbles the phone in his haste to get it out. Can he go to Kraft with this? Sendak? What he's proposing isn't exactly legal. He does know Reese, who knows people in the right department. Remy's done work for the City, for Public Health. But this algorithm is clear: you can bend some rules to save lives.

"Hi, Xander? It's Remy. No, I'm fine. —Listen, I need a favor, and I need it, like, *today.*

REMY'S STANDING IN THE DARKNESS NEXT TO A POTTED SPRUCE, ACROSS THE street from the downtown coronavirus testing center. The center is attached to a hospital, and is almost the last one open in the city. As he expected, traffic has been regular but light since he got here. He's exhausted from watching the hypochondriacs come and go but he can't tune down his glasses, because he needs to see their faces or, preferably, their necks.

It's almost eight o'clock; the place will be closing soon. He'll have to come back in the morning, and anyway he's hungry and his whole nervous system is jangling. Coming here was a long shot in several ways; there are other places you can go to get tested, it's just that they're on the edge of town. And however logical and methodical the killer may be, there's no way to know whether he's taken Remy's bait.

Just as he's turning away in disappointment, a large black SUV pulls into the parking lot next to the center. A jolt of adrenaline sends Remy into the street before he thinks to look both ways; luckily traffic is light. He makes it across okay but with his attention divided, he doesn't see the driver get out. There he is, silhouetted by the center's automatic doors. He's going in as another man comes out. The other guy's suit looks familiar, but not like Kraft's, because it's too expensive.

The two exchange a look, then stop in the doorway; the doors try to hiss close and back up, then hesitantly try again. The two men say a few words, probably about how annoying it is to be tested for the millionth time; then they part ways.

Remy waits until the other visitor drives off, then walks around the SUV, trying to find an angle where his phone can catch enough light. When he's gotten the best shot he can of the license plate, he messages it to Sendak's phone number. Above the photo attachment, he types "Run this plate. May be our kidnapper."

Then he phones her. It rings once, twice, three times, and he's hearing sirens somewhere and the streetlights are popping on up and down the boulevard. It's distracting.

"You've reached Maureen Sendak. Leave a message."

"Ah, uh, Maureen, I mean Detective Sendak, sorry, Remy here. I, uh, I did a thing, you won't like it I think." With an effort he focuses. First, turn down his detail levels; second, take a deep breath.

"Okay. Remember that porch-cam photo of the guy in the SUV? It looked like he was wearing a tracker, and if he is it'll have a contact tracing app on it. They run in the background and they're anonymous, so why would he turn it off? He's cautious, methodical, if you go by what we saw at the crime scene.

"Except here's the thing. There's been no coronavirus cases in the city for weeks. So I know somebody who knows somebody and, I, uh, I had them enter Cawley's wife and daughters into the system. As having tested positive.

"Because most people are still wearing their trackers, right? And even if he took it off at some point, he was around the Cawleys long enough that when we registered them, he'd receive a notification. And so—"

"Hey you!"

Remy spins around to find himself facing a gray, blocky human shape. "Get away from my car!," it says.

Remy fumbles with his detail levels and the blocks are replaced by a stocky, thick-necked man with short-cropped black hair. He has some kind of tattoo on his neck. Remy stares at him for a long moment. Then he blurts, "Where are you keeping them?"

The man's eyes widen and then Remy's on the ground, stinging rings of pain around his left eye. Something knocks the breath out of him; he's getting kicked. He tries to curl into a ball but suddenly there's shouting and the man above him curses. A car door slams; he hears the SUV's engine start and rolls out of the way just in time as it screeches out of its parking spot.

As he's getting to his knees people run over from the testing center—three, four of them? They're all talking at once but he can't understand them. He scrabbles on the ground for his phone. Cracked and dead. He spots his glasses and lunges for them.

They're crumpled splinters, the lenses popped out.

"Are you okay? Come on, we'll help you inside!"

There's more pitiless light in there, and more people and loud voices. Remy backs away. "No, I'm fine, I'll be . . . I'll be fine." He turns and staggers up the pitching deck of the driveway, hunching away from the hissing streetlights and shocked-eyed office towers. Not going anywhere. Just going.

REMY IS A LEAF IN A WHIRLWIND. NOTHING TOUCHES HIM BUT EVERYTHING IS ON him, geometries and noises leaping like panthers. A car's brakes squeal and his vision flashes white; he turns his head and a streetlight's stabbing light sends prickles down his arms. He knows he needs to get home, or at least somewhere safe, but the roads terrify him and every building's doorway is white-hot with glare and detail. By instinct he steers to darker and quieter places.

He's not mindless—in fact, he's thinking furiously. He recognizes familiar signs of shock in himself, he's aware of how he's reacting. But he seems to have split in two. One half is a wailing child, looking for his mother's arms yet terrified of the sandpaper rasp of her hand stroking his hair. The other is a man who got himself off the streets, found a job and even

116

KARL SCHROEDER

respectability; that man knows that he can get the better of this moment. He just needs to regroup.

Up ahead is a bridge, and underneath is dark. Remy staggers down the grassy embankment and onto a broad slab of pavement, then stops dead, blinking at orange and green lozenges, like glowing turtles under the vast leaning slab of the bridge. It's a homeless encampment; the turtles are dome tents with little lights in them, and people are in them lying down, or sitting and talking. There's a campfire with a few people seated around it.

Several heads turn in his direction. He grins weakly. "Does . . . does anybody have a phone?"

"Man, phones get stolen. You need help?" The man is tall and incredibly thin, his features buried in a parka that shouldn't be necessary on a summer night.

"I just need to grab my breath." He must look rough, so he adds, "I got overstimulated. Too much, well of everything. I need somewhere quiet."

"Know all about that," says the man. "Come on down. You can wait your turn at the fire."

Remy gratefully takes a seat on an overturned crate. He rubs his eyes. The man who spoke to him goes away but after a while comes back to lean on the graffiti-layered bridge pillar. "You got anything?" he says.

"I don't carry cash." He pats his pockets. "No weed. I took my meds before I left home."

"No problem. You're still welcome, 'long as you follow the rules."

"Rules?" The fog of noise is starting to lift. Remy looks around, and now it's clear how the tents are laid out in, well, not exactly a grid, but a pattern you can walk between. Tables and chairs are set in specific spaces, mostly where the street light comes in.

"You want the fire, you wait in line," says the man. "There's the fire rule, the water rule, the lookout rule."

Remy nods. "Who makes these rules? Do you vote on them?"

"Naw. We just talk 'em out." He goes away again and Remy sits there, watching the cooperation and order of the encampment unfold in little interactions and in where things are placed.

Near the end of his time at St. Mary's, Remy used to go for long walks. "A tendency to wander," his chart probably said. One day he'd been deep in thought and only looked up when a security guard shouted at him. He blinked and looked around, only to discover that somehow, he'd made his way into the heart of a building site.

"How'd you get in here?" the guard demanded.

"I, uh, just came through the atrium and took a left at the electronics store—"

"Wait!" Another man ran up. "How did you know there'd be a computer store there?" Remy looked, and realized that the buildings were just sketches—concrete slabs, pillars, and some HVAC ducts, all open to the outside air. He hadn't seen that; he'd seen the marble, the seating and lights, and the store. He understood what it would be from its shape and from the kind of power lines and interior walls that had been roughed out.

The architect was impressed, and they'd got to talking. Talking had led to work, inside virtual reality at first, then at unfinished sites where the firm was working to visualize future buildings. Remy discovered design, and coding, and met Xander, and eventually, Kraft.

He had done these things. Therefore, he can find his way home tonight.

A deep calm settles over him, slowly, like snow descending. After a while he turns to look at the skyline.

The city has its own rules, of course. Some are written down. A lot of them support privilege and power and, up until the pandemic hit, they were immovable. The coronavirus overturned everything, but not everybody is happy with the new world.

Something's been nagging at him since he left the testing center. It's like a distant alarm ringing in the back of his mind—something important that he should have told Sendak, but didn't get to. He stares at the towers, idly wonders how much money one of them costs—and remembers.

He seeks out the man who helped him and says, "Thanks. I'm good now, I'll go home."

"All right man. Stay safe."

Remy stalks up the embankment and without flinching turns his face to the lights and the traffic.

ALMOST IMMEDIATELY, A POLICE CAR APPROACHES AND HE WAVES URGENTLY AT IT. It brakes and veers over to the curb. A figure bursts out of the passenger door. That collection of jittery movements and the headlong walk all add up to Sendak.

"Remy! See, I knew he'd still be in the area. Call it in." She comes up to him. "Are you okay?"

"Hi, Sendak. Can I borrow your phone?"

She laughs crazily. "Remy, we've been hunting high and low for you! They told us what happened at the center. We thought you were hurt . . . Wow, that's quite the black eye."

"Is it?"

She grabs him by the arm as he probes delicately at his cheek bone, and leads him to the cruiser. "Listen, we got him! His name's Orelko. You were right, Cawley's wife and daughters were still wearing their tracing bracelets when he snatched them. After you called we put out a BOLO and had his car followed, and he led us right to them."

"Good," he says as they get in the back seat. "I was just coming to see you because there's something else."

He waits because it's dark under the shadow of the bridge and he wants to see her expression when he tells her this part. Remy decides he's going to learn more about expressions. "When the kidnapper went into the testing center, he encountered someone coming out. A man in a suit. I recognized it—I recognized him. But I couldn't place him until . . . later . . . when I was looking at the city lights. I thought about the architects I'd worked with, and the developers.

"Sendak, his name is Langdon, and he's one of the biggest commercial property developers in town. He's been influencing City Hall for years, every-thing from handing out brown paper bags full of cash in parking garages to threatening city planners. The architects I worked for hated him, but he hasn't been able to do that kind of thing in years. At least, nothing they could prove. But now a pivotal referendum on city governance is coming up.

"So why would a property developer with a huge stake in how the city is budgeted, be coming out of the same coronavirus testing center that I set up to trap the kidnapper?"

Her eyes widen. "Oh . . ." He thinks he likes this expression. A second later, though, she's frowning. "It's purely circumstantial. It'll never hold up in court."

"But you caught this Orelko person. When you tell him you know Langdon hired him, he'll want to cut a deal."

"Hell, yeah!" says the cop who's driving.

Sendak slumps back in her seat. "Maybe. Either way, you did good."

"One other thing. You'll want to delay the referendum until we can talk to Cawley. Because maybe he really did code a back door into the voting software. Maybe Langdon knows about it; where were those mysterious payments to Cawley's accounts coming from? Maybe Cawley got cold feet. He refused to play anymore, so Langdon had him snatched to learn the passwords, or whatever it is he's using."

"Well," Sendak is smiling again. "Whatever happened to 'it's impossible to hack the vote?'"

"If there's a back door, it wouldn't be."

"So you're still a radical liberal?"

"I don't know, actually. I might just go for the citizens' panels this time," Remy says.

"What? Why?"

"Just something I saw."

"Hey, I hate to burst your bubble," says the driver, "but where are we going?"

"You must be tired," says Sendak. "We'll take you home." But Remy shakes his head.

"I don't want to go home yet."

"Why not?"

Remy thinks about it. He's found his algorithm, and it's not about tuning down the bewildering, maddening howl of the world. It's not about simplifying. It's about letting all that complexity and chaos knock him into the orbit of the right people.

"It would just be nice," he says, "to come to the station. To see Kraft, and you and your office.

"To meet the people I work with, and the rest of the boys down the hall."

9 MIXOLOGY FOR HUMANITY'S SAKE

D. A. Xiaolin Spires

OVER THE SOUND OF UBIQUITOUS BUZZING, MOM YELLED FROM BEYOND THE SCREEN door, "Rikuta, come out and help the planting drones."

I put the test tube into the holder, as the concoction fizzled. "But, Mom, I'm busy." I called out for the cleanerbot and it swung in and wiped off the puddle from the tatami floor. The cleanerbot's light blinked as it ran into the table, a series of gurgling melodies escaping from its speakers, repeatedly knocking more of the sparkling amazake drink I made onto the tatami. The smell of sweet fermented rice filled the room as the spill spread. "Gotta fix this broken thing."

"Rikuta!" Mom's voice roared. I turned off the cleanerbot, wiped up the rest of the spill myself, careful to move aside the fluffy zabuton I was sitting on so it wouldn't get soaked. I threw the towel over my shoulder.

I raced over to the back door, jammed feet into slippers and hiked up my pants. I saw my dad in one of the plots, back bent and knee-deep in muddy water and beelined him. I wasn't really keen on planting the seedlings but once Mom's voice hit those registers, I knew she meant business. I also knew it meant a lot to her to have this family time together.

Around us drones descended onto the wet paddy, their metal pincers piercing through the water's surface and sticking the seedlings in. I grabbed a handful of tender seedlings from the cart, wrapped them in my towel and tucked the whole thing into my pants like a makeshift quiver. I stuck my bare foot into the paddy and felt an immediate wave of cold overtake my body as the water reached my calves. Chilly mud crept between my toes. At least it was warm out. Drones buzzed around me as they completed their rows of green. It smelled of organic life. My foot released with repeated sucking sounds as I moved to an unfinished row and stuck the seedlings in. Dragonflies fluttered past me, their buzzes next to my ear louder than the drones. I completed row upon row, racing with the drones, until my back hurt.

MY BACK HURTS AS I LIFT THE TENTH KOJIBUTA, THE WAFTS OF SWEET FERMENTATION coming from the cedar box that holds the rice and the fertile fungus, a heavenly marriage of a marinade. The aspergillus oryzae mold spores have done their job incubating in the kojimoro and I smell the koji's wondrous pungency. I'm distracted by my throbbing back, however, and rub my lower back through my lab coat. I bend over the koji, raking my hands through the rice mixture for a bit before I let my automata buddy Kushi handle it. When I was a kid, Mom would tell us to get the wooden rake and use our legs to get into the raking, but Mom was okay dealing with back pain and I'm not.

Kushi does the job with his giant hand and metal fingers. As he rakes, his mechanical arm advancing and retreating, I take a break. I step outside and am about to open a bottle of last week's homebrewed sake. Before I can twist off the cap, I sniff in Kushi's direction. Now that I'm sitting and comfortable, I smell it. Something foreboding. I put down the unopened bottle. Something's not right.

WE RECYCLED BATCHES OF SAKE, WHEN THEY WEREN'T CLEAR ENOUGH, AROMATIC enough, or fermented enough.

"Something's not right," Mom would say. She complained of an off-smell sometimes. We reconfigured the drones and she made us all run through sanitation procedures. "Sniff the batch, and everything that touches it—your hands, your clothes, make sure it all smells right," she said. "Never forget to judge your sake, thinking of ways to improve."

I SNIFF AGAIN. I STEP BACK INTO THE HUMID KOJIMORO. THERE, THAT'S IT. I WALK to the back of the room and the smell hits me again, stronger. It's a bit off, a faint acridness tucked into sickly sweetness. I had hand-selected new strains of rice and added the Kwik Kultivation Krystals before steaming the rice and all went well. But, now I feel like my throbbing back's giving me some kind of warning. I check on the koji.

They look okay, but the smell . . . it doesn't lie.

I hurry back to Kushi, turn him off and stare at the mounds of koji before me. A sinking feeling fills my chest. I had so anticipated this moment, but now my smile's faded and I face the reality of risks realized. I sniff in deep. There it is. That off-putting, lingering aftersmell. The koji was not sublimely "rotten," as it should be, but just dreadfully so. I shake my head. I scoop up some koji and in frustration, let it drop through my fingers and plop to the ground. Decomposition gone awry.

I step outside, grab my sake bottle, and twist it open as I sit on my patio chair. I pour a glass and sip. I sigh, thinking about the mess. Another batch for compost. I stare out at the submerged paddy fields in the distance, the green tips peeking out of the surface, waiting to emerge into rice stalks. I just wasted so many of them—numerous rice plants destined for decay.

But no point in brooding. I'll get back to my 3D graphs and charts again, crunching numbers for the formulas—like the cyclical nature of life, just as another harvest season will come and activity will blossom on the fields, I tell myself. That's what Ena would say.

THE RHYTHM OF THE COUNTRYSIDE WAS IN CYCLES OF WORK AND GROWTH, AND waiting. Once the seedlings were all in and growing, our family waited. Come fall, we harvested the golden yellow stalks from the drained paddy. Mom made us beat some stalks against bamboo slats while drones next to us zipped through the threshing process. I invented some other faster methods, with gears and pedals, but Mom insisted this was the way for the sake—that we had to at least do some of the work ourselves to keep up the tradition. We milled and steamed the rice and mixed it with koji with our hands. Then we mashed it all and tossed in sake yeast. This was all done over a period of days—no machines, just arms pushing wooden paddles to get the shubo right.

Mom even skipped the adding of lactic acid that kept the unwanted bacteria at bay, saying she wanted it straight up old style, using the air's natural lactobacillus instead of the Sokujo method.

"Fast is for the impatient," she said.

She also quoted Thomas Edison at me—genius is 99 percent perspiration and 1 percent inspiration—but she knew that for me genius is 99 percent impatience—and who knows what for the other 1 percent.

I couldn't really disagree. I wanted things done fast.

She wouldn't have it. She savored all the steps.

When we were finished making the sake, we streaked each drone with a fingerprint of the liquid, our own family ritual, in addition to hanging a traditional ball of cedar leaves that signified successful sake production.

And after more waiting, for the sake to mature, we took some bottles into our home and clinked cups and sipped under the warmth of the heated kotatsu. My parents only allocated one small ochoko's worth of sake for me. I would nurse it for the night. While we drank, I harbored rebellious thoughts—dreaming up ways to hasten the fermentation process but keep the savory richness of the alcohol that passed down my throat like fire.

THE WARM TASTE OF YUZU AND SAKE FLOWS DOWN MY THROAT AND I LET OUT A satisfying, "Ahhhh."

I turn on my holovid and nod at my cousin Aimi. Ever since my wife passed, she has been my trusty taste-tester.

Aimi takes a swirl, letting the aromas fill her mouth. She then gulps, her eyes closed. "Too bitter. Needs something bright."

"Mint?" I ask.

"Maybe." She puts it down. She opens her brown eyes wide, taking in all the details of the drink. "Or maybe it's the yuzu rind oversoaked. And this cloudy one? That's next?"

"Yeah. Have a cracker first." She bites, swallows, closes her eyes and sips. I turn off my holovid and sip, too. I don't want her to see my reaction and get biased.

I put down the sake cup. This was my wife's favorite tasting cup, with the blue underglaze. Ena was the best at tasting. I could see her now, her piercing brown eyes staring at me as she takes a sip from the cup. She had quite the appetite and love for adventure and gusto in her life. After her judo championships, she would down breaded pork chops and crispy pick-led takuan alongside straight sake and some mixed drinks. Even with her athleticism, she had a delicate, discerning palate. She'd gulp sports drinks for the electrolytes but only after diluting them. Sports drink and alcohol companies led her through facility tours, trying to get her face for ads, but she refused, saying it was a conflict of interest with our bar establishment.

She was an eclectic drinker, sampling all kinds of drinks, until she lost her taste buds from the second ANVID respiratory pandemic and then passed away from complications while rehabilitating from the disease. Her lungs had been severely damaged, she had a stroke and problems with memory. It pained me to watch her change. She became weak, barely able to stand, let alone execute any judo throw, and at the end, drank only rice porridge. Sometimes she would nurse a bowl of porridge while watching judo moves, trying to recall technique names. The tubes they put in her for breathing even after removal disturbed her ability to swallow, so it would take her hours.

My parents felt bad for me during her illness, and served as my taste testers for a while, but they were never fond of trying my concoctions, since they thought the old ways were the best.

Aimi took over. At my wife's holofuneral—virtual because of the pandemic—she heard about my need for a taster and offered. She's a huge gastronomist.

"Okay, what about that one?" I pointed at the cup she just emptied.

"Pretty good. Nice and dry. Could use a touch of sweetness."

I mark down her words. I enhance and focus in on her eyes. Sometimes her eyes gravitate to the one she likes best. Ena used to say to watch the eyes for intent. I see Aimi flash a glance at the cup with the "ka" katakana letter written on it. That was the one with the newest koji version.

She returns the vessels to the delivery drone, which packs and sanitizes them and flies off for the next delivery.

"Sure," she says, wiping her hands on her skirt. "And so, which is the control, and which are the ones with the flash ferment? And what changes have you made?"

"Well, I can't tell you that."

She shakes her head. "I'll just have to wait for the new line to come out at your bar."

I smile. "Yes, will do. Here to please." It's true.

It's why I opened the bar. All I want is for people to drink sake and be merry. But, the merriment hasn't been so widespread lately.

MY MOM'S LOOK OF MERRIMENT AT SAVORING ALL THE STEPS OF SAKE-MAKING WAS contagious. Even when I was anxious to get the drones to do all the work, I saw her putting her full attention into all the details. She called it chanto suru, doing things properly, and it was part of ikigai, that which makes life worth living.

I responded that efficiency and alacrity are what make life worth living. Increased and swift performance as ikigai. She just shook her head and handed me the wooden mash paddle. "Go and blend."

Blend I did. We made the fermenting mash moromi in three stages, adding hatzusoe (more rice, koji, and water), letting it sit as odori so the yeast can make merry, then brought in nakazoe and then tomozoe, all stages of adding rice, koji, and water. Everything was active, lively, and bubbly: starches becoming sugar, yeasts taking this sugar and converting it to alcohol and CO_2.

I had to admit, like my mom, there was part of me that savored the process of doing it "properly." I enjoyed the sound of the liquids sloshing about as I mixed, my wooden paddle breaking the waves of this little ocean. Yet, even with that small joy, I always thought it could be done faster.

As a symbolic gesture pushed mostly by my mom for the sake of tradition, we handled a portion of the moromi- and sake-making ourselves, filling up the fermented moromi into permeable bags and pressing them using cedar boards. But we also left the bulk of the processing for the stage-specific drones—their incessant arms mixing the moromi, pressing discrete amounts to separate solids and liquids and taking up the resulting sake into tubes, pasteurizing and moving the sake into storage for it to mature. The machines made all sorts of noises, sucking and pounding, dripping and draining. It was all a whole ecosystem there in the sakagura.

I tapped my feet to a different rhythm. I was sure I could speed up the tempo of all the machinery and make the whole process of making sake more convenient while maintaining quality.

USING AIMI'S TASTING NOTES AND THE EVALUATIONS I'VE HIRED A FEW PEOPLE TO run, I reformulate the recipes to enhance quality and convenience. Typically, the traditional sake mixing and brewing process takes about ninety days. I want to bring processing down to a week, and have a dehydrated powder ready for instant sake.

By day, I pass time. I read books, drink, run laps, and do martial arts rolls and falls. I fix and update cleaner and service drones at the gym and the owner pays me a few yen for it alongside a free gym pass. I don't mind hanging around there. They sterilize everything after every use and people are careful.

I'm so used to being Ena's uke, her throwing partner, that I miss the feel of the wrestling mat under my skin. It smells like her at the gym. Perspiration (under the sting of antiseptic) and persistence. I'm one of the ones who've returned to the gyms, even after the latest epidemic wave of GRAVID that drove them to close for a few weeks.

By night, I run the bar.

By dead of the night, I experiment in the food lab I rent out. Rent's cheap at this hour. I've managed to shorten the production process, freeze-dry the liquid with state-of-the-art equipment, and reconstitute it.

I barely sleep anymore.

IT'S QUIET AT THE BAR, SO I EXPERIMENT. I DUMP A PACKET I CALL "KWIK KOJI" TO make an instant sake. It has zero sugar, but the savory richness of a junmai that has been brewing for months. I combine it with another powder of rice flakes and throw it in water. It fizzes, releasing a sour smell. I throw in a touch of the famous sea salt from Ako with nigari. I label the batch and put it in an everstate fridge, which keeps discrete portions of food and drink at whatever temperatures I set the small cubbies.

I make another and shake in lychee and pineapple for the Sun Lush, to Lila's order. Lila is a holosocial queen and discusses food for diabetics. I watch in anticipation as she pulls the perspiring glass toward her.

She pulls up her mask, sips, and exhales.

"When will this hit the shelves?" She stares at the drink, shaking it. Her satisfied look is sublime. "It's so strangely tasty. Like instant ramen, it's as if formulated to make me crave it."

"Well, it kind of is. Zero sugar, after all."

"I can't believe it. Zero sugar," she whistles. "I miss this flavor. It reminds me of somewhere tropical, like Okinawa."

"We have an awamori version in production."

"I'll be back for that." She looks around at the stools around her. "Pretty empty, huh?"

"Nothing new. It gets busier later at night." It's not a lie, but it's not exactly the truth. It's another slow night, and I expect only a few more customers to straggle in.

She nods and takes another sip. She sinks into her seat, with a dazed but happy look. Her blushed cheeks and closed eyes seem almost blissful. No wonder she has over half a million followers. She has such vivid expressions.

The sake's rolled out only in my bar, but already it's gotten some publicity. A few small holocelebs like Lila. She opens an eye and says, "Would be a nice evening experiment at home, a puff of fizz. No chance you'll be releasing the powder kits to supermarkets soon?"

Since the first epidemic wave of GRAVID, some of these holocelebs keep asking about a commercial release.

"Sorry, not yet." A cleanerbot rolls like a coin down the bar, spritzing. I collect her empty cup and chuck it in the sanitizer.

I guard the insta-sake production method with layers of security. I've already gotten numerous calls from investors interested in taking a share of the brand. I've always turned them down. I've also turned down requests to send the powder over as samples. Competitors haven't had a chance to try reverse engineering since it's only available at my bar.

When she leaves, promising to return soon, I nod. These celebrities are always looking for new experiences, so I have to keep up with new drinks. Despite being busy with my experiments, admittedly, business isn't great. A few of the regulars have returned, but there's still a sense of caution in the air.

At the end of the night I tally up sales, and I groan. At this rate, the bar will go under.

I need to get the numbers up.

I CALL UP AIMI LATER THAT NIGHT AND TELL HER ABOUT THE CUSTOMER COUNT.
"You're going to go bankrupt," she says. She's in the midst of doing stretches, about to teach her cycling class.

"Thanks for the frankness. I can see that."

Aimi purses her lips, the 3D filter lipstick bobs into place as an overlay a split-second behind, as she puts on sweat wristbands. "Y'know, it's too bad. Because people want to drink. They miss the bar experience. MyPub Meal Kits don't cut it. They're just not ready to do the crowd thing. Everyone's hurting."

I know. I'm hurting. I miss Ena.

"I have my class in three minutes so I have to go, but if there was only a way you could have it be holo. I mean, I know you can't, since it's a drink. You can't taste on the holo. But, if only you could bring the bar experience to them. The quarantine parties are never satisfying because they don't get the full bar experience. They don't get the skilled bartender crafting house cocktails. Omotenashi. That hospitality factor that makes the customer feel like a customer. I know my students could use a good drink together served right to them after their spin."

"Especially after you yelling at them."

"Encouraging," she says, laughing. "I don't yell. I encourage."

I join in on the laugh as she logs out.

MY LAUGH FALTERS, AS I THINK ABOUT WHAT SHE SAID. THE QUARANTINI PARTIES don't have new expert drinks coming in. Sure, there are alcohol delivery kits, but people complain that the limes are warm and the mint leaves wilted. Plus, the last thing they want to do is to serve themselves—a part of the fun is watching skilled hands mix it, pour it, and bring it right to them. Omotenashi: great service that makes you feel pampered. That's what's lacking.

For a while, the situation on the ground had seemed hopeful. People left the MyPub Meal Kits behind. They were coming to bars again. The elastic silicone sipper made by a local university engineering department looked like it could work. I had participated in the effort by bringing the department drinks for the research and later using our bar as an in situ lab. We had a bit of a local flourish of social interaction, with research participants gathering, placing elastic silicone filters over their mouths and in their noses, cradled by their lips with adhesive and with tiny hooks that latched onto nostril hairs and walls. These inserts had a small device that filtered air and we tried the ones that had fittings and latches to position straws right into them, keeping liquids coming in and viruses out. So the young human subjects could drink and chat, the latch catching as you pulled the straw out so the filter cut-out would move back into place.

It seemed to work with mixed results until a few accidental swallows and choking incidents eroded trust in the technology. Besides the adhesives losing stickiness, people found the masks uncomfortable. They were constantly readjusting and removing them. There were also cases where the epidemic spread despite proper use of the coverings, suggesting the synthetic fibers for the silicone filters weren't as effective as they thought. It was a mess, and distributors had to recall the devices soon after rolling them out. Hopeful bar owners grumbled and I was distraught.

We went through COVID-19 and -22 when I was young, and were successful with vaccines at each iteration but it took a while. Then came ANVID-33 and -36 and now the GRAVID series. People developed strategies for coping. In the engineering and commerce world, they moved up the holo tech faster than imagined and drone delivery speeds took off.

People also tried Portable Personal Bubbles (PPBs), but that was a celeb fad that failed miserably. They were incredibly expensive and stiff. The wearers couldn't move far beyond their power source since the battery drained fast. Those who could afford to rent them complained they were hard to manipulate and hot as hell. The batteries kept dying. Celebs said they felt like they were swallowed up by a hippo, moving like molasses, and that they'd prefer to interact through holoscreens rather than wrapped in plastic casing. Some even panicked, having trouble breathing in them.

With PPBs put to rest, GRAVID-37 took a huge toll on the population. Those infected got unexpected rashes as well as respiratory issues and chronic fatigue, and there was no viable solution in sight. Pharmaceutical companies and experts despaired. A viable vaccine was remarkably difficult to achieve and it took a few years.

We're still waiting for a vaccine for the latest bug, GRAVID-38, and we're impatient. I, perhaps, am one of the most.

I fiddle with a double jigger, rolling it between my fingers as I think about possibilities, ways forward—quick, safe, and easy measures for people to take to get a drink served.

I look at my jigger, thinking of measuring spirits and shaking drinks as customers look on in rapt anticipation.

Omotenashi.

What if I brought the bar experience to them?

I GATHER PARTS FROM BROKEN CLEANERBOTS AND SERVICE DRONES AND SOME old machines at the gym. I scavenge more parts from a junkyard nearby. I remember my cleanerbot, the old one from my parent's house in the countryside, that would bump into things. It had a shaking mechanism to deploy these old aerosol cleaners they sold at the mart. They don't sell the aerosol cans anymore because of environmental regulations, but our bot still had that shake programmed in. It was a bit outdated.

I give my parents a holocall. It takes them a while before they pick up. They don't like using these things. Mom picks up as she's fixing up an ikebana work of art, twisting a sakura branch to the perfect angle, part of her activities in attempting to achieve ikigai. "Just come over and get the antiquated thing. It's still here. It's next to a load of your old clothes, chemistry sets, and junk. I don't think it works though. Just didn't have the heart to throw it away since I knew you liked it."

"Liked it! That thing always malfunctioned!"

"Yeah, but didn't you say you liked the sounds it made?"

Mom has a good memory. I did. The phantom sounds of its gurgling pentatonic melody that played as it shook fill my ears. I'd forgotten about that.

She snaps a branch in half and chucks it behind her. The newest cleanerbot snatches it up. "I'll send it over. And your old chemistry sets. They're sitting around here, gathering dust."

I protest about saving the delivery drone extra work, but she logs out. Oh well, I'll just throw out the chem sets when they arrive.

After the call, I sketch out designs and order more parts from the hardware holostore, my mind racing.

WHEN MY OLD CLEANERBOT ARRIVES, I CHARGE IT UP. AS THE STRANGE MELODY drones on, in my mind I see the flowing waves of verdant blades of rice in the paddies, and the heady smell of fermentation in our old shed. I live in that nostalgic space for a moment before I go into plan-execution mode. I say goodbye to our old family cleanerbot and hello to my new tech.

I drill, cut, shave, and attach. I solder and bend. I even add in pieces of my childhood chemistry set—repurposing the durable test tubes. A couple of drones help me out but I do most of the work by hand, enhanced with a home improvement gauntlet that reduces injuries and enhances strength and grip.

It takes me days and I've ignored all my calls. I miss five calls from Aimi, two from my parents, and a dozen holonet celeb requests.

I attach a small retractable slab to the front of the metallic figure before me. That will be the counter.

I put powder packets into its compartments and turn it on for a test run. The bot empties packages, mixes, adds water with an attached hose, mixes again and shakes. As it shakes, the floor vibrates and I feel the trembling up through my feet and calves. It tinkles out its strange melody as it pours out the concoction, while another appendage reaches in and grabs a straw and places it gingerly into the cup. A compartment ejects an umbrella and a satsuma. The bot grabs these with the same appendage and adds them to the cup. It places the cup on the metal rack.

The drink stops fizzing and rests.

I take a sip. I grimace. It needs work. The proportions and balance are off. The drink tastes watery and weak. I can still feel the residue of powder and grit on my tongue. The shaking needs more rigor. The satsuma slice falls right onto my lap, as it wasn't wedged in well to begin with. The bot looks silly with inelegant protruding parts. It needs a shinier coat and better decor.

I put down the drink, wipe my mouth with my sleeve.

My first drink from my first robosake mixologist.

It might be crude, but we'll get there.

AFTER THE MANY STEPS OF ADDING KOJI, STEAMED RICE, AND WATER AND THEN strained through pressing, my family got crude sake. The liquid was milky and viscous. My mom insisted on clear sake—she wanted to recreate the experience of sipping the refreshing waters of a winter creek.

For that, we had to wait longer. Always the waiting. The crude sake would sit in tanks, filtering, pasteurizing, and maturing. We let the immersed drones do their thing, and waited for the day its aromatic smoothness would grace our taste buds.

Once done, we started the process again for the next batch, the cycle of working and waiting.

AIMI HAS HOOKED ME UP WITH HER NETWORK SO THE FIRST ROUND OF SHARED SAKE Socials is with her cycling group. The SKIM-1s (Sake Karakuri Imagination

Mixologists), tucked into packages, roll in by air drone. They are gently dropped and the students open the packages in unison as they project themselves on holos. They all delight in the SKIM-1 countenances, cute and doll-like in the karakuri automata tradition of the seventeenth to nineteenth century, but metal and still robot enough not to hit the uncanny valley.

At the request of the SKIM-1s' vocalizations, the cyclist students sit back down in their seats in different homes. Out of the robot mixologists' shoulders, a panel opens up and they project a short menu. After taking orders, the SKIM-1s deliver mixes, ripping packets of kwik koji and brisk yeast, throwing in flavor profiles to order and attaching to water pipes to rehydrate within their chest cavities. They dip, stir, and check the solutions. The students all have their holos of each other up and they're laughing, having a ball.

I can see their legs vibrate as the SKIM-1s do the rigorous shake that activates the flash fermentation mechanism, and this elicits more laughter. The SKIM-1s all emit that same strange melody, which I've altered to be more lively than dour, as they pour. They fill up ecologically friendly, molded dried squid cups enhanced with keep-cool tech and then add umbrellas and fruit. From the holos, I see one SKIM-1 overpours and the drink spills. I groan. Its cleaning mechanism activates.

The customers drink and that's where I lean in and take notes. The students seem to be excited about the flavors, saying mostly "Umai" but without much other context, just laughing about the experience. Once they finish, they take tentative nibbles out of the cup, some saving the rest for later. We leave the SKIM-1s there for a while, in case they want to order more. Once it seems like they're done and busy chatting, the SKIM-1s fold back into transportable shapes, get repackaged by the drones, and are flown away.

The success of the pilot run stirs up interest. We tweak, change the cocktails around, update the recipes and troubleshoot quirks. We add more melodies to the repertoire and smooth out the movements.

Before I can digest that my dream is coming true, my small army of SKIM-1s have full schedules, and are getting split up and sent to different parts of town. I've signed deals with a larger delivery drone company, StripedCat, to get them where they need to go. All my initial security worries dissolve. The deliveries come in a seal-all pack. If someone who is not the recipient tampers with the package, an alert gets sent back to the sender and authorities. My hesitation to send out my recipes is erased as event after event goes smoothly. Even the SKIMs are made tamperproof themselves, and are equipped with face scanning and age confirmation devices.

I worry less about my bar clients, hire a manager to handle those operations, and put my full attention into the Shared Sake Socials.

WHEN WE DRANK THE FINISHED SAKE, MY MOM INSISTED THAT IT BE A SOCIAL EVENT. She used to invite Ena and me after we'd moved to the city and were no longer involved in the sake process. We'd come back to our rural town for the ritual. Ena would regale my parents with tales of martial arts—perfect tosses in competition and triumph over those who picked on her outside the mats.

Even two years ago, when Ena's health was declining, no longer positive with ANVID but still suffering from the consequences of it, my parents brought the sake to us. They put a drop in her porridge, after confirming it would have no interactions with her medication. "For old time's sake." I tried shooing them away at the door, telling them they shouldn't be there, but they declared their tests were negative and said it was their right to see their daughter-in-law. We sat around in masks, sitting at a distance but sharing that one bottle.

For once, it wasn't Ena telling stories, but my parents, clinking sake cups and digging deep in their imaginations for tales that would charm us into feeling better.

OUR SMALL COMPANY, IMAGINATION MIXOLOGY, HAS A GROUP OF PEOPLE WHO monitor the live feeds of these holos. I duck in every once in a while, as I still like to be "on the ground."

Our new and improved SKIM-2s have been deployed to more and more locations. Now we're prefecture-wide. We've increased production, but we're still working with a limited group of employees, as I'm still guarded about our recipes; I have all of the new hires sign nondisclosure agreements. Luckily, the SKIM-2s can't divulge recipes as they are equipped with the most advanced set of redundant security systems. The memory log is immediately deleted if there has been any tampering and coupled with the benefits of StripedCat's security features, there hasn't been an issue.

Everything has been going smoothly and even the bar has been doing better, with people feeling more relaxed as the weather warms up.

Aimi's on board full-time as our director of operations, coordinating drone flight schedules and simultaneous Shared Sake Socials. I've retreated to the role of inventing new recipes and improving the body and aftertaste of the flash ferment and ingredients, as well as cooking up new flavor profiles for various versions.

But I'm restless. I wish I could get my bar back into shape, get people interacting, laughing, and drinking—all in one spot. I thought my bots and these parties on the holo were social enough, but there's still something eating away at me. I miss running my hands down the bar counter, the sound of chatter and the dishwasher, the smells of colognes and perfumes all intermingling. I want to work toward that goal, but I wonder how.

I pull a jigger from my pocket and roll it across my knuckles. My mind churns. I consider ways to get involved. Perhaps partner with sanitizing companies? Or volunteer with companies developing vaccines? I don't think it would bring me back my bar or my customers, but maybe it's worth a shot—if nothing else it will quell my restlessness. I recall Aimi mentioned something about a pharmaceutical company and I make a note to ask about volunteering opportunities.

AS I'M SETTLING DOWN AT HOME WITH A NEW GINSENG DRINK WITH TRACES OF ginkgo nut and seaweed, I get a message to enter into the holospace that Aimi currently is in. I down my drink and log in.

It's a party—of course, they're always parties—but this time, I see familiar faces. Two to be exact, among about twelve. The spokesperson of Nakamura-Clemont Pharmaceuticals and CEO Ito Yui. I have seen them on the news. Their freeze-dried vaccine has been chosen to be released to the public and received federal approval. They're drinking cocktails, suda-chi sakejitos, from our much sleeker SKIM-2s and chatting through the holos. As I mingle, a drone arrives at my door bearing another SKIM-2 to serve me drinks.

I'm enjoying the convivial atmosphere, the celebration and the handi-work of the SKIM-2s (such skilled pouring and precision placing of straws and green wedges)—when the spokesperson pulls me aside and Yui draws me into a corner space. I can still hear the muffled sounds of laughter.

"Congratulations," I say. "It's quite an achievement."

"Thank you," she says. She nods at me to take a sip of a sakejito my SKIM-2 has made for me, and I do. I make a note to ask about volunteering before giving her my full attention. She gestures to the crowd behind the masking net. "I asked Aimi to invite you here not just to partake in the celebrations, but also so we could thank you for bringing this party to life. Our researchers have been working day in and day out to make the freeze-dried vaccines work and they deserve this."

"You're welcome," I say. "It's a pleasure to honor the people who have worked hard to make this vaccine happen."

"We'll still be needing your services as we have many milestones ahead and our employees need a way to celebrate. This is only a small portion of our staff. We have many challenges facing us and these socials give them some reprieve between intense meetings."

"Challenges?"

"We are testing ways to release the vaccine to the public. We are disseminating vaccines to hospitals and conducting home visits, but the deployment is still slow."

"Might I suggest StripedCat? I have nothing but good things to say about their delivery services."

"Yes, we are looking at a number of distribution services. My staff is weighing the benefits and risks of each."

Through the holo, she gazes at me with an intensity that reminds me of my wife before she would execute a judo throw. The holo doesn't dilute the effect at all. I see the fervor and depth of intention behind the bronze eyes.

Yui's voice shifts in tone, edged with impatience. "I only wish that the vaccines could come to them. The old, the weak. Some can't leave their houses. And medicine can't administer itself. The costs for the ambulance services to bring the vaccines to them have been hefty."

Her relentless gaze rests on my drink and moves up to meet my eyes. She tilts her chin, and raises her eyebrows questioningly.

I detect a slight vibration beneath my feet, picked up and transmitted by the holos, the signature feel of the cutting edge mixologist's cocktail shake in one of the physical rooms of these pharmaceutical researchers. From behind the masking net, one of the SKIM-2s plays its signature melody indicating the pour.

I would help. I am going to volunteer, I told myself.

I saw a vision then.

My SKIMs deployed, draining not sake into the mouths of clients but concoctions administered into muscles to stir up antibodies. My enterprise—and my impatience—redirected to partake in a global effort to minimize the effects of the pandemic. Each client treated, not entertained—and injections, not mini umbrellas, that signal the end of the interaction.

I can hear the voice of my wife calling me, asking me to help her, as she got thinner and thinner, her usual muscular physique reduced to a gaunt skeleton.

It can't be more than my imagination making me think that the holo has been enhanced or warped, but I feel a strange connection, like I am in sync with Yui's thoughts.

"Yes, yes, I see. SKIM-2s are quite versatile, implementing various drink designs and deployments."

"They indeed are." She takes a sip from her own sakejito, her lips on a thin straw pulling up liquid. I imagine something else tube-like, a needle entering into a muscle, a thick one like a deltoid, the flow of the liquid preparation absorbed into the bloodstream, coursing with the red blood cells. Vaccines.

I pass her credentials to my direct hololine.

"Let's talk more after the party," I say. I feel in accordance . . . with what I'm not sure. But it feels right, proper. It must be the feeling my mom calls chanto suru.

In the universe, something clicks into place.

ENA USED TO TELL ME THAT WHEN SHE EXECUTED A PERFECT THROW, EVERYTHING clicked into place. The body is squared up, the opponent rides up right where she wants them to and the toss itself is not difficult.

Just a quick turn and pull and they're right where you want them.

THE CONVERSION HASN'T BEEN SO DIFFICULT. THE FREEZE-DRIED VACCINES NEED to be reconstituted. Then, with care, administered.

I confer with medical engineers, Aimi, and biopharmaceutical higher-ups. We repurpose the mechanical shake of SKIMs to fit the parameters to rehydrate the DNA molecules. The vaccines are powdered and their color and constitution look a lot different from my kwik koji and brisk yeast lines—they certainly don't emit that hallmark fermented smell. Instead, the vaccine powder—immune-dust as we call it—seems almost inert, with little smell at all. So little presence for something so critical to a robust society.

We decide to automate the administering of the vaccine with redundant feedback loops to reduce errors. A team of operators would handle reprogramming the bots, refitting the manipulator designed for positioning straws and pointy umbrellas to positioning the needle for the injection.

We iron out the kinks in trials and test runs. Then we deploy them to a host of volunteers.

THE FIRST TWO TRIAL RUNS FAIL. THE HONING DEVICES WEREN'T EXACTING AND WE need a method to calm patients.

I start losing sight of what it's worth. All this—life. Holding on so dearly when my dearest friend and partner slipped away from me.

My ikigai slipping. What was it anyway? Did I ever have one?

I think of Ena's mantra: "When you get thrown, take the fall. Then get up. Keep moving until you see your chance. It's not about expediency, it's about getting the right move in."

I put aside my sake cup. I think of new mechanisms of delivery for the SKIM-2s. I get up, clear some space. There's a chance here somewhere, I just have to find it.

Get the right move in.

I'm impatient. We have to move quickly to save more people.

I REPROGRAM THE SKIM-2S TO GO ALONG WITH THE SKIM-3S AND SERVE ALCOHOL OR any mocktail or drink on the menu. Then the SKIM-3s swoop in to deliver the shot. These injection givers make use of the mixologist's distraction.

Unlike the socials with the SKIM-2s, these events are not gatherings and the atmosphere is apprehensive, but there's a feeling of release when the needle pierces skin and delivers the concoction, much like when the cocktail hits the throat. You can almost hear the audible sighs.

And the action's fast. Blink and you might not notice it. The delivery of the inoculation is as quick as one of Ena's signature throws. Getting them right where you want them.

Aimi said to nix the music. We don't play a jingle anymore. Not for the injections. It's enough that the vaccine receivers get a small drinkable treat.

Cocktail and inoculation, all rolled up into one event.

A cause for celebration.

WE PARTNER WITH THE BIOPHARMACEUTICALS IN RELEASING THE VACCINES IN A wider form. Bars open again and people are eager to socialize. Maybe we're in the calm between storms. Maybe the virus will mutate. Maybe we'll get lucky (or savvy) and we'll be back to business as usual for a long while. In the meantime, we have the skilled SKIM-3s, should we have new vaccines needing some tried-and-true delivery methods.

Back in the bar, I welcome my first customer, Lila, put together as always. She can't quite get enough of my drinks. I smile, tossing a shiso leaf into a sake-infused drink a SKIM-2 usually makes, now brought to life by my own hands.

She leans in and gives me a peck on the cheek, takes a gulp from the glass and the look on her face could make headlines.

She takes a few more sips in silence. Wiping the perspiration from the glass, she says, "This is almost as good as the way SKIM-2 makes it." She punctuates her tease with a wink.

"Almost as good, huh?" I say. I pat a SKIM-2 near me. "What can I say? They're programmed by the best." The bot's on standby, there mostly to keep me company, but it stands erect, as if in a salute. I can't help but be proud.

"The best." She chuckles. "Of course they are. The best programs I've ever sipped." She takes another gulp and mixes the liquid with her stirrer. "That's why I'll be asking you for an interview. Let's talk more once I'm done with this drink."

She closes her eyes and takes another sip. Then she gets up.

Ena's voice plays in my head as I watch Lila work her magic. "Get up. Keep moving until you see your chance." Lila has certainly put that into practice.

Lila leaves me to chat with her influencer friends, as she should, embracing each of them with a long hug while still holding up her cocktail. They take a few selfies with their drinks together, eager to share their collective presence to the world.

AFTER I WIPE DOWN THE BAR, I RETURN HOME AND TINKER. I PULL OUT MY OLD chemistry set, what's left of it, lost in thought.

Feeling all the grooves of the miscellaneous pieces, flasks, and beakers, helps me contemplate possibilities. A thought comes to mind and I stir and blend, bringing in more sophisticated equipment and tubes.

I craft a powder, a chaser made with the sweet and tart flavors of takuan and infused with electrolytes. It would complement a sake with a strong rice aroma and a deep umami, one that goes well with Ena's favorite breaded pork dish.

"This is for you, Ena, for pushing me to forge on."

I do a quick reprogram of a SKIM-2 and it serves out the drinks, tinkling its melody as it pours them into dried squid cups: the sake, pure, without adulteration, followed by the electrolyte chaser. I take a sip. The concoction's not perfect yet, but it would be great for an athlete. Chasing away dehydration and fatigue.

I think of all the people we've helped with the vaccine. I think of how they won't have to deal with what Ena had to deal with. What we had to deal with together. The anxiety and dread as the disease took its toll. I think about all the good times with Ena and my parents, the small family we cobbled together.

SKIM-2 serves another round of drinks.

I peer at the butsudan, at the picture of Ena's smiling face next to the memorial tablet. I place an offering of satsuma and steaming rice. For good measure, I position by her photo SKIM-2's output of a small cup of rich junmai sake. Next to that, I set down the electrolyte chaser it shook and poured.

You're my first customer, Ena. I'll serve this at my bar next.

I imagine her smile after practice, sweaty but vivacious at the bar counter, keeping me company as I finish work. She recounts judo moves as she puts me in a playful choke and plants a kiss on my cheek, her other hand reaching for a quenching cup of sake.

I can't help but think that's ikigai. Getting together with your loved ones, sharing a drink.

And for a moment, I forget about speed or execution and the utter convenience of kwik koji—it's about being together for it all and savoring each instance once there.

I dip a finger in sake. I caress her cheek, and holding my finger there for what seems like an eternity, smearing the glass of the frame with a fingerprint of my home-brewed concoction, knowing she'd be happy for me.

I wish I could say the smile in her photo gets wider.

I smile back and get ready for tomorrow, just another day at the bar.

Indrapramit Das

0

Brishti had a memory that seemed unreal but wasn't, of an army of giants carrying an entire forest on their shoulders and backs. She couldn't remember her mother, but she remembered this. The giants had carried the forest to the city, and pounded old roads with their great fists, tearing asphalt and concrete like cloth, filling trenches with fresh soil to plant the trees they'd carried.

People watched from the valley of buildings around them, many wearing face masks. Some shook their heads or shouted as they watched their roads vanish. Others clapped and cheered as they watched the forest come to their plague-haunted city, to bear fruit and breathe for its choked denizens. Brishti couldn't remember who had held her in that moment, listening to the tolling of their fists, warned to keep a distance by the flashing lights on their bodies.

One of those giants would become Brishti's father.

I

It was well into the age of plagues that Brishti was born again. It was a time of warnings, of sirens blaring across the skies, alerts sparking across networks to warn people of pandemics, wildfires, superstorms, flocks and swarms that darkened the sky in panic. The streets of Kolkata were emptier than they had been for centuries, with most of its millions huddled at home or in rows of garibaris, old fossil-fueled cars reclaimed as interim homes for those who didn't have any. Hundreds of thousands had vanished to overcrowded crematoriums, ghats, and burial grounds.

During superstorms, the roads were rivers. As one of these cyclones roared into the megacity from the Bay of Bengal, unhindered by the sunken Gangetic delta, a lone child clung to a bobbing branch in one of those rivers. She shouldn't have survived that maelstrom, but some atavistic impulse, some holy hope, had kept her clinging to that branch, saved only by her scant malnourished weight on the shattered tree limb. As the child tumbled through the city on her branch, the wind strengthening with each passing second, she floated near a giant who stood in the waters, epaulettes of light flashing on its shoulders and bursting in starry spray across the flowing floods and rain-slashed air.

The giant saw her.

The giant swept one great arm down and snatched her off the branch, taking the child to their chest as a mere man might hold a tiny kitten found in a gutter. And the giant's chest opened up to reveal their beating brown heart—a man, who took from the giant's hands the child, his skin quickly shone by the rain to match the gleam of his new charge. The giant's glass-webbed ribs shut again, to seal in their confines man and child, as well as the little girl's first memory of the new life she was hurled into by the storm. It was, perhaps, a memory only imagined later when her father told her how it had happened—the memory of her first time inside the giant, from cold to the warm gush of the giant's breath against her, steam fogging the panes of their transparent chest, the earthy smell of the man's soaked limbs holding her to his chest, the softly blinking lights that lined the inside of her great savior as they stood waiting. "You're safe, you're safe," the man told her over and over again, like the words of a song.

He would tell her often that he'd had named her Brishti, *rain*, right then and there, rain outside lashing the giant's skin, rain inside running down their skin and turning to fog on instruments and windows. Brishti knew he hadn't named her in that moment. It didn't matter—it was true in the same way that he was that being of ultra-strong but lightweight metal and carbon fiber that had rescued her. In that moment she was born Brishti, daughter of a giant and a superstorm, even if neither of them knew it yet. He wiped the caul of rain from her dazed face and smiled at her for the first time.

THE GIANT SPENT THAT NIGHT WALKING THE STORM-LASHED CITY, REMOVING FALLEN trees, cables, and posts from the street, their outer body sometimes sparking when live wires shocked it, dimming the lights inside.

Brishti spent that night curled against the giant's heart, sat in his lap, shivering despite the heat inside, which the man had turned up to dry the both of them, having no clothes to replace her tattered t-shirt and shorts. He'd wrapped a threadbare blanket and towel around her.

The giant waded Kolkata's streets, sweeping searchlights across the waves and hurtling squalls. The giant's heart lent the girl the heat of his blood as he piloted his greater body, his arms moving in comforting concert with the limbs outside, the wired braces around his limbs sometimes pushing against her with a comforting assurance. She had no mask. She could have been infected with any number of the novel pathogens scouring the world, her foreign body a hazard to the greater one of the giant and their heart. But the giant's heart kept her in their shelter, let her arms unfurl slowly from a tight curl against her chest to an embrace around his torso, cold hands tucked between his back and his seat, head against his ribs. She was the rain against his chest. Inside, outside. She could hear his heart beat, even above the hum and hiss of the giant's sinews, the roar of raindrops against their body.

THE NEXT DAY, BRISHTI WATCHED HER RESCUER HELP CLEAR THE STORM-STRUCK megacity with other giants, all the while sitting in his lap. She learned the face of the giant's heart by light of day—his fearsome but graying muttonchop beard, insomniac eyes bloodshot, bald pate always glistening with sweat, heralding a surprising ponytail of curly hair tied with a rubber band. His white tank top was grayed by extensive use.

They never had direct contact with other humans, only seeing giants and vehicles, or people, in the distance, at their windows, descending up or down the mountainous spires of multi-stories on tensor cables from their balconies, tending to the vertical gardens hanging off the buildings. It came back to her, this land recreated by the giants—roads turned to forested paths and groves, buildings forming verdant vales and geometric hills bejeweled with windows, the distances of emptiness given to the city by the plagues filling with vegetation. The giants had wandered Kolkata like gods, transforming the land, grasping in their titanic hands an opportunity to draw the wilderness back to cool the Earth's raging fever.

Brishti watched keenly through the giant's transparent chest, as their hands righted the fallen trees that could be salvaged, and embedded their exposed roots into heaped earth again, packing the soil around their trunks. Around her, the man's smaller arms moved in the same way, hands dark and calloused like the bark of those trees he was restoring, but so delicate in their movements. His body of flesh and blood looked frail in comparison to the one that enclosed them, his limbs tough but wiry.

They never left the inside of the giant, though it began to stink of damp. Brishti wondered if they would be inside the chest forever, watching the city pass by. The giant spoke to the other giants through their instruments, voices crackling disembodied over speakers, coordinating efforts. Sometimes, the cousins of the giants—solar and biofuel cars and lorries—passed by along the roads, cousins also to the still rows of garibaris. Reformed like the giants themselves were—some had been used for military and police, in past lives. As Brishti watched the city, she knew that it was her home, though she had no other clear memories of her life before, except of the giants planting the trees that were everywhere. The storm, or something else, had knocked them out of her head.

Sometimes masked people came out of buildings, and walked out into the roads to give thanks to the giants. They came with offerings of fruit and vegetables from the rooftop gardens of their high-rises—capsicum, tomatoes, apples, mangoes, cucumbers. The giant would squat low to respect these pilgrims. The civilians would wave through the glass, brush their palms against the giant's limbs, and leave their offerings of food in a small mouth below the giant's chest, which was flipped open from the instrument panel inside. Offerings to gods. Brishti remembered this. This was the country they lived in. Giants were gods too, in some of the stories. The giant swallowed these offerings. But inside, the giant's heart ate nothing. So Brishti ignored the gnawing in her gut. She drank from the water tap he'd shown her among the instruments.

Brishti didn't speak. The heart needed to beat, so the giant would move and help the people of the city, the ones inside their garibaris and high-rises and ancient crumbling houses that had survived the age of development by donating their plots of land to reforestation, their centuries-old structures hidden by trees. It was work that required a deep attention.

As the sun receded behind the city, windows began to glow through the foliage trailing down from rooftop farms and gardens and snaring the remnants of useless billboards whose faces wept with rust. The roads and paths of Kolkata glistened in the firefly glow of alor gach, the bioluminescent trees and plants that had replaced most streetlamps, their light-flecked leaves giving the impression of stars rustling close enough to touch.

In the quiet, under a sky ripped cloudless and moon-shot after the storm, the giant came to rest at the shore of one of the many streams and canals of Kolkata, which were only a few years or decades old at most. Along the water, there were garibaris parked in their permanent spots, solar-powered lights glimmering behind their brightly curtained windows, the shadows of their residents flitting like moths trapped in paper lanterns.

The humming of the giant's body died down. Insects drummed against the glass of their chest, a stringed charm of dried chilis and lemons twirling in front of the panes. The giant's heart picked Brishti up off his lap and sat her down in the extra seat next to his. She looked nervous to finally leave his lap. He pushed a lever on the instrument panel.

The ribs of the giant's chest hissed open a little, letting a cool draught of air inside.

"You can speak, child?" the giant's heart asked, turning to her. "You understand Bangla?"

She nodded.

"Do you have a name?"

She said nothing.

"That's alright. What about a home I can take you back to?"

She shook her head.

"You are lost."

She nodded.

"And found," he peered at her. "Do you remember anything? That the world is sick? That you should stay away from people?"

She nodded.

"Good. Good. This," he waved his arm. "This is a mekha. I, too, am mekha. You understand this?"

She nodded.

"The mekha allows me to be one with god, so I may give service to the people of Kolkata, help them in this age of plagues. Our bodies," he patted his chest. "They can't protect us. But this body can. It is an emanation of god. In here, you are safe. You are one with god."

She said nothing.

"Ah! Are you hungry?" he said, and his stomach growled to follow his words.

She giggled.

He smiled at her. "I am a fool. I forget not everyone is like me. I have been alone for a long time. I go long hours without eating, you know . . . when I am one with my mekha. Look at me babbling. Words won't fill your little stomach."

He freed himself of the braces that connected him to the giant's body, collapsing them with practiced movements and letting them hang in the air above the seat. "Remember the food those people gave the mekha? It is their thanks. Now we eat it." He played with his instrument panel, his fingers dancing across the mystery of switches. Something hissed and clanked

147

in the guts of the giant. He bent down and opened a hatch below the console, revealing a cache of fruits and vegetables fed to the giant by grateful people over the day. There was a citrus scent of disinfectant in the air. He handed Brishti an apple, and took one himself, biting into it. Brishti did the same, juice squirting on to her dirty face.

"You're . . . a boy or a girl?"

Brishti paused as if to think about this, and nodded.

"Boy?"

She shook her head.

"Girl. Of course. Stupid me."

She crunched on the apple.

"Do you have a . . . a mother and father?"

The words tumbled out of her mouth with bits of half-chewed apple, as if she hadn't been silent all day, her voice small and cracked in the tight space of the giant's chest, assertive in its desperation: "You are my father."

He looked at her, his chewing stilled.

She continued devouring her apple, not looking at him. As if she were suddenly afraid of looking at him, for fear that he wasn't actually there.

He tapped her shoulder gently. He noticed the tears rolling down her cheeks now, mingling with the juice on her lips, salt and sugar that she licked quietly. She concentrated on the apple, and nothing but the apple, taking huge chunks out of it with her teeth. He waited a moment, and tapped her shoulder again. She looked at him fearfully with her big brown eyes.

"You are right," he said, softly. "I am your father. By god's grace, I am your father."

The giant's body pinged in the silence as it cooled. The girl looked down at her mostly eaten apple. Her hands were shaking.

"I remember you," she said, voice wavering.

"You do?" he asked cautiously.

"I saw you and the other giants carry the forest on your shoulders. You planted it in the city."

He looked out of the giant's ribs. Indeed, there it was—the "forest," entwined into the labyrinth of the city. He and all the mekhas in Kolkata had walked hundreds of kilometers across Bengal to a tree farm and transplanted the harvest to the city, replacing smaller streets with groves, seeding the empty spaces of fields, racetracks, golf greens, and club lawns into forest land for new villages of public housing. He couldn't remember how long it had been since that great march, carrying young trees like umbrellas against their shoulders, along endless highways emptied by the age of plagues. It had been one of many marches, performed over decades, before he became a mekha. The last one had been five, six years ago, maybe. The girl was older than he'd expected, if she could remember that. He barely remembered Kolkata when it was less reclaimed by forest, when cars moved in armies down the streets like he and his fellow mekhas had during the forestation march, when people flooded the footpaths like water did after the storms. Like his parents. People who, in another time, would have had to risk death and walk thousands of kilometers to their distant villages, when pandemics hit and they were left with no jobs or help by uncaring governments. His parents had no giants to walk for them on those harsh migrations, no free housing to give them shelter, not even makeshift villages of repurposed cars, no urban forest from which to gather communal food.

"We moved the forest," he agreed.

"Because you are a giant," said the girl. The apple in her hands was whittled to its core.

"Are you scared of me?" he asked. After all, the word she used, *daitya*, could also mean monster. Perhaps that was what the word father meant to her, he thought, with fear in his heart.

She shook her head. He couldn't tell if there were still tears fresh on her cheeks, because her face was so grubby.

"You don't mind being a giant's daughter?" he asked, his body heavy with exhaustion, limbs aching from the work of the day. He hadn't been this close to another human being in a long time. He had never shared this space inside his mekha with another, ever.

She shook her head again.

His relief was so palpable that he had to wait a moment before he spoke again. He had never wanted a child. But the thought of sending this girl out beyond the safety of his mekha's body terrified him, an idea that was a corruption of all the mekha stood for, all he stood for in his place inside it, as a servant of god and of the people of this wounded land. He stood, and reclined both their seats. "Sleep now. You need to rest."

She leaned back without hesitation, still clinging to the apple core. He took it from her fingers, to add to the biofuel compost cache. She was snoring softly in seconds. He shook his head, cursing his single-minded will, the fact that he hadn't remembered to let her sleep in the side seat earlier in the day. As a mekha, he had a duty to do the work of repair, rescue, and cleanup after the cyclone. But logic evaded his self-judgment. How could he have not let her sleep or eat, after everything she had been through? He found himself once again struck by a fear—that she would dream of her parents, of her real father and mother, if she had ever known them, and wake and remember them. He shook his head to banish this uncharitable unease.

She jerked awake with a gasp. Her little hand found his larger hand. He enclosed it. "Don't leave!" she said.

"No. This is my body, my mekha. This is my home. You are part of this body now, as am I. I cannot abandon my body. I will not go anywhere, I promise you," he said. Her breathing slowed, eyelids drifting down as she fell back to sleep. He unfolded the blanket, and covered her entire body with it. He looked around at his mekha's chest, the neuronal flicker of its internal lights, its cabled nervous system and hydraulic musculature surrounding them. He wondered whether it too felt this new heart inside their chest. Water glittered on the panes between the mekha's ribs, catching the soft organic light from the alor gach. The city was calm now.

He was a giant.

The girl was small for her age, from the way she talked, her memory of the march. Probably nine or ten. He touched the wall of the mekha in silent thanks, for being the body it was, for saving this child. For making him into a giant, though he had never felt less like one than in that moment. He felt like an open wound, in a way that awakened his senses.

"By god's grace. A daughter," he whispered, looking at the sleeping child. "My daughter."

TO BRISHTI, THE HEART OF THE GIANT BECAME DAITYA, OR BABA.

II

Brishti, in all her smallness, became one of the giants.

She was a spark in their solitude during fresh plagues like this one, when the mekha were among the only ones on the roads of Kolkata, along with the rest of what the inside-people called *robotlok*, the essential workers who ventured outside in smaller exoskeletons and HEV suits that were second skins rather than second bodies. The chatter of the robotlok was constant. They would take job requests from the barirlok, the insiders, over their comms, and joke with each other in between, to stave off loneliness.

As they roamed the city, Brishti sat in her father's lap, following the movements of his limbs, the giant's limbs, the dance of his hands across the instruments, learning how he was both heart and brain to the great body that surrounded them. He often repeated that the mekha was an emanation of god. At other times he would point to the stenciled tattoos all over its body in Bengali, Hindi, Urdu, Japanese, and explain how it was designed by international technology collectives, made in factories here and owned by the government. But to Brishti, it was clear that the mekha was him. He was the life of the giant, and she learned how this was truth.

She learned to use the tiny toilet embedded in the back of the cockpit, which was attached to a biofuel processor, cleaning it in turns so it didn't stink.

She learned that the mekha had no religion but their own.

She learned how they bathed out in the open, in forest groves, turning on the mekha's hose and standing under the giant's open hands. Daitya would always turn around to give her privacy, asking her to hum loudly so he would know she was right behind him as they scrubbed themselves under the cold spray.

She learned how they made the mekha breathe disinfectant, gushing vapor like breath in winter, trailing clouds of it as they walked the city's valleys.

She learned how they unfurled the mekha's solar sails when they were low on biofuel or charge, the absorbent membranes iridescent, reminding her of dragonfly wings.

DAITYA SHOWED BRISHTI THE CITY THE GIANTS HAD MADE ANEW.

The streams the giants had dug with their titanic hands out of old roads no longer used, redirecting the anger of the rising Hooghly, filled with fish they could snatch from the waters and eat after roasting them in the palms of the giant, under the flames of their mounted torch.

The hilly ranges that the giants had raised from the flat land of the city, layering fertile earth over the vast mounds of garbage being digested by microbes in Rajarhat and New Town, stepped villages of huts and terraced farms replacing refuse, peaks graced with the floodlights and huge mesh origami of insect farmers' traps.

The forests the giants had planted along the arteries and spaces of the city, the groves they had pulled forth from grassy field and torn concrete, where wild deer, horses, and goats were bred, hunted, or tamed by the urban villagers who lived in the bans, the woods of the Maidan, Victoria, and St. Paul's. Self-repairing biocrete huts and garibari clusters huddled around the old Christian cathedral and the memorial palace to the queen whose empire had once ruled this land. Both buildings were now plague hospitals, and places of worship for people of any and all faiths.

IN HUNTING SEASON, DAITYA SHOWED HIS DAUGHTER THAT ALL BODIES HAVE THEIR potential for violence. In the mekha, in low power mode with all their lights off and engine low, he stalked a cheetal, one of the local deer, through Victoriaban one dusk, when sunset crumbled in gleaming shards through the eaves. When the beautiful creature was in the sights of the giant's ribs, Brishti's father raised his hands, and so did the mekha. An invisible volley of hunting darts killed the cheetal instantly.

Daitya regretted this instantly, not because he hadn't hunted deer before and sold their carcasses to butchers in the Muslim communes of forest villages, but because his daughter burst into inconsolable tears when she realized what had happened to the cheetal.

They carried the cheetal in the giant's arms to a baner gram, one of the forest villages. There, it was exchanged for leaf-wrapped meals of kebabs and cricket flour roti left in the giant's mouth. Daitya tried to share the meal with Brishti, but she refused, the meat a reminder of the death they had caused.

In that moment, Daitya remembered clinging to his mother during one of the labor uprisings, so many years before Brishti was born, watching in terror as a giant not unlike the one they sat in sprayed scalding teargas over the crowds, and another swiped a huge hand through them, sending bodies flying like they didn't matter. They had barely escaped.

"You're a horrible monster," said Brishti to him, and to the mekha, no doubt. *Daitya.* Still the same word she normally used with such joy. Different meaning.

"Brishti. A mekha will never hurt any animal unless the body is used to nourish others. And I would never hurt another person, ever, with my body or that of the mekha. You know that, don't you?" he asked Brishti as she cried. "Just like the body of god we inhabit, and our bodies, that cheetal's body is serving a purpose. His body didn't expire in vain. It goes back to this city, this land. People need to eat. To make clothes and blankets for winter."

Brishti didn't acknowledge her father's words, only begrudgingly snatching the rotis and not the kebabs. He watched her eat through her tears and suppressed a smile. He had lied—he *would* hurt another person or animal, with his body or that of the mekha, if it meant protecting her. He ate the kebabs as her sniffles died down to a sulk.

In a few years, Brishti would be helping her father target the cheetals during hunting season, and praying over their bodies before their delivery to the village butchers. She would soon deny she had ever refused the kebabs made over the firepits of the city's bans.

WHEN THEY HAD WANDERED LONG ENOUGH IN SERVICE, THE GIANTS OF KOLKATA returned to the mekha depots scattered throughout the city. There, the mekhas would periodically gather inside cavernous warehouse garages. Workers in gas masks and HEV suits would examine the giants and provide surgery on them if needed, sparks flying like glowing blood, lubricant oil seeping across the floor like bodily fluids, filling the air with an acrid scent. Their disinfectant tanks would be refilled, their backup batteries charged, their bodies trailing cables like hair.

They would usually spend the night at the depots, when all the mekhar hridaya, all the hearts of the giants, would talk to each other over their radios while lounging in the open chests of their mekhas, smoking weed beedis that twinkled in the shadows. Brishti thought it a beautiful sight, all the giants kneeling and quiet, praying in peace while their hearts chattered. Glowing earrings of worklights hung from their sides, illuminating their freshly polished and stencil-tattooed arms in the gloom of the warehouses. During these visits, Daitya would tense up, always holding Brishti's hand, telling her not to wander off.

Sometimes the other hearts greeted Brishti over the comms. She was an open secret. They knew about her from the radio chatter in the city, but it was only at the depot they saw her clearly. On these rest stops she would wear one of her father's lungis like a long skirt, instead of her shorts, along with a t-shirt, and she'd tie her now long hair into a braid. She was welcomed by the tribe. They waved from their mekha's chests and told her father how lucky he was to have found her, with a hint of envy in their voices. But they were loyal to each other, and no one informed the state that one of their own had broken the rules attached to their greater bodies—namely, that they couldn't share the mekha with anyone else. Luckily for them, the age of plagues had diminished the surveillance networks of governments, broken by the very cataclysms they'd aided by using their billion eyes to look at the wrong things. In this fragile and healing world, trust had far more value than it had in the collapsing time before the age of plagues.

Since Brishti's father, like all of his lonesome tribe, was mekhar hridaya, the heart of the mekha, Brishti became affectionately known as mekhar atma, the soul of the mekha. Theirs was the giant with both heart and soul.

153

SOMETIMES DAITYA WOULD BRING THE MEKHA TO THE CRACKED HIGHWAYS BEYOND New Town at night, where the dark green lakes of algae farms glistened under the moon. His hands guiding Brishti's, they would increase the speed of the mekha together. The giant would run down the open road until the inside of its chest was shaking violently, making Brishti laugh, safely strapped into the seat. The packs of wild dogs who wandered the highways would join the race, howling and barking alongside the pumping mechanical legs of this strange beast, which they knew not to get too close to.

III

The forest flowed, the city ebbed.

The plagues waned like the shadow of the moon, always sure to return.

AS BRISHTI GREW OLDER, AND HER BODY GREW WITH THE YEARS, THE MEKHA stayed the same size, still a giant but less of one to her. She became, more and more, a part of this god's body, a twin heart and soul to her father, mimicking his moves, absorbing his knowledge of the being that sheltered them. As she grew more confident inside the mekha, her father grew less confident about the future he had bestowed upon her, wondering if he had imprisoned her in the cramped chest of a giant for all her days. She was a teenager, and deserved a life of less solitude than being one of the mekha.

Whenever he brought this up, she would go silent with rage. Later, she would blame him for trying to get rid of her, the only times she could bring him to tears deliberately. But Brishti couldn't hide the way she looked at the young people in the villages they delivered supplies to. Daitya recognized the longing in her eyes as she watched them play in the distance, or walk up to the mekha's open mouth to leave offerings. Sometimes they would look up and wave to Brishti. She would wave back but retreat into the chest of the giant with uncharacteristic shyness.

One day, Daitya asked Brishti, "Do you feel like, living with me, that you're missing out on being with other children?"

She frowned as if this was an absurd question. "I am mekhar atma," she put a fist to her chest. "My life is here, I don't need anything else."

He smiled at her. "I know. But . . . it's normal to want to be with others your age."

She shrugged and looked away, evening light through the panes of the giant's chest catching the curve of her cheek. "You aren't with others *your* age." He felt these words, sharper than she realized. "I'm not *normal*. I'm like you. We live to serve the people of the city."

"You're a child, Brishti. You shouldn't have to live to serve—"

Brishti's head whipped around, eyes wide. "I'm not a child! We are the heart and soul. We are one with god together here, you said," she said, her voice wobbling.

"Of course you are. Of course we are, I didn't—"

"You don't want me to live with you anymore," she snapped, eyes shining.

"No," he pleaded. "I could never think of leaving you. But this is not a space for two people to live in. There are opportunities out there."

"You are mekhar hridaya. You can never leave this body. It's your home!" Brishti said, shaking her head. "You told me that, you promised. Which means the only solution is for *me* to leave."

"I don't want you to leave. I want you to think of . . . of a life outside. Outside this giant. I helped build this city, with its forests, these rivers and villages, with this giant. It is not like when I was small, and those without wealth would be doomed to die on the roads, or work for nothing. There are forests to live off, villages to settle and lend your labor to, where you could meet others your age, and grow with them."

"I will not leave the giant that saved me. The giant won't abandon me, even if you will, Baba," she said, not hearing him at all, because she was a teenager, and terrified of losing him.

"Okay, I am sorry," he said, over and over, and didn't bring it up again. But he couldn't forget the look on her face when she looked to other children beyond the shared body of their giant. He couldn't forget what he had denied himself as a teenager, struggling to survive at the dawn of the age of plagues.

DAITYA CONTACTED GOVERNMENT HQ OVER THE RADIO ONE DAY, WHEN BRISHTI was bathing under the open palms of their giant. They no longer bathed together, because she was too old. Though Brishti had little notion of privacy because of the way they lived, even she would come to appreciate some time alone, or even separated by just the barrier of the giant's chest, since she had never left the shadow of the giant. She still hummed loudly, by habit, or to assure her father she was outside the giant, still there.

It felt like a betrayal, but Daitya forced himself to tell HQ that he had a daughter now, and that she lived with him.

Their next trip to a mekha depot was their last with their giant.

Daitya lost his home, the body that housed him. He felt a self-loathing so powerful it nearly buckled his legs when Brishti looked at the reclaiming officers at the depot, the realization that the open secret was now no secret at all, that she had become the infection in the giant's body, expelled along with her father from their place in god's body.

"Please, please, please, I take very little space, please don't take away my baba's home," she begged the officers. They looked sympathetic but firm behind their masks. Daitya went to tell her the truth, to calm and comfort his daughter and absorb her anger. But he saw her holding on to the giant's leg, the worn, soiled leg of the body that had been his for so long he couldn't remember, the body that had saved her life. Brishti, born of a superstorm and a giant. Her face mask had slid off on her tears. Looking at this, Daitya collapsed at his daughter's feet and broke down in shuddering sobs. Brishti's own sorrow vanished in concern as she crouched and held him. She had never seen him cry with his body, his tough, exhausted body. Only ever his eyes, when she blamed him for trying to get rid of her. He shook in her arms and begged forgiveness, and she realized what had happened, that he had done the opposite of get rid of her, like she'd feared so many times.

Though she was of the mekha, one of his tribe, he didn't want her to be. He didn't want her world restricted to the rib cage of a giant that did not grow with her.

IV

Shorn of his outer body, Daitya the mekha became just a father raising his teenage daughter in a small village in the forest of the Maidan.

Shorn of her outer body, Brishti the mekha became a young woman, taller than her father now and more formidable, a butcher and huntress with bow and machete. Clad in sari and gas mask, she rode out of the forests of central Kolkata on horseback with cryocaches full of meat, out to the less verdant valleys of high-rises, delivering the meat to open-air markets, sending the caches up hoisting cables to the balconies and windows of barirlok.

Though Brishti's hands remembered the motions controlling a different body, she loved riding horses through the forest paths with her friends, some of whom fell in love with her. She fell in love with some of them. She slept with some of them under the stars, drunk on this private intimacy new to her, thrilled by the mythic danger of tigers that sometimes wandered this deep into the city, annoyed by the real danger of insects.

Sometimes, Brishti's dreams made of her a giant running through the forest.

With the passage of time, Brishti forgave her father. Her father, who found others to love besides her: the married couple who shared their communal hut. The quiet husband a butcher, and the garrulous wife a garden-farmer. They shared their bed with Daitya, who learned their trades, and shared his body in ways he had never done before. Their daughter, a child, became as a daughter to him, and as a sister to Brishti.

By the grace of god, a family.

BRISHTI GOT OFF HER HORSE AND LOOKED OUT OVER THE MEKHA SCRAPYARD. A graveyard of giants rusting in the rain, sinews overgrown with vines, chests heartless and filled with nests of birds and jackals that flitted across the grounds like spirits. Finally at rest, their limbs sprawled in disarray. Brishti's contact, looking like a crow in her black cloak and gas mask, pointed the way through the winding labyrinth of bodies. Brishti led her horse carefully, not wanting her to get hurt on the rough ground.

The contact pointed at a giant, still kneeling with dignity, not disrepair. Newly arrived at the yard.

Brishti's breath hitched. She didn't have to check the serial number tattooed on the giant's arm. This body, given of god, once had a heart that had sat behind those open ribs, a heart who became her father, and christened her the soul. It was her body kneeling there in the rain. A retired mekha belonged to no one. She had as much right to it as salvagers and recyclers. Was it fixable? She would take that chance.

Her contact held up two gloved fingers as a reminder. Two goats for a lead on one dead giant. Fair. Brishti nodded, tethering her horse to the broken limb of another mekha. She climbed into the giant's ribs. Into the dank, dark chest. Her body remembered, traced the neural pathways of her father's movements across the broken console. She could feel wind whistling through the giant's body. Breath. Rain pattered on the broken glass of its chest. Of their chest. Brishti remembered her father's heartbeat as she leaned her head on his chest, after he saved her. Her dear father, who had sacrificed his body for her, the body of his god. This body was no longer his. She understood that now, even if it had taken her a while.

But her father had taught her well. The giant had a new heartbeat now.

"Let me save you this time," Brishti said.

11 VACCINE SEASON

Hannu Rajaniemi

THE SMALL AUTONOMOUS BOAT SKIPPED OVER THE GRAY WAVES. THE ENGINE howled in mid-air with each jump. Every jarring landing made Torsti taste the protein bar he'd had for breakfast. The overpowering fish smell in the boat didn't help.

For the thousandth time, he imagined what would happen when he arrived at his destination. He would jump out of the boat and run down the pier. His grandfather's lanky form would reach down and embrace him. One shared breath and it would be done. Torsti would never have to be afraid of losing him again.

A cold spray on his face brought him back to the bucking boat. Jungfruholmen Island lay up ahead.

It was early autumn. From a distance, the blazing leaves of the trees made it seem like the island was on fire. The boat sped past the granite wave-breakers that guarded it, toward wave-polished coral-hued cliffs crowned with twisted birch and pine. A familiar pier jutted out of the stony half-moon of a beach.

In a few minutes, the boat bumped against the pier gently and came to a halt. Torsti climbed out carefully and secured his loaned vessel to a metal ring with a length of rope. There was no sign of Grandfather. The windows of the squat sauna building by the pier were dark. What if I am already too late? he thought. What if he is already dead?

A path covered in rotting leaves and pine needles wound into a patch of trees, up the cliff and toward Grandfather's cottage. Torsti followed it, shivering in the wind.

The hiisi's churn was just past the trees, in the middle of a large hollow. It was a gaping hole in the rock, fifteen feet in diameter. After a ten-foot drop, bottomless dark water lapped at the spiral-grooved walls. A stream of meltwater from a glacier had drilled it into the granite by rotating gravel, millions of years ago.

Torsti's stomach tied itself into a cold knot. He had been five years old when he first came to the island with his parents to celebrate vaccine season. On a summer evening, with the red smear of the sun on the horizon, Grandfather had brought him to see the churn. In hushed tones, the old man had told him that the churn was actually an ancient portal to the stars. If you threw a rock into the spiraling grooves in just the right way, alien machines activated and opened a wormhole to wherever in space and time you wanted to go. He had closed Torsti's fingers around a stone and told him to try.

Torsti had taken an eager step forward and looked into the churn. The vast depths had looked back, like the entire island was a monstrous eye and the churn its pupil, inhuman and black and fathomless, like Death itself. The stone had fallen from his hand and he had run away in tears. Even now, seven years later, he remembered the shame of it.

And I remember *you*, the churn seemed to say. I haven't changed. I am the past. I am the future. I'll get you in the end.

"No, you won't," Torsti muttered under his breath.

Branches rustled, and his heart jumped. A tall figure loomed on the other side of the churn. It wore dark overalls, gloves, and some kind of helmet. In the shadows, its face looked skull-like.

Then it stumbled on a pebble and set off a small avalanche into the depths of the churn. It let out a muffled curse in a familiar voice.

"*Perkele*," Grandfather swore. He was wearing a battered face shield over a cloth mask, but his bushy eyebrows were unmistakable.

This is it, Torsti thought. He tried to will his legs to move, but the terror of the churn still held him in its grip.

Grandfather raised a hand. "Don't try to come any closer, boy," he said. "I mean it."

Torsti stared at him helplessly. The old man huffed and adjusted his mask. This wasn't going to work, he realized. The vaccine replicating in Torsti's upper airways was engineered to be infectious, but just like the old Pandemic One virus it was based on, it still needed close contact to spread, especially outdoors.

Very slowly, Torsti took half a step forward.

"Stop right there," Grandfather said, "or I'm going to run." His voice was thin. It was hard to see his expression behind the mask and the plastic face shield, but his eyes were wide. He is afraid, Torsti thought. He has never been afraid of anything.

"I'm going to rest here for just a moment," Grandfather said. "You stay right there." He sat down on a boulder and massaged his leg, not taking his eyes off Torsti. "Did your mother send you?"

"No!" Torsti said. "Why are you dressed like that?"

"Well, I think it should be obvious. I don't want to catch your damn vaccine, that's why."

"Why not?" That was the question that had been haunting Torsti for two years, ever since his mother had told him that they wouldn't be visiting Grandfather during vaccine season anymore. He was surprised by how fierce his voice sounded. "Why did you stop talking to us? What did we do to you?"

Grandfather ignored him and took a phone from his pocket. He tapped at the screen laboriously—typically, he hadn't had the opto interface infection either, and had to use all his devices by hand.

"Doesn't look like you are shedding that much," he muttered. "Thank goodness for kids' immune systems." Then he looked up, narrowing his eyes. "If your mother didn't send you," he said suspiciously, "then how did you get here?"

This wasn't the Grandfather Torsti remembered from the vaccine seasons past, the one who had played hide and seek with him and built a castle from sticks and pine cones in the secret grove on the eastern tip of the island. This was someone else.

"I skipped school," he said, swallowing back tears. "Then I took a train to Hanko. There was a fisherwoman Rnought introduced me to. She lent me her boat."

"Why on earth would somebody do that? Who the hell is this Rnought?"

"It came out last year. It's a serendipity AI to speed up vaccine spread. If you already caught the vaccine, it matches you up with people who want to be immunized and can help you with something, or the other way around."

One of the benefits of living in Helsinki was catching every new vaccine days or even weeks earlier than the rest of the country, and Torsti had gone to the big launch party at the Senate Square with his parents. And the new vaccine was so popular that the fisherwoman had jumped at the chance of helping Torsti get to Jungfruholmen, in exchange for a verified transmission.

"Sending a twelve-year-old out to the sea on his own, just like that." Grandfather said, shaking his head. "Everyone has gone mad. When I was your age, we couldn't always trust the machines to save you. That's what's wrong with this world, it's too safe."

"No, it's not," Torsti said. "It's not safe. People still get old. People can still die."

"Unless they get this bloody vaccine, is that it? A vaccine against death?"

It wasn't a fix for death, not really. Torsti knew as much. But it was the next best thing. It was the last in the long series of vaccines the Global Immunity Foundation had been releasing for decades. Backed by a group of billionaires, they had invented transmissible vaccines to stop Pandemic One—a controversial move at the time, but necessary when more than half of Americans and countless others around the world had refused to be vaccinated against COVID-19. After an initial uproar, the Foundation had been hailed as heroes after they stopped Pandemic Two in its tracks, saving countless lives. In the two decades since, the Foundation's vaccine releases had been coming out on a regular basis: first, updates against emerging coronaviruses, flu, dengue, pre-pandemic zoonotics. And eventually, protection from the big ones, non-transmissible diseases—heart disease, Alzheimer's, and cancer.

Now each vaccine release was a global event, a cause for celebration. At Senate Square, this one had rained down on a cheering, dancing crowd from dispersal drones amidst a bioluminescent fireworks display. Pre-infected choirs had sung it onto onlookers from the steps of the Helsinki Cathedral. The new vaccine was a senolytic: it trained your immune system to kill the zombie cells that accumulated in your body with aging. You wouldn't live forever, but you would stay healthy much longer—no one knew how long. There were still mice alive from the first experiments, decades ago.

Torsti had clinked glasses with Mom and Dad when their phone sequencers confirmed their infections—champagne for his parents, Pommac for him—and then hugged and kissed passersby, all in vaccine season masks—feathers, crowns, and horns, but always leaving the mouth and nose uncovered. And then, all of a sudden it was as if he was watching the revelers from behind a pane of glass, cold and distant. How could they celebrate when there were those who would be left behind?

Like Grandfather.

"Is that what this is about, Torsti? You don't want me to die?" Grandfather asked.

Torsti stared at him. Grandfather really didn't understand. But maybe it was unfair to expect him to. Unlike Torsti, he hadn't grown up with Mom coming home and talking about her job at the Long Reflection Committee. Over and over, she had explained what a special time this was in the human history. Things no longer hung in balance, existential threats—pandemics, bioterror, rogue AIs—had been overcome. It was time to look toward the deep future and decide humanity's destiny.

Torsti had loved it, and had devoured everything the Committee published that Mom let him read. He had even started contributing ideas to the Committee's open simulations that mapped out possible futures, millions of years ahead. He had spent countless hours wandering through the virtual worlds, until his parents disabled his opto. And even then, his imagination kept going, conjuring images of things to come.

GRANDFATHER DIDN'T REALIZE THAT THE VACCINE WAS JUST THE FIRST STEP. THE Committee scenarios were clear. If you extended your life by just a decade or two, the next set of longevity technologies would come along—not just to prevent aging but to restore youth—and so on. Longevity escape velocity, it was called. If you made it just a little bit further, you could travel to the stars, live as long as the universe itself.

Grandfather was letting all that go, because he was mad at Mom, for some reason Torsti could not understand. And that made Torsti angry, angry enough to do desperate things.

He opened his mouth to explain, but there were so many words that they just sat heavy in his chest, all jumbled up and stuck together, like a pile of twisted iron nails.

"No," he said, finally. "I want you to live."

"Well, that's very touching," Grandfather said, not understanding the difference. "But as you get older, you'll understand that there are some decisions people have to make on their own. I have made mine, and I have to live—and die with them." His voice broke, just for a moment. Then he continued in a harsher tone. "I don't need a silly little boy coming here to take that away from me, just because he doesn't understand how the world works.

"Now, I'm going to send a message to your mother." Grandfather tapped at his phone laboriously. "We have our differences, but I don't want her worrying herself sick. I'll take you back to the mainland in the morning. With two boats it should be safe. You can sleep in the guest bed in the sauna, I already set it up—I'll disinfect it all afterwards. And here's a bunch of surgical masks." He set a small pile of flat blue objects on the rock next to him. "I want you to wear them."

He stood and started back up the path. "Come now. Since you're here, you can help me chop some firewood. It gets cold at night."

"You knew I was coming," Torsti said. "How?" He had left his phone at home, and the ubiquitous surveillance of the old days had been banned at the start of the Reflection.

Grandfather shrugged.

"You have to be prepared," he said. "Your Mom messaged me and told me you had gone missing. We don't talk much, but some things you always share with family. I called an old friend at the Foundation, asked for transmission data. They barcode the viruses, you know. They don't talk about it, but you can actually trace the contacts with the phone sequencers. It is still so early in the season that you left a pretty clear trail."

He knew, Torsti thought. He didn't have to let me come this far, he could have told Mom much earlier. He *wanted* me to come.

He followed Grandfather up the path toward the main house, keeping a respectful distance. Fallen leaves whispered beneath his feet, and he breathed in their earthy smell.

There was still hope.

THEY WALKED AROUND THE MAIN HOUSE TO THE FIREWOOD SHED. GRANDFATHER hauled out an armful of logs to the chopping block, and then his phone rang. He twisted awkwardly, trying to get it out of his pocket. Torsti moved forward to help, then remembered himself. The old man let the wood clatter to the ground, swearing, and pulled the device out.

"It's your mother," he said, frowning. He tapped it and held it up toward Torsti. "I think she just needs to see you are all right."

Mom and Dad peeked at Torsti from the tiny screen. Mom's eyes were tired, and her chestnut hair clung to her head, unwashed. Dad had an arm around her shoulders, tugging at his braided beard as he always did when he was anxious.

"Torsti," Mom said. "I know I said you should have more adventures, but this is not what I meant." She looked so small, so far away on the screen, so different from the full-sized opto projections he was used to.

"I'm fine, Mom. I'm coming back tomorrow." He glanced at Grandfather, who was holding the phone. The old man's eyes were squeezed shut as he listened.

"Tell . . . tell your grandfather thank you for me," Mom said.

"I will."

"Bring back some of that islander bread," Dad said, a fake cheer in his voice. "We'll see you soon."

"Can I talk to your grandfather a bit?" Mom said.

Torsti nodded and waved.

Grandfather walked away, holding the phone to his ear.

"Yes, of course," he said. "No, it's no trouble. Of course. You both take care now."

Grandfather ended the call, wiped the screen surface with a small alcohol pad and pocketed it. His face shield was clouded with steam. Sniffing, he swept his shirtsleeve across it.

"All right," he said. "Let's chop some firewood."

In practice, what it meant was that Torsti chopped the firewood, at Grandfather's amused direction. The handle of the axe stung his hands with every blow, and more than once he ended up having a log stuck to the axe blade and then bashing it against the block, lifting the whole thing like a giant, clumsy hammer.

"No, no, no," the old man said. "There's a trick to it."

"What is it?" Torsti asked, huffing. There was a painful blister in the middle of his left palm. The surgical mask he now wore was moist with his breath.

"You have to catch the edge," Grandfather said. "You go with the grain of the wood. It's pointless to fight against it. It should feel like the wood wants to split. Come on. Try again."

Torsti carefully positioned the birch log on the block and swung the axe. This time, he hit it just right, with the tip of the axe blade, and the log flew apart in two pieces effortlessly. He looked at it, surprised.

"See?" Grandfather said. "That's the problem with everybody, these days. They don't know the tricks anymore."

Torsti looked at him. It felt strange to talk to someone wearing a mask that completely hid everything except the eyes. In a way, it felt more distant than seeing Mom on a screen. What is *your* trick, Grandfather? he wondered. Which way does your grain go?

"Where did you learn that?" he asked carefully.

"Well, now. It would have been in the time of Big Corona, back when your mother was little," he said. "Not the virus, of course, not Pandemic One. The Coronal Mass Ejection Event, the solar flare. Nothing but wood to keep the heating going, back then. Had to learn quickly how to chop it."

"What was it like?" Torsti asked, starting to gather the split logs into a pile. He knew the facts, of course. A massive blast of charged particles from the Sun had slammed into the Earth's magnetic field, frying every electric circuit. But it felt like this was something Grandfather wanted to talk about.

The old man's eyes were distant.

"Oh, it was a mess. You had satellites falling from the sky. No Internet. No electricity for six months. It was worse than the Pandemics. At least then we had ways of talking to each other. The Big Corona really isolated everybody. It was in the middle of the winter, too. People hoarded firewood. Even now, I keep too much of it around. Not good for my carbon credits, but once you go through something like that, your habits change."

"I was in my forties. But it was only then that I learned how to be a grown-up. There is something about protecting your family that changes things. Not that anyone understands that, these days. After it was over, I made sure I *prepared*. Learned first aid, bought this place here, made sure we had canned food for years. Maybe I overdid the protecting with your mother a little bit, that's why she grew up so wild. But you do what you have to do."

His mask twisted, just a hint of a smile beneath.

"You know, we had this old chest of drawers, mahogany, from your great-grandmother. One night I took it to the back yard and chopped it into pieces. It kept us warm for a night, but your grandmother never forgave me for that."

He sighed. "She loved the northern lights, though. We saw the best ones ever, the night it happened. We were all in a panic, trying to find candles in the pitch black, and then she told me to look outside. The city was all dark, and the sky was ablaze, with every color you could think of. We took your mother and went outside, stared at it for hours. It was the most beautiful thing she had seen in her life, she said, and because of the way she looked at it, it was.

"That's what I miss now, her way of seeing things. I see the aurora here, in the winter, sometimes, but it's just lights in the sky.

"We can't really know, but that was probably what killed her, us going out there. The cancer wave that came afterwards, all those particles, messing with everyone's DNA. I got lucky, roll of the dice. Your mother was fine, the Foundation rolled out the cancer vaccines by the time she started school. But your grandmother . . . "Grandfather looked away, at the choppy sea beyond the trees. "She drowned on dry land, in the end," he said quietly. "Her lungs filled with fluid."

Torsti stared at Grandfather. He didn't know much about his grandmother, but her paintings and drawings were all over the cottage, small landscapes and quirky manga-style cartoons. He felt the terror of the churn's black water rise in him again. To get rid of his disquiet, he chopped at the last log, hard. It flew apart violently, and the axe got stuck in the block.

"So that's why," Grandfather said.

"That's why what?" Torsti asked.

"That's why I don't want your vaccine. I don't need to see the future. AIs and space colonies and Dyson trees and all the things your Mom spends her days thinking about for the Long Reflection Committee. Lights in the sky, nothing more. I don't need to see it."

He got up. "Let's gather these and get the fire going for you, hmm? It's going to be cold at night."

THE SAUNA SMELLED OF DRY WOOD IN A WAY THAT SEEMED TO RETAIN ITS WARMTH. It had a small front room with a low bed where Torsti had slept during previous island visits. It had one of Grandmother's drawings, a tiny watercolor and ink of the view out toward the sea from the sauna window, framed by the wavebreakers.

"You'll have to stay outside while I get the fire going," Grandfather said. The old man went into the sauna itself and kneeled painfully by the stove, assembling kindling and wood into careful layers.

Reluctantly, Torsti got out of his way. He walked to the pier and looked out to the sea. As Grandfather had predicted, the wind had picked up. The trees on the cliffs danced, and heavy waves crashed against the breakers. It looked just like Grandmother's painting, a window into the past.

So much would be lost when Grandfather died, entire worlds Torsti had never known. I have to find a way to do it, he thought. I have to bring him to the future with me. If I leave, I might never see him again.

It is just lights in the sky, Grandfather had said.

That's the problem, Torsti thought. He can't see the future. But maybe I can show him.

He went to the boat and picked up a coil of sturdy rope from its storage locker. Then he gathered a few round pebbles from the beach and went back to the sauna. Grandfather came out, dusting his hands.

"All right," he said. "If you add a few logs before you go to sleep, you should be warm and snug now, even if the north wind blows." There was a regretful look in his eyes. "It's too bad we can't actually use the sauna together. Shame to waste a good löyly." Then he frowned, seeing Torsti's expression. "What is it, boy?"

"I want to show you something," Torsti said. "Let's go up to the churn."

THE HIISI'S CHURN LOOKED EVEN DEEPER AND DARKER IN THE FADING LIGHT. Slowly, Torsti walked right to its edge. The fear moved in him now, as if the deep water was reaching out from the churn with a cold hand and squeezing his heart.

He laid the coil of rope down on the ground and tied one end carefully around a boulder. Then he drew his hand back and tossed the first stone into the churn. It bounced off a wall and vanished into the black water.

"What are you doing?" Grandfather asked.

Torsti threw another stone. This time, the angle was better, and the stone actually caught on the grooves, spun around the churn bore before falling into the water.

"I want you to travel with me," he said quietly. "Remember? It can take us anywhere."

Grandfather watched him, eyes unreadable, almost invisible in the dim light.

"So let's go to the future. A thousand years from now."

He threw another stone. He was getting better at it now, and now the stone slid along the grooves almost a whole circuit. His palms sweated. The images from the simulations flashed in his head. Squeezing them hard like the stones in his hand, he forced them into words.

"Look," he said, motioning Grandfather to come closer. "Here we are. Not many people live on Earth. Maybe you are still here, on the island, but when we come visit you, it's from the artificial worlds in the asteroid belt, every one of them unique and different. I—I might have wings, since I live in a low gravity world, and I have to wear an exoskeleton to walk around. Mom is no longer just thinking about the future, she is building it. Dad is a mindweaver, trying to get big group minds to get along, helping them to find the balance between the parts and the whole. We still celebrate vaccine season. But now it's just a ritual for family, like Christmas used to be."

He threw another stone. This one was better: the round stone bounced and followed the grooves, almost all the way down.

He looked at Grandfather. The old man sat on a rock now, leaning his chin on his hands, watching Torsti.

"It's a million years from now. Everybody comes back to Earth during vaccine season, once a century. There is no disease anymore, so the vaccines are memetic: *ideas*, entire systems of thought, ways of being, different kinds of consciousness. Mind vaccines against despair and war and fear."

He looked up at the pale October stars. "The wormholes open in the Lagrange Points, and they come. Some—some come in ships; tiny ones, living spores that carry minds in molecules that then grow in soil and turn into bodies and minds; large ones, ones made from dark matter or with a black hole in the heart that can cross between galaxies. Others are already here, in virtual realities inside diamond machines; but they make bodies to visit Earth and the people here, because it's vaccine season. So they can remember where they come from."

Now Grandfather stood close. I'm not doing it right, Torsti thought. He still can't see.

He gritted his teeth, strained to see the deep future and hefted the final stone.

Grandfather took his hand.

"Torsti," he said gently. "It's all right." There was a smile under his mask. "You are a good boy, you really are. I *know* you can see these things, I know you can. You will do things I never imagined. And . . . it's enough for me just to know that.

"Now, let's go back. It's getting cold. I'm going to make some food, and tomorrow I'll take you home."

The churn's hollow voice mocked Torsti in his mind. *You can imagine all the futures you want, boy. But they are not real. Only endless dark is real. Your Grandfather knows that. Nothing will exist. Only I will remain.*

"No," Torsti said. "I *am* going to show you."

He withdrew his hand from his Grandfather's and threw the last stone. It hit the grooves of the churn perfectly, spinning around the bore, rattling like a ball in a roulette wheel.

Then he jumped in after it.

For an instant, he was suspended in mid-air, could almost touch the walls of the churn. Maybe it is really a wormhole, he thought. Then the water rose to meet him and pulled a cold hand over his head.

Torsti had never learned to swim, in spite of Mom and Dad's attempts. So he just lifted his arms and floated, disappearing beneath the surface. Water filled his mouth and lungs. It was like breathing in cold space. The dark filled him, and suddenly it was like he was hollow, a container for the universe itself.

He saw the future. Artificial worlds strung around stars like strings of pearls. Wormholes connecting galaxies like synapses between neurons. Currents of dark matter redirecting the movements of superclusters, slowing down the expansion of the universe, preventing the Big Rip that threatened to leave each photon alone in its own bubble. And then, new universes, budding off from the first one, entire new realities with their own laws and constants and life, a forest growing from a single seed. A multiverse, made from minds and wonder and surprise, no longer dead and cold, lighting up, inside him.

We are the vaccine, he thought. We are the vaccine against the dark.

And then it all blinked out.

THE COUGHING BROUGHT TORSTI BACK. IT FELT LIKE BEING CHOPPED AT WITH AN axe, right in the chest. The universe came out of him in tiny big bangs of phlegm and cold brine.

Finally it stopped, leaving him freezing and shaking all over, but alive. Torsti opened his eyes. His Grandfather's silhouette loomed over him, against the evening sky.

"Don't try to move," the old man said, crouching next to Torsti on the granite. He lifted up his phone, pointing the camera at Torsti, and the screen lit up his face.

He wasn't wearing his mask. His thick silvery hair and salt-and-pepper beard were dripping, and he had a pained look on his face. The lines were deeper than Torsti remembered, his cheeks were hollower.

"Grandfather," Torsti wheezed. "I saw it."

Relief spread over Grandfather's face, smoothing the wrinkles.

"Thank goodness," he said. "You stupid, reckless boy. What if I hadn't been strong enough to haul you up that goddamned rope?" He held up his phone. "The Hanko Medical Center AI said you were going to be fine, but I almost didn't believe it. You should be glad I still remembered my rescue breath training. How are you feeling?"

Torsti's ribs hurt, but he felt better with each breath. Slowly, he sat up. He was soaked through and shivered in the wind. Grandfather wrapped his coat around Torsti, and then hugged him tight, wiry arms around the boy's shoulders and back.

"I saw it in the churn," Torsti whispered. "The future. I really saw it."

Grandfather pulled away and looked at Torsti.

"I believe you," he said. "You have it too, don't you? That way of seeing. And I never realized. What a strange thing."

His voice was thick. Then he held up his phone, clearing his throat. "Well, I guess I'm going to see the future too, now. This damn thing confirmed transmission."

"I'm sorry," Torsti said. "I took away your choice."

Grandfather sighed.

"You did no such thing, boy," he said. "You can't take what wasn't there in the first place. My choice was made long time ago. I just wasn't ready to admit it."

He helped Torsti up. "Let's go to the sauna," he said. "All these vaccines or not, you don't want to catch your death."

They walked down the pine needle path together, toward the sauna and the warmth.

CONTRIBUTORS

Madeline Ashby is a futurist and science fiction writer based in Toronto. She is the author of the Machine Dynasty series from Angry Robot Books and also *Company Town* from Tor Books. She is a contributor to *How to Future: Leading and Sensemaking in an Age of Hyper Change*, available soon from Kogan Page Inspire. She has also developed multiple science fiction prototypes and scenarios for Intel Labs, the Institute for the Future, SciFutures, Data & Society, Nesta, the WorldBank, WHO, and others. You can find her at madelineashby.com or on Twitter @MadelineAshby.

Indrapramit Das (aka Indra Das) is a writer and editor from Kolkata, India. He is a Lambda Literary Award winner for his debut novel *The Devourers* (Penguin India/Del Rey), and a Shirley Jackson Award winner for his short fiction, which has appeared in a variety of anthologies and publications including Tor.com, *Slate, Clarkesworld*, and *Asimov's Science Fiction*. He has lived in India, the United States, and Canada, where he received his MFA from the University of British Columbia.

Cory Doctorow (craphound.com) is a science fiction author, activist, and journalist. He is the author of many books, most recently *Radicalized* and *Walkaway*, science fiction for adults; *In Real Life*, a graphic novel; *Information Doesn't Want to Be Free*, a book about earning a living in the Internet age; and *Homeland*, a young adult sequel to *Little Brother*. His latest book is *Poesy the Monster Slayer*, a picture book for young readers. His next book is *Attach Surface*, an adult sequel to *Little Brother*.

Adrian Hon is CEO and founder of Six to Start, co-creator of the most successful smartphone fitness game in the world, Zombies, Run! He is the author of *A New History of the Future in 100 Objects* (MIT Press, 2020) and has worked with the British Museum, Disney Imagineering, and the Long Now. Before becoming a game designer, Adrian was a neuroscientist and experimental psychologist at Cambridge, UCSD, and Oxford.

Rich Larson was born in Galmi, Niger, has lived in Canada, the United States, and Spain, and is now based in Prague, Czech Republic. He is the author of the novel *Annex* and the collection *Tomorrow Factory*, which contains some of the best of his 150+ published stories. His work has been translated into Polish, Czech, Bulgarian, Portuguese, French, Italian, Vietnamese, Chinese, and Japanese. Find free fiction and support his work at patreon.com/richlarson.

Gideon Lichfield is from London, where he began his career on the science desk at *The Economist*, then spent stints as a foreign correspondent in Mexico City, Moscow, and Jerusalem before winding up in New York City. He was one of the founding editors at the business publication Quartz and worked there until 2017, when he became editor-in-chief of *MIT Technology Review*. He has taught journalism at New York University and has written (not very good) short science fiction as a fellow at the Data & Society Research Institute.

Ken Liu (http://kenliu.name) is an American author of speculative fiction. A winner of the Nebula, Hugo, and World Fantasy awards, he wrote *The Dandelion Dynasty*, a silkpunk epic fantasy series (starting with *The Grace of Kings*), as well as *The Paper Menagerie and Other Stories* and *The Hidden Girl and Other Stories*. He also authored the Star Wars novel *The Legends of Luke Skywalker*. Prior to becoming a full-time writer, Ken worked as a software engineer, corporate lawyer, and litigation consultant. Ken frequently speaks at conferences and universities on a variety of topics, including futurism, cryptocurrency, history of technology, bookmaking, and the mathematics of origami.

Malka Older is a writer, aid worker, and sociologist. Her science-fiction political thriller *Infomocracy* was named one of the best books of 2016 by Kirkus, Book Riot, and the *Washington Post*. She is the creator of the serial *Ninth Step Station*, currently running on Serial Box, and her short story collection *And Other Disasters* came out in November 2019. Her opinions can be found in the *New York Times*, *Nation*, *Foreign Policy*, and *NBC THINK*, among other outlets.

Hannu Rajaniemi is a cofounder and CEO of HelixNano, a venture- and Y Combinator-backed biotech startup developing a COVID-19 vaccine. Hannu was born in Finland. At the age of eight he approached the European Space Agency with a fusion-powered spaceship design, which was received with a polite "thank you" note. Hannu studied mathematics and theoretical physics at University of Oulu and Cambridge and holds a PhD in string theory from the University of Edinburgh. He cofounded a mathematics consultancy whose clients included the UK Ministry of Defence and the European Space Agency. Hannu is the author of four novels including *The Quantum Thief* (winner of the 2012 Tähtivaeltaja Award for the best science fiction novel published in Finland and translated into more than twenty languages). His most recent book is *Summerland* (June 2018), an alternate-history spy thriller in a world where the afterlife is real. His short fiction has been featured in *Nature*, *Slate*, *MIT Technology Review*, and the *New York Times*. Hannu lives in the San Francisco Bay Area with his wife, neuroscientist Zuzana Krejciova-Rajaniemi, and their vizsla puppy Neo.

Wade Roush is a technology journalist and audio producer based in Cambridge, Massachusetts. He is the author of *Extraterrestrials* (MIT Press, 2020) and editor of the 2018 edition of *Twelve Tomorrows*. He hosts and produces *Soonish*, a nonfiction podcast about the future, and cofounded Hub & Spoke, a collective of independent podcasts. He has been a staff writer, editor, and/or columnist for *Scientific American*, *MIT Technology Review*, Xconomy, and *Science*, and was the founding producer of *Technology Review*'s *Deep Tech*

174

podcast. In 2014–2015 he was acting director of MIT's Knight Science Journalism program. He has a B.A. in history and science from Harvard College and a PhD in the history and social study of science and technology from MIT.

Karl Schroeder is an award-winning Canadian author and professional futurist. Of his twelve published novels, two have won Canada's Aurora Award for best sci-fi novel of the year. Karl came to prominence as one of the vanguard writers of the "new space opera," but after obtaining a master's degree in Strategic Foresight he shifted his attention to near-future fiction. Now he writes about positive solutions to issues such as global warming, using his foresight skills to inform his science fiction—and vice versa. Karl lives in Toronto with his wife and daughter.

D. A. Xiaolin Spires steps into portals and reappears in sites such as Hawaii, New York, various parts of Asia, and elsewhere, with her keyboard appendage attached. Her work appears in publications such as *Clarkesworld, Analog, Strange Horizons, Nature, Terraform, Uncanny, Fireside, Galaxy's Edge, Andromeda Spaceways* (Year's Best Issue), *Diabolical Plots, Star*Line, Factor Four*, and anthologies of the strange and beautiful: *Ride the Star Wind, Sharp and Sugar Tooth, Future Visions, Deep Signal, Battling in All Her Finery*, and *Broad Knowledge*. Select stories can be read in German, Spanish, Vietnamese, Estonian, and French translation. She can be found on Twitter @spireswriter and on her website daxiaolinspires.wordpress.com.

Ytasha L. Womack is an author, filmmaker, independent scholar, and dance therapist. Much of her work centers around Afrofuturism, new futures, and the use of the imagination for change. Her book *Afrofuturism: The World of Black Sci Fi & Fantasy Culture* is taught in universities around the world. She's the author of *Rayla 2212* and *A Spaceship in Bronzeville* and directed the award-winning dance film *A Love Letter to the Ancestors from Chicago*. A Chicago native, she was an inaugural resident at artist Kehinde Wiley's artist residence Black Rock in Senegal. Her debut graphic novel *Blak Kube* will be released in 2022.